Folly Beach Homecoming

John C. Lasne'

John C. Lasne'

Finding Jack

It was the Fall of 1967. Summer was over; the tourists had abandoned the island, the amusement park was closed, and the beach had a slightly forlorn look. Mary took all this in as she crossed the bridge and traveled the length of Center Street. She had never been to Folly Beach, but her mother had spent many summers there in her youth.

Mary had not come to Folly for surf and sand; she was there to deliver a Valentine's card. A card that should have been mailed over thirty years before, and had it been mailed, everything would have been different. Mary was on Folly Beach to deliver the card herself.

Along the way, Mary was destined to meet many people living on that small island. Some of them became determined to help Mary with her quest. Everything could be made right, she knew. It was just a matter of finding Jack.

Folly Beach: Homecoming

3nd Edition 2022

© 2016 by John C. Lasne'

ISBN-13: 978-1530001552

All rights reserved. No part of this publication may be reproduced or transmitted for commercial purposes, except for brief quotations in printed reviews, without written permission from the author.

This book is a work of fiction. Events or incidents included in this work are products of the author's imagination and are used fictionally.

The characters in this novel are fictional. However, there are several based on people I knew while growing up on Folly Beach, relatives of mine, and some new friends I made when I started this project.

Cover and illustrations: Public domain photos and computer graphics by John C. Lasne'

Contact information:
Phone or text 864-230-3036
Email john@jlasne.com
Website www.jlasne.com

Published by John C. Lasne'

John C. Lasne'

Author's Note

They say you can't go home, but I bet the people that utter that phrase didn't grow up on Folly Beach.

I was born on Folly, in my Grandmother's house in 1949. The first sounds I heard were the crashing waves and cries of seagulls. My first smells were of the salty air, fish, and marsh grass. The trips I made on foot and bicycle from my house to the home of my grandmothers, Lottie Blanton, would number hundreds. My Uncle Bud, Preston Blanton Jr., passed on to me the desire to learn as much as I could about everything. Mr. Jesse Porter was a second father to me. The love and time he had for "his boys" has been a guide for many things in my life. I learned the value of hard work from my father, Louis (Frenchie) Lasne, as I spent many hours on his shrimp boat and in his upholstery shop. My mother taught me to love books and art. I could continue naming names, but I don't think I could do justice to them all.

I left Folly Beach many years ago, but it has never left me. Maybe most people remember their childhood home the way that I do. I'll just say this, there is no place on this magnificent planet that I would have rather grown up. Folly Beach I know has changed a great deal, some for the better and some for the worse. One thing will never change, however, Folly Beach will always be a magical place.

Dedication

This book is dedicated to Maebelle Barnette Bazzel and her late husband Milton 'Bubba' Bazzel.

They are the kind of people that make Folly Beach the special place it has always been.

It is my hope that this book and others to come will bring good memories to Maebelle and all the others out there who love Folly Beach.

Maebelle and "Bubba"

John C. Lasne'

Chapter 1

"You look terrible!" He knew they were the wrong words as soon as they left his mouth.

"You always have such a way with the ladies, Carl Thompson." Mary frowned, reached out, grabbed the front of his shirt, and pulled him into the house.

Following her into the living room, he realized why Mary looked as if she had stayed up all night; she had. The small room was littered with papers; some were neatly stacked, while others were placed haphazardly on the coffee table and in a chair.

"I take it I did not need to borrow my brother-in-law's truck today," Carl said while smoothing the front of his shirt. "I thought you broke our movie date so you could pack some of your mother's things for storage. It looks like you did more unpacking than packing."

"I'm really sorry, Carl, but you won't believe what happened." Her voice was so laden with exhaustion that Carl could not be upset with her. He took Mary by the arm and led her to an empty chair. He then carefully cleared a spot on the sofa across from her and took a seat.

"OK, Mary, give me the whole story. Could you tell me what happened here last night?"

Mary smiled wearily and sat back in the chair. "I am sorry, you know, about the truck and the date and all, but..." She picked up a neatly stacked pile of papers and handed them to him.

"Do you know what these are?"

Carl took the papers and glanced at them.

"Letters?" He asked.

"These are love letters. Love letters my mother got from a man I have never even heard of."

"You mean your mother was having an..." Carl started.

"No! My mother was not having an affair... I'm sorry, I didn't mean to yell. She received these letters before she ever met me, I mean my dad..." Mary covered her mouth as a yawn she could not suppress came to the surface.

Carl put up a hand to quiet her, placed the papers on the table, and stood.

"Mary, wait a moment. Let me make a cup of coffee. We could both use one, and then you can tell me all about these mysterious letters."

Without waiting for an answer, Carl headed for the kitchen. When he reached the door, he looked back and saw Mary relax and close her eyes.

"Thanks, Carl, I could use a cup of coffee."

"When was the last time you washed this coffee pot? If the Health Department got wind of this kitchen they would close it down." Not getting an answer Carl swished the old coffee out of the pot. He then busied himself with making a freshly brewed pot.

"I used the high caffeine stuff this time..." As Carl entered the room balancing the two cups, he saw that Mary was fast asleep. Quietly he set her cup on the only clear corner of the coffee table and took a seat on the spot he had cleared before. As he slowly sipped the hot brew, he studied the young lady asleep in the chair.

Mary Lassiter was twenty-six, five-foot-seven, with light brown hair and hazel eyes. She wasn't model thin, but he doubted she weighed more than a hundred and thirty pounds. Mary didn't think she was pretty, but Carl knew better.

Often, at work, he would find himself watching her from across the room. He was fascinated by the way her smile could light up the whole room; the way her eyes sparkled when she laughed.

Carl smiled and placed his empty cup on the floor next to the sofa and continued to study her. Mary was a reporter at the DC Times, where they both worked. Her last series of articles garnered much praise from the editor. She was definitely a confident, self-sufficient woman, but at the moment curled up in the plush overstuffed chair she looked very innocent, almost childlike.

Actually, she was perfect; at least for him anyway, if he could just get her to see it that way. He was sure he loved her and had even told her so the week before while they ate ice cream after their weekly movie date. They both loved the old classics and a local theater that showed them was just down the road from Mary's house.

Mary had accidentally knocked her bowl off the table when he told her how he felt. She seemed very concerned about helping the waiter clean up, and he had decided Mary did not want to talk about it. He understood and did not push the matter. She was obviously not interested in becoming a wife at the moment.

It had not been an easy year for her with her mother getting sick and Mary having to move in with her. Not that she had minded, because Mary had been very close to her mother. Margaret Lassiter's sudden death had taken everyone by surprise.

The fact that Mary's grandmother was in a nursing home more than fifty miles away didn't help either. Mary made the trip to visit at least once a week and Carl tried to visit as often as he could for support.

Carl knew Mary liked him, but if she would ever want to be more than friends, he wasn't sure. Carl was six years older than Mary, wore his dark hair a few inches longer than current fashion, and stood six-foot-two. He had been offered more prestigious jobs at other newspapers but Carl had chosen to stay where he was; he knew Mary was part of the reason he stayed put. He could not imagine reporting to work and her not being there.

"Face it, Carl, old pal. You are smitten with yon damsel." He said softly to himself.

Carl gave a small smile, shrugged his shoulders, and picked up the papers Mary had given him before falling asleep. He settled back to look through them. Mary shifted position and a stray beam of light through the curtains framed her face, catching Carl's attention.

Forcing himself back to reality, Carl returned to the letters in front of him. He flicked on the reading lamp next to the sofa and adjusted the light so it would not bother Mary. He glanced up only when Mary shifted position, but she remained asleep so he returned to reading.

"How long have I been asleep?"

Carl had been so engrossed in the third stack of letters that he was startled by the sound of Mary's voice. He put his watch in the light and squinted at the dial.

"Let's see, it is 11:30 now, so I would say just under two hours."

Mary slowly uncurled from the chair and stood, weaving a bit. She lifted her arms high and stretched. The jogging suit rose to show about half her belly, a very cute belly Carl observed.

"Why did you let me sleep for so long?"

"You were pretty tired, and besides, it gave me a chance to read some of these," Carl said, holding up the letter he had been reading.

"They are quite interesting. Seems your mother and this Jack Young fellow had quite a relationship."

"A summer romance," Mary suggested.

"Well, yes, but for quite a few summers it seems. Tell me, how did you come across these anyway? Were they in that box? Where was it?" Carl pointed to a wooden box about two feet long and eight inches wide. There were dividers every four inches that formed compartments. The box still held some letters that Mary had not read.

"It was in the attic under some boxes. I had this and figured it must fit something. I started looking until I found this box." Mary held up a small key that indeed fit the size and shape of the lock on the box.

"Where did you get the key?"

"It was really weird," Mary said as she sat on the floor at her friend's feet. In the glare of the lamp, with her hair uncombed and hugging her knees with both arms, Carl thought she looked like a little girl.

"Are you listening?" Mary asked, noticing that Carl seemed to be lost in thought.

"Me, yes, of course. I was just noticing how pretty you looked today."

"Actually, 'you look terrible', were the first words out of your mouth." She tried to smooth her hair back into place as she spoke.

"A couple of months ago Mother called me to her room. She had her jewelry box sitting on the bed. Mother said everything in it was mine, but then she took the box and slid it under the bed instead of giving it to me. She said, 'But not quite yet, dear, not yet.' Then she said goodnight and never mentioned it again. Actually, I had forgotten about it until last night. When I remembered how she had made a point of telling me that everything in the box was mine, I had to sort through it. Mostly there was just some inexpensive jewelry, except for Grams' ring. At the bottom, wrapped in tissue, was this key. You would not believe how many different kinds of locks there are in this house. I had just about given up when I found the box under a blanket in a corner of the attic."

"Why would your mother hide her old love letters? She was just a kid spending summers at the beach. I mean seeing each other a couple of months out of the year couldn't make for too hot of a romance." Carl thumbed through the letters in front of him and pulled out the first one Margaret had received. He held it to the light and began to read.

I have met a lot of girls, but you are the neatest one I ever met. I had the best summer ever with you. Please tell me you will be coming back next year.

"Hardly what you would call a sizzling affair," Carl concluded.

"Carl, he was fifteen, and my mother was only thirteen when he started writing. I bet you wrote some cute love letters when you were a kid."

Carl winced at the cut. "How did you know their ages?"

"I am a reporter, remember? Mother had all the letters organized by when she received them. I found the letter where Jack mentioned mother's sixteenth birthday and worked back from there. What are you smiling about?"

"Like mother, like daughter."

"What do you mean?" Mary asked.

"Only a relative of yours would organize their old love letters. It obviously runs in the family since you are the only one I know that keeps their paperclips arranged by size."

"Are you making fun of me?"

"Me? Not at all." Carl's voice took on a serious tone. "One of the reasons you are such a skilled reporter is the way you are able to organize things in your mind while the rest of us depend on a few scraps of paper, which I lose most of the time."

"You wormed your way out of that quite well."

"Hey, when you chew on your foot as much as I do you get proficient at getting it out. So..." Carl reflected for a moment, "it is 1967 and the first letter was postmarked in

1935, so they met over thirty years ago. You think this young budding romance grew into something more?"

"Their relationship lasted more than six years, and it was much more than casual," Mary answered as she reached into the pile and pulled out another of the letters. "Here, listen to this one. It would be... let me see, yes, this is the letter where he mentions my mother's birthday."

Well, Margaret, you aren't a little kid anymore. You are finally sixteen, sweet sixteen. I wish so much I could be there for the party. Just being there in the room with you would be enough for me. You were really pretty when we met three years ago, but now, you are beautiful. I had copies made of the picture we took right before you left this summer so I could put them everywhere and then I can see you all the time. I had one left so here is one for you.

Love,
Jack

"Quite a smooth talker for one so young. Okay, I guess you could say things had gotten a wee bit heavier," Carl said as he leaned over to take the photograph from Mary. He held the photograph up to the light and then looked at Mary.

"Your mother looks just like you at this age. Very pretty."

Mary took the picture back and placed it next to a pile of other photos. "Is it too late to make up for that first comment about the way I look?"

"How am I doing?"

"You're a fast learner, but you still have some ways to go," Mary smiled and then turned back to the letters stacked around the chair as Carl headed back to the kitchen.

A moment later, Carl handed Mary her coffee and returned to his place on the sofa.

"Jack wrote a letter every week telling my mother about everything that was happening on the island," Mary explained as she took a careful sip of the hot brew and leaned back in the chair.

"Whew, that's a lot of letters. I guess that is why the box is so substantial. Did you say island?" Carl asked.

"Yes, Folly Beach is where my mother used to spend her summers. It is a small island about ten miles from Charleston, South Carolina."

"That's not exactly close to here. Why was your family traveling all the way down there to go to the beach?"

"I guess a lot of families do that. They rent a house for the whole summer in some out-of-the-way place. I never even knew Folly Beach existed before now. I don't understand why my mother never mentioned the beach or Jack. It is so strange." Mary picked up some of the letters and shuffled through them. She chose one and unfolding it, she began to read.

Imagine how lucky I am. My house being right next door to yours, and all. Too bad y'all can't stay here year round. The house seems so lonely being boarded up all winter.

"How come you never ventured down to, what was it, Folly Beach when you were young?" Carl questioned.

"I don't know. Maybe because my father died so young and we couldn't afford it. Maybe the answer is in one of these letters," Mary said, sweeping her hand across the box of remaining letters.

"Jack wrote a lot of letters to my mother and I have to assume she wrote back. They were really young and I guess something happened to break it off. But Carl, they were in love; I don't mean just teenage infatuation, I mean real love. Here, listen to this letter."

My Dearest Margaret,

I know that others cannot understand how we could really be in love when most of the year we don't even get to see each other. But, it is just like you said in your last letter. The heart doesn't measure love the way miles are measured. Even if I never saw you again, my love for you would never die.

"He wrote that when my mother was a senior in high school. I don't understand why my mother kept it a secret for so many years. I am sure she loved dad, but they were only married for three years before he was killed in an automobile accident. I didn't even really remember my father so why wouldn't she mention Jack and why didn't she ever get married again?"

"Both valid questions. What about those?" Carl asked, pointing at the box.

"The letters I have read so far span up through high school, so I imagine those continue on from there. I was just getting ready to start on them when you arrived."

Mary unfolded her legs and stiffly got to her feet. She bent and stretched to try and unkink her body. "It has been a long night. I have read so much my eyes hurt."

"I'll read a couple to you if you would like," Carl volunteered. He plucked the rest of the letters from the old box and returned to the sofa. Mary took her place back in the chair. Carl took the first letter from the pile and removed it from the envelope, unfolded it, and holding it under the light began to read.

Dear Margaret,
Your college registration worked out well, I hope. I had sure hoped you would be coming to the College of Charleston. However, I can understand why your parents want you to stay closer to home for a while. If my father didn't need me to work on the shrimp boat, I would be up there in a minute. He knows I want to come and said he would get a replacement as soon as possible. Unfortunately, there are few men that work as cheaply as I do (free for the most part).

Carl read the rest of the letter, which contained information about what had been happening on the island. Obviously, Mary's mother had gotten to know several of the locals during her visits. When he had finished, he took another from the pile.

My Dearest Margaret,
I miss you so much. I wish it was summer. My life will begin again as soon as you cross that bridge. I admit that I've been jealous of all the guys at college. They get to see

you almost every day. My father plans to hire someone to operate the boat for him. That means I won't have to captain the boat and we can have plenty of time together. In fact, I am thinking of entering college myself. I sent for the information last week. I plan to start after summer if I can. Keep your eyes open for a cheap place for me to live, because I am coming up there to be with you!

"So, the plot thickens," Carl said, sipping his coffee. "Your mother's boyfriend can't bear to be away from her anymore. Moving away from the ocean would be quite a change. Would you like me to read another one? Wait, I have a better idea. Why don't you get a shower and eat something and then we can finish these?"

Mary rubbed her eyes and smiled.

"That sounds like a terrific idea. I am rather hungry; sooooo, how about fixing us some of those world-famous pancakes of yours? But don't read any more of the letters while I'm not here."

"Alright, you get all prettied up and I'll cook us up some breakfast. I am kind of hungry too."

"So we're back to how I look again, are we?" Mary joked wearily, as she headed to her bedroom and a beckoning hot shower.

Chapter 2

Mary let the steaming water bring her back to life as Carl whipped up some breakfast. When she came out of the bedroom, she was dressed in jeans and a cardigan and looked fresh and ready to continue.

Carl had brought the unread letters to the kitchen table and laid them in the middle. Mary reached for one as she finished her second helping of pancakes. Carl tried to give her some more, but she shook her head.

"I couldn't eat another one. They were great, though." She reached over and took Carl's hand and squeezed it.

"You are a true friend, Carl. I can always count on you to be there if I need something."

Carl winced at the friend part, but he just smiled and carried her plate to the sink. Mary was not ready yet to change her life. She was on the fast track and he couldn't blame her for wanting to put her career first, at least for now.

Mary took the letter out of the envelope and began to read it to herself. It was a lot like the letter she read before taking a shower. She folded it up and placed it at the bottom of the pile. The next letter was much longer and she was going through it for the second time when she realized Carl was talking to her. "… and so what exciting things have happened down at the beach?"

Mary took a sip of coffee and motioned for Carl to sit at the table. "Listen to this."

Dear Margaret,

I don't know how to say this. I had planned on coming up in two weeks and preregistering for school, but it won't be possible now. I feel so terrible because it was supposed to be a surprise. My dad has taken a turn for the worse and I have to stay and run the boat. The doctor says he doesn't think dad will get better, at least not enough to work full time on the boat. Mom said she thought he should sell it, but if he did where would the money for them to live on come from? She has told me I can still start school this semester, but I am sure that won't be possible. You will understand that I can't leave now, at least for a while. I don't mean to pressure you, but would you consider changing to a school down here so we could be together?

I love you.
Jack

"Sounds like things are starting to get pretty complicated. He can't leave his parents to fend for themselves. I am sure your grandparents were not thrilled with the idea of their daughter moving so far away to be with her boyfriend," Carl stated. He took the seat next to her.

"He was more than a boyfriend, Carl," Mary said softly and continued to read.

It isn't fun to see the girl you plan to marry so rarely. Have you told your parents yet? I am not sure how they will take it. Sometimes I think they feel like I am not good enough for you. The thing is, they are right. What could I possibly do to deserve someone as amazing as you? If I had all the money in the world, I could not buy this feeling I have in my heart.

All I have to do is whisper your name or remember your laugh and I feel happiness I can't even describe.

Your love.

Jack

"Marry? They were much more than just friends. At least Jack thought so. What happened next?"

Mary carefully folded the letter and placed it back inside the envelope. She made sure to place it back in the pile so that it would be in the proper sequence. She then unfolded the next letter and began to read.

My dearest Margaret,

I miss you so much. I am not sure I understand why you can't come down for the school break like you planned. You didn't say in your last letter if you had told your parents that we planned to get married someday. Is that why you can't come down? I had arranged for Scotty to take over the boat for a couple of days so we could be together. I even walked over to the house and aired it out. I am not sure how to ask this but, well, have you changed your mind about us? I mean about our marriage. I know your father probably thinks I am just a dumb old fisherman or beach bum or something. However, if he only knew how much I love you he might understand.

Mary set the letter back on the table after putting it into its envelope.

"You never met my grandfather did you, Carl? He was really nice, but I can imagine he would be somewhat upset about mother marrying someone that wasn't a doctor, lawyer...."

"Or Indian chief. I get the point." Carl said with understanding. "Do you think they told your mother she couldn't marry Jack? Your mother didn't seem like the type to be denied something she really wanted."

Mary didn't answer but took the next letter near the end of the stack. When she took it out they could both see immediately that it was one page and very short.

Margaret,

Why didn't you answer my last letter? I need to know how things stand between us. Please tell me that you love me so much that nothing can keep us apart. I'll check the mail every day for your letter.

I Love You

Mary returned the letter to its envelope. Carl took her cup and refilled it without saying anything. He then sat back down and picked up the letter that remained unread. "Is this the last one?"

"Yes. Mother put the date she received the letters down here on the corner. That's how I arranged them. Read it for me Carl. I don't think I can do it."

Carl removed the letter and began to read.

My Dearest Margaret,

Folly Beach: Homecoming

Writing this is the hardest thing I have ever done in my life. Please believe me when I say I love you more than anything or anyone I could ever love...

Mary was sitting bolt upright listening so intently that she seemed in a trance. Carl touched her hand and she jumped.

"Are you alright?"

"Yes, I'm fine. Read the rest." She smiled a halfhearted smile and patted his hand. "I'm fine, really."

I have tried to put my feeling into words a hundred times, but I can never find just the right way to say it. I guess I'll have to do the best I can. I had planned for so long to have you by my side for the rest of my life. Maybe you never felt the same way I did and perhaps it was unfair for me to assume that you did. My father is very close to death and I realize now that the job of providing for my mother has fallen to me. College is out of the question for now, probably forever. Luckily, the boat is mostly paid for and in good condition. I have often thought that it would be good for me to get away from here, at least for a while. There are many places I would like to see; things I would like to do. Most of all, I had hoped to join you at school. We both know that is not possible now. I am sure your parents think we are from two different worlds and that neither of us would be happy in the others world. All I know is that I cannot leave here for a long time.

Margaret, more than anything I want to ask you to come to me and be my wife. You could go to college down here. I even believe that you would if I begged you to. I can't do that. Not because I am too proud, but because it has to be your decision, made on your own, after you consider all the consequences.

My dearest love, the choice is yours, even though it may not seem fair to lay it at your feet alone. I'll not write to you again until I receive your answer. Valentine's Day is two weeks from now. If I do not hear from you by then, I'll know the answer and I'll understand. Margaret, my love for you is so great that I would rather live without you, than for you to ever have one regret about your decision.

I do not blame anyone for what has come between us. Having loved you will be more than payment for the pain of living without you. My heart aches with a sadness that is so heavy it nearly drags me to the ground. If our love is not to be, we will both live on; but I do not think I'll have enough left for another.

Margaret, if I do not hear from you, this will be the last letter you will receive from me. If this is the end, I release you from any commitment; but I'll never release you from my heart.

I'll Always Love You
Jack

When Carl looked at Mary, she was staring into space and there were tears in her eyes. He had been moved by the intensity of the letter himself. They sat silent for a long while and then Carl put the letter back in the pile.

"That's it then," Carl said with finality. "Since there are no more letters, your mother must have decided to end the relationship." He got to his feet and placed a consoling hand on her shoulder. "Come on, let me help you pack these up."

Mary did not answer and sat still, her eyes focused on something miles away.

"I know this has all been a big surprise, but remember your mother did get married and seemed like a happy woman. So really it didn't turn out so bad. Almost everyone has a romance that goes south," Carl said, attempting to console her.

Mary gave a halfhearted smile and slid her chair back.

"You're right, Carl, it... well, it just seems so sad is all. They were really in love. You could tell by the letters. I just don't understand what happened. Why would mother just drop him like that? I wish I could see just one letter that she wrote him so I could see how she felt. If only she had told me about him, I could have asked her why." Mary gathered up some of the letters and put a rubber band around them.

Carl picked up a paper sack that sat next to the table and asked. "What is this?"

"That was stuff from Grams' desk. Some old papers and things like that." Mary said in a disinterested voice.

Carl pulled a handful of papers from the bag and leafed through them.

"What do you want to do with these? I mean it is a little too late to mail them now." Carl said as he held up several envelopes kept together by a big paper clip.

"What are they?" Mary asked.

"Well, this one is a telephone bill and there is a water bill and..."

"I don't understand. I paid my bills already."

Carl laughed and waved the bills in the air. "They aren't yours. I have a feeling your Grandmother probably had a hard time explaining the late notices. These were stuck in this bag with a bunch of other papers. I would imagine someone was supposed to mail them, but somehow they got mixed up with the other papers and packed away."

"I'll bet grandfather was mad. He would have considered a late payment notice a personal insult. Mother was the same way. She always paid her bills long before they were due just to be sure they were on time. Anyway, give them here and I'll look through them later and see if there is anything I should keep."

Mary gave a sigh as she placed the letters they had been reading back into the box.

"I guess I'll never know just what happened. I could try and ask Grams, but most of the time she doesn't even know who I am." It had been months since Mary's grandmother had been moved from an assisted living residence to a nursing home.

Mary took the old bills from Carl, and as she did a smaller envelope slipped out and fell on the floor. Carl quickly picked it up and started to hand it to Mary when he stopped and looked closer at it.

"This is interesting."

"What is it?"

"I'm not sure, but I think it is some kind of card and it is addressed to Jack Young."

Mary jumped to her feet and grabbed for the card so fast she spilled her coffee. Carl, began dabbing at the little brown river with a napkin. He heard Mary opening the card as he lost the battle and coffee began trickling to the floor.

Carl looked up to ask Mary to hand him some paper towels but stopped short when he saw her face. She was staring at the card, which had a big red heart on the front. He could not remember seeing her so shaken before.

"Mary. Mary, are you alright?" Carl stepped close to Mary as she read the card in a low whisper.

My Dearest Jack,

Please forgive me for not answering sooner. Mother wasn't too upset when I told her that we were going to get married. Getting married! That sounds so beautiful. She believes I do love you and finally said she and daddy would give their blessings! I am planning on transferring to The College of Charleston next semester.

Mom said this wouldn't get to you before Valentine's Day. She says you might be having second thoughts by then, but I know you won't. She said I should not write you again until I hear from you, in case you changed your mind. I couldn't believe she would think you could change your mind!! After all, you love me almost as much as I love you. I can't wait to be Mrs. Jack Young! Please write back SOOOON! I LOVE YOU! I LOVE YOU!

Your Margaret

Mary did not move for a long moment after she finished reading the card. Carl moved to put his arm around her, but she backed away. He did not take offense because he knew she sometimes pulled into herself when she was upset or faced a serious challenge. At first, it had bothered him because he always wanted to comfort her, but he had learned to accept it.

When Mary did finally speak, her voice shook a little. "She wanted to marry him; marry Jack. She thought the valentine had been mailed. Jack never got this card. What they both must have thought!"

Mary brushed a tear from her eyes and read the letter again. She was exhausted and had lost her usual stalwart composure.

"Mary, why don't you sit down. I have never seen you like this before. Think about it; This card is more than thirty years old. Everything that went on then is ancient history."

"Ancient history! This..." She held the card up. "This was their life! This was their dream! Imagine how they felt, Carl. When Jack didn't get this card he thought my mother was willing to call it all off just like that, without even writing to tell him. Mother must have figured Jack was willing to forget her just because he hadn't gotten the card until after Valentine's Day! She must have thought Grandmother was right and Jack had changed his mind. It's so sad Carl."

As if she realized how close to the edge she had gotten, Mary regained her composure. She walked slowly back to the table and sat down.

"I didn't mean to upset you, Mary. You know with the ancient history stuff. I just meant..." Carl stammered.

"It's OK, Carl, I know what you meant. I shouldn't have yelled at you. You are right, it is old news. It happened a long time ago and there is nothing to be done now. Mother is gone and for all I know, Jack is too."

"He could have a wife and six kids," Carl conjectured.

When Mary looked at Carl he saw something in her eyes he had never seen before. She spoke softly and very calmly, "I don't think so, Carl." Then she smiled and added, "Come on and help me get these things packed up and put away."

Carl helped her gather up the letters without speaking. He could see that her heart was heavy.

After collecting the letters from the table, they spent the next half-hour placing all the letters back into the box in order. When she had finished, Mary slowly closed the box and fastened the lock. To Carl, it reminded him of the slow deliberate way one would close a coffin.

"I guess I should get that truck back. I don't think we are going to need it today, do you?" Carl questioned.

Mary glanced up at the clock and was startled to see that it was already mid-afternoon.

"I'm so sorry, Carl. You went to all that trouble for nothing. Do you think you could get it again next Saturday? I am putting most of the stuff in storage until I decide what to do with the house, probably sell it and get a condo closer to work."

Carl could see that she really wasn't thinking about the house since she never took her eyes off the box.

"Sure, I can use it anytime you want, but are you sure you want to try it again then. Remember, we have the subpoena to testify before the Grand Jury next Friday. You know how nerve-racking those things can be. You can be sure that Senator Billings' attorney is going to try and make it look like we have a vendetta against him," Carl said as he reminded Mary of their court date.

"You better believe I have it in for that slumlord. Here he lives in one of the fanciest places in DC and he rents out low-income housing full of rats and roaches. You can be sure I'll let the Grand Jury know everything. I want big blowups of the pictures we took last month, so everyone there is able to see what kind of place he owns."

Carl was gratified that the upcoming hearing had snapped her back to normal. For the next half-hour, they talked about what they expected to happen at the hearing. Carl pretended not to notice that Mary kept glancing at the box as he continued to tidy the room until he heard her sigh. When he turned back, she had pushed the box of letters over against the wall. Mary stood, stretched and then walked over and gave Carl a big hug.

"What was that for?" Carl asked, a little surprised since Mary was usually reserved in her outward show of affection.

"For being such a good friend, giving up your Saturday and all to help me," She answered with a smile. Carl heard something in her voice that made him bold. He lifted her face by placing his hand under her chin and stared into her eyes.

"Mary, I know you don't feel the way about me that I do about you…"

She started to say something, but Carl placed a finger over her lips.

"There is nothing I'll not do for you regardless of how things go with us. No pressure. Understand that I am here for you no matter what. Now, I don't want you to say anything. Just nod your head if you understand."

Mary affirmed that she understood by nodding in agreement and then they both smiled.

"Why don't I take the truck back and pick you up around seven and we will get something to eat?" Carl suggested.

"That is a nice offer, but if you don't mind, I am going to crash early tonight and make up for the sleep I didn't get last night. I'll just pick up a little around here and eat a sandwich or something."

"I can stay and help for a while yet," Carl volunteered.

"No, you have done enough already. You go home and I'll be alright." Mary responded, not really sure that she wanted him to go, but knowing it was the best thing for him to do. She was just too mixed up and emotional right then to pursue these feelings she was having for him.

Mary took his arm and walked him to the door. Carl was almost out the door when he stopped and turned back to Mary.

"You know, if we were married, I would already be home," Carl said with a big grin.

"No pressure, huh?" Mary laughed and shoved him outside.

Carl was halfway to the truck when Mary called out to him. "Want to take me to lunch tomorrow?"

Carl pretended to think hard while scratching his head before he answered.

"How about we catch early Mass and take a trip out into the country? The weather is supposed to be perfect tomorrow. There are a couple great restaurants I have heard Jerry talk about. I'll give him a call tonight and see if he has any suggestions."

Jerry Willabee was the entertainment writer for their paper and was renowned for his ability to find out of the way places that were more than worth the trip to get there. Carl had a 1967 Camaro convertible he loved to drive out to the countryside and the two of them had spent many Sunday afternoons cruising the rural roads outside of the city.

"It's a date," Mary answered with a warm smile.

Chapter 3

Sunday morning began as every September day should, and got better by the hour. By the time Carl and Mary were on the road, around 10 am, it was warm enough to enjoy riding with the top down. There were few other cars on the road as they headed out of the city. The powerful V-8 rumbled softly as the scenery turned from buildings and parking lots to trees and farmhouses. It had always amazed them both just how quickly one could leave the hustle and bustle of the Nation's Capital behind. Mary reclined her seat back a few inches and closed her eyes. When Carl took a corner fast, she was pushed against the door. It was always this way when they were on a country drive.

For the first half hour, he would push the car well past legal limits. It was as if he were taking the frustrations of the world and challenging them to a race; a race he intended to win. She was not worried as the rear of the car slid when he punched the throttle out of a turn. Mary had seen his bookshelf loaded with a number of trophies he had won in American Amateur Road Races.

After a few minutes, she opened her eyes and watched him maneuver the car. Carl was intent on driving and was totally unaware he was being studied. Mary knew that was the way he was; when he was concentrating he seemed able to block out everything else but what he had to get done.

She thought back to the first time they met. It was the second semester of her senior year of college and this handsome man had walked into her journalism class as a guest speaker. Although the reporter was only a few years older than some of the students, everyone was so impressed that a "real" reporter from a "real" newspaper was coming to talk to them.

Carl had talked about the excitement of being a reporter and how he believed that everyone had the right to know what was going on in the world. He had also warned them about the boring aspects of the job. He told of the endless hours on the telephone trying to line up an interview or tracking down facts that might end up being useless. All the negatives seemed to pale next to the love the man speaking to them had for his job.

Mary had approached Carl in the hall after class and introduced herself as a potential journalist. He had been polite, given her a business card, and told her to let him know when she was ready to begin her career and he would try to "help her."

She smiled as she remembered the look on his face when six months later she was standing at his desk holding that same card. Mary was sure he had never expected to see her again, but he recovered quickly. As she got to know him she learned that Carl had a knack for appraising the situation and making snap decisions.

"So you really want to be a reporter? Well, let me have a moment with the editor while you take a seat at the desk here." Carl said, with a knowing smile. He had dealt with this situation before.

Mary had barely seated herself when Carl plopped a huge Metropolitan DC phone book down in front of her and said.

"While I am gone you can help me out with a story. Make a list of all the Smiths that live on the north side of the metro." Carl said with a slight smile.

Surprised, Mary opened the book to the Smiths and was amazed to see there were several hundred and street addresses were given but they were not broken down by area.

"How can I tell which area of town they live in?" Mary asked with exasperation.

Carl had already grabbed his jacket and started out the door. He called over his shoulder.

"Maps in the bottom left drawer."

Carl returned an hour later carrying an immense bag of Chinese food, which he set down on the desk in front of Mary.

"How are we doing?" He asked.

Mary slid a large yellow notepad across the desk in his direction.

"Here is the list arranged in the quickest line of travel from here and back, forming a kind of circle so it will take the least amount of time. I also made a note on a couple of these as to the possibility that you might not want to go there without a backup. They are in some rough areas and..."

Carl smiled and slid the bag of food in her direction. "Young lady, you are hired."

"But I thought you had to talk to the editor first," Mary said surprised.

"No need. He already told me I could hire an assistant when I found the right one." Carl answered as he began unloading the bag.

"And I am the right one?" Mary asked, feeling almost giddy.

"You may be too right. As efficient as you are, someday I might be working for you." Carl answered as he opened a box of Chow Mien.

Mary laughed and peered into the bag. "Did you get any egg rolls?'

From that moment on they had become a team. Mary, with her meticulous organization and planning, and Carl, with his instinct and fearless pursuit of a story, had proved to work perfectly together.

The Camaro's tires squealed as Carl rushed the car into a sweeping corner. He downshifted to third gear and held the car in his lane. As the road straightened Carl punched the gas pedal to the floor. Mary felt herself being pushed back into the seat. She could not keep from watching the speedometer as it quickly climbed: 70...80...90...100...110... The car was still accelerating when Carl suddenly lifted his foot. Mary felt the pressure ease as the speed decreased until they were traveling exactly the posted speed limit. Carl's hands relaxed on the wheel and all tension had left him. When he turned to look at Mary he had a little boy smile on his face. "Was that fun or what?"

"You noticed I didn't spend a lot of time on my hair this morning. But seriously, wouldn't you get a million-dollar ticket or something if you got caught going that fast?" Mary asked; glad to be traveling at a sane speed again.

"Don't fret the ticket thing. I have connections with all the cops in the area." Carl said and Mary was not surprised. In fact, every police officer within a hundred miles of the city knew who Carl was.

Mary gave a little shudder as she remembered what had happened the year before.

Carl had received a tip from one of his cop friends that there was going to be a big bust early on a Saturday morning. A chop shop had been set up in an abandoned warehouse. Mary and Carl were sitting in the front row of a car lot where they could see all the action. His new Chevelle blended in the other cars. They had a view straight down the street with the warehouse on their left and the police on their right.

One of the officers was moving toward the door for the warehouse office when a shot rang out and he slumped to the middle of the road. Several other cops started to rush to his aid but were driven back by a hail of bullets.

The next instance, Carl reached across Mary and pushed her door open. "Quick! Get out!" He ordered as he shoved her from the car.

As soon as she was clear Carl started the car, slammed it into first, popped the clutch and floored the gas pedal at the same time. The car smoked the tires as it left the lot and jumped the curb.

Mary could only watch, stunned, as Carl shot down the street. He slammed on brakes and slid to a stop between the downed policeman and the bullets that were coming from both sides of the street. Carl slid across the seat, pushed the passenger door open, and dropped to the ground next to the injured man as the police stopped shooting.

A hand grabbed his collar and one of the officers dragged him to safety as another did the same to his wounded comrade, protected by Carl's car. The criminals decided they couldn't win the gun battle and the gunfire suddenly stopped. As they were led from the building in handcuffs Carl walked over and looked at what was left of his car.

"Are you crazy?" Mary yelled as she rushed over to him.

"I wonder if my insurance covers something like this?" Carl wondered out loud.

Carl was praised for his heroic action, but in his usual manner, he shrugged it off. The car dealership that had sold him his Chevelle offered to take it in trade for the car he was driving now. His son was a rookie on the police force and had been in the shootout. Despite his protest, Carl was handed the keys to his new car in an even trade. Needless to say, everyone on the police force was grateful for what he had done and they showed it.

Mary was brought back to the present by the rap of the dual exhaust as Carl shifted down a gear.

"I have a bit of a surprise for you," Carl said as he turned off the small country road onto an even smaller gravel road that quickly disappeared into a grove of immense trees. The branches of the trees intertwined to form a canopy that almost blocked out the sun. This was a new road to Mary, although she would have guessed that Carl had taken her down every road in the countryside at least once. She was about to quiz Carl again about where they were eating when she saw a sign. It was shaped like a boat of some kind and on the side was painted the words "Captain Hap's Landing."

As they rounded a curve a dilapidated building came into view. It was situated on the edge of a small lake of clear blue water. As they drew closer Mary could see that the building was only built to look run down, but was instead rather new. It was finished to look like an old fishing dock complete with the recorded sounds of sea birds.

Since they were early for lunch nearly every parking spot was available and Carl pulled the Camaro right up to the front door.

"Where did you find out about this place? I have never even heard of it before." Mary asked, taking in the décor.

"Well, believe it or not, I came across it last night while I was doing some research," Carl explained.

"You were researching seafood restaurants?" Mary asked.

Carl hesitated for a moment and then gave a mischievous smile. "Well, actually I was searching for information on Folly Beach and this place was in a short article."

Mary smiled as she remembered the way his place had looked the first time she had dropped by with takeout for them to eat during some research on drugs in the area middle schools. Books and magazines filled shelves and notebooks were stacked in piles around all along the walls. Carl even had a microfilm viewer. She never knew how he could find anything, but he could always put his hand on any information he needed.

"Before you say anything, let me ask you one question. How long did it take for you to open that box and read the letters again after I left?"

Mary started to protest, but instead she touched Carl tenderly on the arm. "I intended to put the letters away, I really did. I just couldn't get the whole thing off my mind, though. It all seemed... I don't know..."

"You wish you could do something, but you know it has been so long that there really isn't anything you can do?" Carl finished.

"You do know me too well Carl," Mary said, blushing slightly.

Carl looked at her intensely and said, "Mary, I'll never know you well enough. Not well enough for me, anyway."

Before Mary could say anything he undid his seat belt and added, "I tell you what. Let's talk inside. We should have our pick of tables if we don't wait until the Baptist get out of Church."

Carl got out and Mary waited for him to come around and open her door. He liked playing the gentleman, and she enjoyed the special attention. She had often marveled at how different her friend could be on a given occasion. He was tough and fearless, sometimes, seeming unafraid of physical danger, and yet she had seen him cry when a child was injured and there was nothing he could do to help.

Carl shut the door and they started toward the restaurant. Abruptly he stopped and stepped back to the car. He reached down into the back floorboard and pulled out a large yellow envelope. He held it up for Mary to see. "I almost forgot."

"What is it?" Mary asked curiously.

"You'll see. Look, they are waiting for us." Carl motioned toward the entrance where a pretty blond wearing jeans and waders stood smiling.

"Welcome to Capn' Hap's," She said with a toothy smile. "Is this your first visit with us?"

"Yes, we came out from the Capital. This is a very unusual place." Carl answered as he motioned for the girl to lead the way.

Mary observed everything as they followed the girl into the building. Old fishing nets hung from the ceiling, filled with sea shells and other nautical things. Oars hung on the walls and polished brass lamps lit the inside of the building. The wood was rough-hewn and looked old.

"Would you like to sit inside or out on the boat? Since you are the first ones here you have your choice. The boat is very popular and the weather is perfect today." The girl suggested.

Mary was about to ask what kind of boat there was to eat on when she spotted it. A fairly long dock stuck out into the lake and at the end of the walkway a large white boat was tied. It was, at least, fifty-foot long and was high in the front and a flat deck toward the back. Cables and ropes, as if a spider had spent the evening creating a crazy web, seemed to go everywhere and nowhere.

"What is..." Mary started to ask.

"A shrimp boat," Carl said knowingly.

"Shrimp boat. How do you know what a shrimp boat is? Have you even ever seen a shrimp boat?" Mary asked suspiciously.

"Ahh no, but... I can read. Remember I told you how I found this place? Well, the article mentioned that the restaurant had a shrimp boat tied to a dock on the lake. I thought you might like to see what a shrimp boat looked like in real life. Besides, the article said that this very boat had once been tied up, I think that is what you call it, at a dock across the river from Folly Beach. I thought you would be interested, you know with what you read about Jack and all." Carl explained.

While they had been talking, they had been following the girl in the big boots down the dock and now they stood in front of the shrimp boat.

On the deck, three sets of tables and chairs for two were arranged far enough apart so that there was privacy. In the cabin that sat toward the front of the boat, they could see another girl, dressed similarly to their escort. Carl assumed she must be the waitress.

"Will this be alright with you?" The first girl asked.

"Yes, this will be delightful," Mary answered and then walked across a gangplank that went from the dock to the boat. Carl guided Mary to the table that was nearest the rear of the boat.

"Will the stern be ok with you?" Carl questioned.

"The what?" Mary asked.

"This is the stern, or back end, of the boat. That is what you are supposed to call it so everyone won't think you are a landlubber. See, I told you I can read." Carl explained.

Mary laughed and sat in the chair Carl had offered her. "I must say I am impressed."

"Oh, that's nothing. The front of this thing is called the bow. The side that is toward the lake is the starboard side, and the port side is next to the dock. If you like I can tell you about the mast and transom and other nautical stuff like that?" Carl explained, proud of his newfound knowledge.

"It is very fascinating, but why not wait until we order? Our waitress is coming." Mary interrupted.

As Carl took his seat the waitress laid a menu in front of each of them. After she had taken their order they sat looking out across the lake without speaking for several minutes.

"You can't just pack them up and forget them, can you? The letters, I mean?" Carl asked knowingly. Although it was a question, Carl's tone was more of a declaration.

"I tried, Carl, but it is like... well, like some of the stories we have worked on. You know, we get just enough information to make us wonder what the rest of the story is. It's like the puzzle you talked about that time you came to my class. Do you remember?" Mary asked.

"In a room, an unfinished puzzle is sitting on a table. It has been completed just enough to be interesting, but not enough to show what the picture is. Most people will look at the puzzle and wonder for a moment and then just go on about their business. Occasionally someone comes along and sees the unfinished puzzle and has to know how it will look finished. If all else fails that person will sit down at the table and finish the puzzle in order to know. They have no choice; it is imperative to know what the puzzle is destined to be. That person, the one who can't walk away, has a journalist's soul." Carl repeated the little analogy he had given when he had visited Mary's college class.

"That is how it is with these letters. I have to know more; is Jack still alive, how would he react to the truth, what he is like, the things I never knew about my mother and her childhood, all that and more. It's just like that puzzle Carl; incomplete. I know it would be almost impossible to find all the answers, but I just feel I need to try."

Mary stopped talking as the waitress appeared with their food. The seafood tasted even better than it smelled, so both of them took the time to eat some of everything they had on their plate. Neither one of them had said anything for a few minutes when suddenly Carl snapped his fingers and reached under his chair. He pulled out the large envelope he had taken from the car and opened it. Then he slid out a smaller envelope.

"I almost forgot. I thought you might like to take a look at these." Carl said, holding the envelope up for Mary to see. He took some photographs held together by a large rubber band from the envelope and laid them on the table next to Mary's plate.

"What are these?" Mary asked, as she carefully picked up the photos.

"Take a look, I think you will be pleasantly surprised," Carl said with a smile.

Chapter 4

The photos showed a dilapidated multi-story building. Trash was piled high on the curb outside and several decaying cars, sans wheels, squatted on the road. Throughout the building were broken windows, giving the impression that it was a war-torn country. Other photos showed the same building from different angles and from the inside. An immense rat stared at the camera, seemingly unafraid, from the steps in one shot. One photo showed the inside of a where the plaster had fallen from the ceiling and walls. In one corner a filthy mattress lay on the floor with a young girl sleeping as cockroaches crawled across her bare legs.

"Senator Billings' complex?" Mary asked, with rising excitement and disgust.

"Exactly. A real vacation resort. And not only that, remember the honorable Senator swore in his deposition that he had purchased said resort as an investment. He had never even been within a mile of the aforementioned complex. Well, take a closer look at this." Carl said as he pulled another picture from the envelope and handed it to Mary.

Carl leaned over and pointed at one corner of the photo. "See that car? Looks a bit fancy for that side of town wouldn't you say?"

Carl passed another photograph to Mary. This one was larger, an obvious blowup of the car he had pointed out.

It was rather grainy, being enlarged so much, but she could make out a long black automobile with dark tinted windows. One of the back windows was rolled down and you could see that a conversation was taking place. This conversation was between a man in the car and two burly, rough-looking characters. The face in the window was very fuzzy. Mary stared at it and a smile crept across her face.

"It's Senator Billings!" Mary exclaimed loudly, and then covered her mouth and looked around. It appeared there was no one else on the boat, which she was happy to see.

"I stopped by the office last night and looked through some of the photos that Fred took when he was on a stakeout. Do you remember Fred? As a freelance photographer, he worked with us on a few projects. I had him take photos of every person that came within two blocks of the building for a week. Bob Jackson blew several of them up for me after I realized who might be in the picture. I can't wait to see the good Senator's face when I show up at the hearing with these. In case you didn't recognize the two gentlemen standing talking to the Senator the one on the right was arrested and charged with beating up an old man; an old man that happens to live at Living Gardens Housing Complex, and the same old man that took a petition door to door trying to get something done about the conditions." Carl finished his explanation.

"This is great! That slime ball just might get what is coming to him this time." Mary said triumphantly.

"We will know in a couple of weeks. My sources say there will be hearings on the entire matter. Finish eating and I have another surprise for you." Carl instructed.

They finished eating just as cars began filling the parking lot. In a few minutes, there would be a long wait for a table.

"Can I get you some dessert or coffee?" The waitress asked as she took their empty plates.

"Coffee sounds good to me, how about you Carl?" Mary asked.

"I hate to keep anyone else from having a table," Carl said.

"There is a small table at the bow that is too small for eating, but perfect for coffee. Would you like me to show you?" The waitress suggested.

The lunch rush was now in full swing but their new table was the only one on the bow and they enjoyed the isolation.

It was a beautiful day and Mary felt more relaxed than she had in a long time. She didn't want to think about mysterious romances or lost love. However, everything from the day before kept pushing its way past her other thoughts to the front of her mind. Sitting on the deck of a shrimp boat, Mary couldn't help but wonder if her mother had been on a boat just like this one with Jack. Carl had said her name several times before she realized he had been talking to her.

"I'm sorry, Carl. I guess I was daydreaming. This is such a wonderful place. You said you had another surprise for me." Mary said.

"Actually, I have two surprises. The first is this..." Carl once again retrieved the large envelope from under his chair and laid it on the table. "In that envelope is all, I repeat all, the information available on Folly Beach that I could find."

Carl shifted into his formal speaking voice as he began quoting statistics from a sheet of paper he pulled from the envelope.

"Folly Island, the proper name, is only six and one-half miles long and just one-half miles wide at its widest point. It used to be a lot bigger, but it is a barrier island. Thus, its sole purpose in life is to wash away, something it has done quite well over the years. The first mention of Folly Island was in 1696 and...let's see, the population has ranged from a couple dozen to a high of around thirteen hundred over the years. Those are the full-time residents, of course. During the summer months, it grows quite a bit."

"Like when my mother would go for the summer," Mary added, getting excited.

"Exactly, in fact, there are more empty houses than people some of the time." Carl agreed.

"You are amazing Carl. One minute you tell me I should just put all this behind me. The next thing I know you are an expert on the life and times of Folly Beach." Mary laughed, as she reached for the envelope.

"Hey, I am a reporter remember? Besides, I am not emotionally involved, so I can be objective, right? I am not an expert by any means. Most of the information I could gather was about local politics as such..." Carl reached back inside the envelope and pulled out several sheets of paper. "I did find a couple of interesting pictures. This one is of the boardwalk that stretches along the front of the beach."

Mary eagerly took the photo and studied it. She could see some people lying on the beach and others either leaning against the railing or walking around. The photo was dated due to the dress, particularly the modest bathing suits.

"It looks pretty much the same now, except for the bathing suits. I saved the most exciting for last. Here is a newspaper photo taken of a group of kids around the same time as this summer romance your mother was involved in. And here are a couple of photos of how it looks now."

Mary looked at the prints Carl had laid on the table in front of her. Jack began to point out some things in the most recent photo. "See behind them here is the boardwalk and the pier. They were having a surfing contest and you got extra points for 'shooting the pier'."

"Shooting the pier?" Mary asked.

"Yeah, that means you try to thread your way through the pilings that hold up the pier while riding the wave. If you make it everyone thinks you are a talented surfer." Carl leaned back and stretched as if he were relaying information for the hundredth time.

"And if you didn't?" Mary asked, not sure what Carl was talking about.

"According to the article that appeared with the picture you get a trip to the hospital for a couple of hundred stitches from being cut by all the sharp shells that grow on the pilings," Carl answered.

"And is that fun?" Mary asked incredulously.

"Look at their faces. They are all smiling so I guess they think it is. These guys were all part of some kind of surf club or something." Carl explained.

Mary squeezed Carl's hand and then let go. "Thanks so much, Carl. It seems like you are always helping me. I'm afraid I have gotten used to it and forget to tell you sometimes."

Carl started to say something, but he just shrugged his shoulders and slid the envelope across the table to her. "Keep this stuff. I have copies of everything. It was no big deal, really. It was sound research practice, that's all. Now for the second surprise. Remember I told you I had two? Here it, or rather he comes now."

Carl rose and motioned to a man that had just boarded the shrimp boat. As the man approached Mary had the feeling that she was looking at a living painting of an old-time sea captain. The man was slender and moved with a quick, stiff gait. His white beard was neatly trimmed and hung just above his chest. He wore a dark blue coat with gold braid and a crisp white captain's hat perched perfectly on his head.

"Mary, may I introduce Captain Haptumus Rafferty," Carl stood, shook the man's hand, and nodded at Mary. "Captain, this is Mary Lassiter."

The captain quickly removed his cap, displaying a full head of thick white hair. He tucked his cap under his left arm and gave a crisp bow. "My pleasure; my pleasure indeed, Ms. Lassiter. You may both call me Capn' Hap, everyone else does. I have grown accustomed to it. May I join you for a moment?"

Folly Beach: Homecoming

Carl motioned for the man to take his seat as he moved back to lean against the railing.

Once he was seated the man addressed Mary. "Well, young lady, I understand you are interested in a slightly out-of-the-way place called Folly Beach."

"How did..." Mary stammered.

"Oh, your fella here," Capn' Hap began.

Carl had to smile at the comment. He shrugged his shoulders as if to tell Mary he had no idea where the man had gotten the idea he was her fella.

Hap continued, "called me in the middle of the night and said he was looking for a local expert on the island. To tell you the truth, I thought he was a bit touched. Then he told me he was a reporter and I knew he was... touched that is. I have nothing against reporters, mind ya, but I am never quite sure just how far they are stretching the truth."

The man across from her winked and showed a row of sparkling white teeth. She liked him and found herself quite comfortable in his company. "Have you been to Folly Beach, Captain, uh, Hap?"

"Just shorten that to Hap or Capn', whichever takes your fancy, and yes, I have been there. Actually, I lived across the river from the island for a long time. My granddaddy ran a charter fishing boat, then my daddy, and then me."

"So you went fishing every day for a living?" Mary asked.

"Took people fishing, there is a big difference. I never did much myself, fishing that is, but lots of folks come down from the city and want to try and catch a world-record fish of some kind. They figure fishing from a boat twenty miles offshore gives them a better chance, so I was always glad to give them a shot at it." Hap answered.

"Was it like this boat?" Carl asked, motioning to the deck where they sat.

The boat you see here is a shrimp boat. The crew on this kind of boat doesn't usually take visitors out with them. They are out there to catch shrimp, not to wet-nurse a bunch of city folks that are afraid to bait their own hook." Hap explained.

Carl laughed, and decided like Mary, he found it easy to like this fellow. "You are right, Captain; I would be one of those city folks that had never been out on the ocean, although I can bait my own hook."

"Well, it is about time you got some education. A boat like the Four Saints here usually carries a crew of two. The captain and a striker. The striker does a little more work than the captain, but not much." Hap explained.

Mary felt like a schoolgirl again and had to resist the urge to raise her hand to ask a question.

"Four Saints? Do all boats have names?" Mary asked. "I knew Navy ships did.".

"The Coast Guard requires that most commercial boats have a name and number so they can identify them. The name of a boat like this might change when a new owner takes over, but one as famous as this one, well…. I don't think anyone would even consider such a thing." Hap explained, in an easy manner. He was obviously used to explanations concerning boats.

Carl felt his reporter's blood coming to the surface and he edged a bit closer. "This boat is famous?"

"Not around here, of course, but back on the coast, yes. You would have a hard time finding anyone that fishes, shrimps, or works the docks along the coast of South Carolina that hasn't heard of this boat." Captain Hap said as he leaned back in his chair. He watched a buzzard circle over a small field on the other side of the lake. He was silent for a moment and Carl sensed that the man was reaching deep into his memory. When he finally spoke his voice was different, almost reverent.

Chapter 5

"When Capt. Blackie died a few years ago, there were a lot of folks at his funeral. There was a time, however, when there would have been no more than a handful." The old seaman began his story.

You see, Capt. Blackie wasn't always the likable fellow that he was known to be at the time of his death. Time was when he wouldn't even give the time of day without being paid. Something happened to Capt. Blackie changed all that.

To explain the change, I have to start with Wills Creek. That is a place where some of the shrimp boats take on ice and offload their catch. The Four Saints used to tie up there too.

In case you did not know, boats and ships are almost always referred to as she, even if they have a masculine name. Anyway, as I was gonna say, the West Wind slowly rocked back and forth as a pleasant onshore breeze drifted across the marsh grass. The captain of the small commercial fishing boat helped his passengers, one at a time, onto the deck.

First was a slightly balding dentist, next came a middle-aged male school teacher, and then finally a rather heavy-set fellow who only volunteered that his name was

Jake. After checking his watch for the day, the captain notified his passengers. He said that if the remaining guests didn't show up in five minutes, they would be on their way without them. After all, he had been paid in advance, and they knew that prime fishing time was early morning.

Jake grunted a little later that it had already been seven minutes and were they going to be on the way. If not, he wanted his money back. He hadn't paid seventy-five dollars to sit at the dock all day.

After one last look down the dock, the captain announced it was time to leave. He was just about to cast off the last line when he heard running on the dock. As he looked up, he saw a young lady towing a dark-haired young boy across the rough planks.

As the captain helped them onto the boat the lady, Betty, explained that there were only two of them because her husband had become ill the night before. Nothing serious she explained, probably just a mild case of food poisoning. Anyway, her husband wanted his six-year-old son, David, to make the day trip even if he himself couldn't.

Jake muttered something about hating kids while the captain quickly ran through the safety rules. The last rope was cast off and the West Wind headed out for a fun day of fishing twenty miles out in the Atlantic.

By the time they cleared the inlet, Capt. Blackie, on his shrimp boat, The Gin Fizz, had been at work for hours.

He dropped the nets for the third time that day. He yelled at his deckhand for the tenth time that morning and stalked into the cabin for a cup of coffee thick enough to eat with a spoon. He was planning on being out for a week this time and already he was in a foul mood. But then, of course, that was the only mood he ever was in.

Everyone was doing fine aboard the West Wind until that is, the teacher started throwing up. Betty and the dentist felt fine before the teacher arrived, but found they had to spend some time over the rail once the teacher began. Jake just glowered, Betty's son thought it was funny, and the captain just broke out the 7-Up. It was his favorite cure for seasickness, and it must have been effective because after a few sips everyone settled down.

By mid-morning, the boat rocked gently, its engine silent, and the fishing party cast their lines over the side. Jake caught the first one, and the dentist could have sworn that he almost saw a smile on the big man's face.

In a fairly short time, the ice chest was full and everyone settled back to eat the bologna sandwiches the captain furnished for lunch. The teacher leaned back and patted his stomach, feeling much better than he had earlier in the day. Looking around, he remarked that they must be far out since he could not see the shore.

The captain was just about to say that they were indeed nowhere near land when he heard a thumping below deck. When he pulled up the engine cover his heart leaped to his throat. The banging came from his small toolbox, which normally sits right next to the powerful diesel engine. As it floated, it struck the deck support.

The West Wind was sinking, and sinking fast. The dentist looked over the captain's shoulder, saw the water, and almost fainted. The distance from the water to the deck was decreasing fast and everyone realized the boat was going under.

Without saying a word, the captain rushed to the cabin, pulling the teacher with him. They emerged with an inflatable survival raft just as the stern of the fishing boat began sinking.

The captain had never used the raft before and he prayed silently that the small bottle of gas that would fill the raft was sufficient. Tossing the yellow parcel over the side, he yanked hard on the cord. Before their eyes, the blob turned into a six-man rubber raft.

Jake was the first one in, and it seemed that he was almost reluctant to accept Betty's son as she thrust him at him. Seeing that all his passengers were in the raft, the captain turned toward the cabin. He needed to call the Coast Guard, but he didn't have time. The teacher yelled for him to jump. The captain leaped, sprawling on the floor of the raft as the West Wind disappeared

For a long moment, the six people sat silently, stunned by what had happened. It had taken less than five minutes. Betty hugged her small son close as he began to softly cry.

Jake was the first one to speak. He said that the next time he went fishing he was going on a boat that would float for more than a couple hours. The dentist asked how long it would be before someone started looking for them. The captain said he wasn't sure because he hadn't told the dockmaster that he had an excursion that day. The captain had not even told anyone which direction he would be heading. In fact, he had ventured into an area that other charters seldom visited.

There were several old shipwrecks on the bottom in that area, and they didn't like losing fishing lines. He didn't say it, but he knew his friends might think he had taken a trip down to Florida. This was something he had talked about for the last couple of weeks.

Two days later, they found themselves bobbing up and down on the swells twice as far from the shore as they had been when the West Wind had sunk. A couple of times they saw Coast Guard planes in the distance, but none of them came in their direction.

The captain took stock of their emergency supplies and was not happy with what he found. Two cans of rations and only three small cans of fresh water were all that remained. The sun blazed down on the hapless survivors, burning them.

Another day passed and the dentist, the teacher, and the captain did all they could to make Betty and her son comfortable but it was almost impossible. There was one biscuit and a half can of water left for them to live on.

Hunger, thirst, and the hot sun can cause even the most honorable of men to do things he wouldn't even think of otherwise. The dentist and the captain began to argue over how they would split the remaining water. Jake threatened to throw them both over the side if they didn't shut up. The teacher started to cry. Soon all the men were yelling at each other.

They stopped as a very soft, sweet sound began to come from Betty's parched cracked lips. Rocking her unconscious son in her arms, she sang "Amazing grace, how sweet the sound...." The men stopped their fighting and listened to the words as the sun sank from view. In the

Folly Beach: Homecoming

last rays of light, every one of the men sat, watched, and listened.

There was no moon that night and no one heard or saw the captain slip over the side of the raft and quietly float away.

The next morning Capt. Blackie spotted a small yellow raft. Pushing his engine to full throttle, he quickly pulled alongside.

How strange it must have seemed to him to find a young woman and her son alone, floating miles from shore. The barely conscious woman told him about the boat sinking. However, she didn't understand what had happened to the four men that had been in the raft with her and the boy.

After putting the woman and her son in the bunks and ordering the deckhand to watch them, he turned his boat to shore. Blackie lit his pipe, took a puff, and then shuddered; the kind of shudder that comes from deep within, like a huge cold hand wrapping around you, chilling you to the bone. Blackie was a man of the sea and he understood what had happened to the men. One by one they had slipped, unseen, over the side and floated away from the raft. Each one thought that by giving his life the others might live; that somehow the water and food would be enough if their share was given to the others. Capt. Blackie wept, and he was forever changed.

Now, I know you are thinking this here story sounds like some kind of movie or something, but I am telling you it is the Gospel. Captain Blackie became a new man. He never treated his fellow man the same again. In fact, the

John C. Lasne'

very next morning he painted over the name Gin Fizz and then carefully lettered the words *Four Saints*.

Chapter 6

Carl and Mary sat silently after Captain Hap had finished his story. When Mary finally spoke her voice was almost a whisper. "This is really that boat, the Four Saints?"

"Yes, it is Missy. I bought this boat after Captain Blackie died and moved it up here." Hap glanced toward the rapidly filling parking lot and said, "It has been a pleasure, but I 'spect I better get back to the dock."

"Wait!" Mary said loudly when the Captain got up to leave. "I'm sorry, I didn't mean to shout. Before you leave, I have one other thing I would like to ask you. Did you ever know anyone by the name of Jack Young?"

The Captain squinted, rubbed his beard, and repeated the name several times to himself. Suddenly he snapped his fingers and surprised both Carl and Mary. "I'm not saying I did, but I just might have. Maybe, I'm not positive. It has been a while, you know. Let's go take a look."

Hap took the bill from the table and stuck it in his pocket. "It's on me. Not too often do I get to tell one of my stories to such an interested audience. Besides, maybe one of your friends can give me a favorable write-up in the restaurant section of your paper."

Taking the captain's arm, Mary asked with a smile, "Are you trying to bribe the press?"

"Works for me," Carl said as he left a big tip and followed after them.

Both of them glanced at the bow of the boat as they moved down the dock toward the main restaurant. Four Saints stood out in grand letters for them to read. Neither Mary nor Carl spoke as they made their way down the dock. Both of them were thinking about the story they had just heard. Carl made a mental note to have one of the editors contact the captain about doing an article on his place.

When they reached the main building Capt. Hap led them through a maze of now-filled tables. He greeted several of the couples and families that recognized him and thanked them for coming to his place. He stopped in a narrow hall that led to his office and pointed to a double row of framed photographs that lined the walls.

"Each one of these is a different boat. Most of them are shrimp boats like the Four Saints. Here is the fishing boat I ran for all those years. You can tell from my hair it was taken a long time ago. You see, each picture has the signature of the captain and the date."

Mary and Carl both moved closer to the hanging photos. The light in the small hall was not very bright, but they could see the writing. Most of the signatures were very challenging to read, almost scrawled.

"You don't find too many shrimpers with a good hand for writing; too many calluses and too many hours mending nets. If you folks will pardon me, I need to greet a few of the regulars. Take your time and look all you want. I'll check back in a short while and see how things are going. Many of these boats have tied up around Folly Beach at Andre's dock at one time or another, so maybe you will find what you are looking for." With that, the old captain straightened his coat and sauntered out to greet the patrons.

Carl looked at the dozens of photos that lined the hallway and suggested he start at one end and Mary at the other. As they began studying the photos, they realized the captain had been right; many of the signatures were almost impossible to read, although the names of most of the boats painted on the bows and sterns were legible. At least the year could be determined from the dates. After about twenty minutes Carl figured they might be out of luck. Most of the boat captains were far too old to be Jack or, at least, the age he should have been when most of the photos were taken.

Suddenly Mary called out to him. "Carl, I think I have something!"

Mary was standing in front of a photo at the opposite end of the hall. His attention was drawn to the photo she was looking at as he moved over to her. She looked at him and he could see the excitement in her eyes. Carl glanced at the signature and quickly realized it would be of little use. It was easy to distinguish the Jack part, but the last name was smeared beyond recognition.

"Well, did you folks have any luck?" Capt. Hap had returned to their side and leaned over to study the photo.

"What happened to the signature? I can't read the last name." Mary asked.

"Sorry about that, young lady, but these pictures were stored for a while and a couple of them got some water damage when the roof leaked. This could be your Jack fellow, though. Have you ever seen a picture of him before?"

Carl lifted the envelope he was carrying and replied. "We have a photo taken when he was young. That guy in the picture would be around the right age based on the date. How many Jacks could there be that run shrimp boats anyway?"

The captain laughed. "Well, I wouldn't know all of them, but right off the bat, I can think of more than a dozen. Now, if you knew the name of the boat he was captain of we would be a lot closer."

Mary blurted out, "LouLou! The boat was named LouLou! It was in one of the letters. Remember Carl? Jack said that the boat was paid for and, at least, they didn't have to worry about that."

Captain Hap looked at the name that was plainly visible on the hull of the boat. "I'm sorry, but this one is named Miss Margaret."

He was surprised to see Mary smile. "Margaret is...was my mother's name. I mean, she recently passed away. That is how I got started with this whole thing. I found love letters from Jack to her."

Hap nodded, understanding. "I would say that you might have yourself a match. That there fellow in the picture could be your Jack. It would be a long shot, but I learned a long time ago, anything is possible."

"Unless," Carl chimed in, "Jack sold the boat to someone else named Jack and that is who is in the picture."

Mary turned to Carl and put her hands on her hips. When she answered him she sounded none too happy. "Carl, one would think you don't want me to find Jack. What do you think the odds are that Jack sold his boat to someone with the same name and age?"

"Mary, I am the one who brought you here. Remember? I just want you to use your skills and take all the options into account. We don't even know if this is Jack's boat or not. The only name we have is LouLou, not Margaret. I admit it is quite probable that this is the boat and that guy in the picture is Jack..."

"And, I might add," Captain Hap added, "it wouldn't be too likely that he would have sold the boat; that is if he planned to keep on shrimping. She looks to be in pretty decent shape and it wouldn't make much sense to get back into debt."

Carl put his hands up in defense and then turned to Captain Hap, "Alright. I give. Is there anything else you can tell us about the photo? Like where it was taken or anything like that?"

Captain Hap moved closer and stared hard at the photo. He rubbed his chin for a moment, then turned, stepped into his office, rummaged through his desk drawer, and emerged with a large magnifying glass. He studied the photo closely for a long minute before he spoke.

"My most likely guess would be Jacksonville, Florida. Yep, that would be my guess. Those Navy ships in the background are the giveaway."

"What dock in Jacksonville?" Mary asked.

"I'm sorry, Missy, but I couldn't say. Could be one of a dozen. Wish I could help you more, but it has been a very long time since I have been down that way."

"I understand. I don't know how to thank you for all the time you spent with us, and for letting me see these." She indicated all the photos that lined the hall.

"Glad to do it, but there is one thing you can do for me." The Captain said with a sly smile.

"Sure, anything," Mary answered.

The Captain gently removed the framed photo from the wall and handed it to Mary. "You can take this with you for a while. It might help you with your search somehow and I need to remove all of these for a couple of weeks. I am planning on adding several more tables so this wall will have to move." He smiled and turned back to the dining room.

Before he disappeared around the corner, he looked back over his shoulder and added: "Missy, I wish you the best of luck. Let me know how it all turns out, either way."

Then the old sea captain excused himself and returned to running his restaurant.

"Well, Missy." He perfectly mimicked the old sea captain's voice. More than once, he had found this natural talent invaluable when he needed to obtain information from a source who would only speak to one person, and that person was not him. "Shall we head back to the big city?"

During the drive, Mary could not stop talking about the discovery of Jack's boat, named after her mother. Carl was soon won over by Mary's enthusiasm and excitement. He could only pray that something positive would come out of the whole thing.

Chapter 7

Monday found the two reporters very busy preparing for the Grand Jury appearance and their testimony against Senator Billings. They ate burgers at their desks and spent hours organizing and reorganizing their notes. There was not much time for anything else, and when Thursday afternoon finally arrived they were relieved. Friday morning, they would be in the closed Grand Jury room giving their testimony.

"How about stopping by Leus for a bite of Chinese before we head home?" Carl suggested as they made their way out to the employee parking lot.

Mary yawned and stretched her arms over her head. "Chinese sounds good to me. I want to get to bed early tonight, so eating out sounds good. I have gotten tired of pizza and tacos."

"Yeah, I'm ready to eat at a table instead of my desk for a change." Carl agreed as they made their way out to the parking lot.

"Mary, I wonder who those two guys are over by your car?" Carl asked, noticing two large men leaning against the side of her green Volvo. They wore dark glasses even though the sun had begun to dip below the horizon.

"For some reason, I don't think they are salesmen," Mary answered with apprehension in her voice. She edged a little closer to Carl. As they approached her car the men stood erect and faced them. They did not seem the friendly type.

Mary took her keys from her purse to open the door. "Can I do something for you guys? Or were you just admiring my car?" She spoke clearly and with more confidence than she felt as she looked around and saw that there were no other people in the parking lot.

Neither man cracked a smile. "Mr. Thompson, Miss Lassiter could we have a word with you?"

"We are a bit in a hurry if you don't mind," Carl replied as he passed the men to open the car door for Mary.

"This will only take a minute." One of the men said as he stepped in front of Carl and started to place a hand on Carl's chest to stop his forward motion.

The man was tall, standing a couple of inches over Carl's six-foot-two height and matching his broad shoulders. Mary figured the stranger was at least twenty pounds heavier than Carl, who was a hundred and ninety-five pounds.

Carl, with one swift motion, grabbed the man's thumb and twisted it, bringing his weight down on the man's arm. With a sharp cry, the man twisted his body to relieve the pain and found his arm twisted behind his back. This movement brought the man's body between Carl and the other man, who had placed a hand inside his jacket and had begun pulling something out. Swiftly, Carl reached inside the right breast of the helpless man's jacket where he found the pistol he somehow knew would be there. Sliding it out, Carl pointed the menacing-looking weapon at the sky, his finger resting lightly on the trigger. The other man slowly removed his hand from inside his jacket. He held a leather badge case at arm's length, so Carl could see what it was, and flipped it open. The bright silver badge read FBI. The identification card below the badge bore the name of Special Agent Leroy Stanford.

Carl glanced at Mary, who had moved behind him, and then back at the man.

"What is this all about?" Carl asked, still holding the man and the gun.

"I would be happy to explain things if you would release Agent Carboli." Stanford said quietly, replacing his badge casually.

Carl released the arm of the other Agent and took a step back. Carboli had a scowl on his face so Carl reached past him and handed the revolver, butt first, to FBI agent Stanford.

The man smiled and then handed the gun over to the other agent, who replaced it in his shoulder holster. He then straightened his jacket and stepped over to stand beside Agent Stanford.

"Agent Carboli is a newcomer to the department, so you will need to forgive his abrupt manner." The man smiled an easy smile and Carl relaxed.

Mary moved Carl's side and asked, "Why did you frighten us like that? We thought you were some of Senator...."

"Senator Billing's men." The agent finished, "No, Miss Lassiter, just the opposite. We have been assigned to, well, assist you until the hearings are over." Agent Stanford knew what the next question would be so he continued, "We don't have any reason to believe you are in danger..."

"But," Carl interrupted, "You had reason to meet us out in the parking lot like this. Were you checking Mary's car for bombs? Isn't assist a nice word for 'protect'?"

"The young ladies' car is just fine, and as I said we don't have any real reason to believe either of you is in danger."

"Then why all this?" Mary asked, still a little shaken.

"Well, actually," Agent Stanford said with a smile, "all we really wanted to do was let you know we would be around for a few days." Stanford's smile faded a touch. "Listen. We don't expect the Senator to even consider doing anything to either of you, but…."

Carl sensed what the agent wanted to do so he said, "Don't worry, this is 'off the record'. Just be straight with us, okay?"

"Senator Billings has had a slight money problem the last couple of years and has…."

"Should you be telling them this?" Agent Carboli whispered nervously into the other agent's ear.

Stanford did not look at him but instead met the gaze of the couple in front of him. "I have never met either of these reporters before, but…" He nodded at Mary. "They have a right to know what is going on. I am a pretty reliable judge of people, and I believe Mr. Thompson when he says this is all off the record."

Carl gave a slight grin and said, "I know how, and when, to keep quiet, and Mary does too. Now, what is this all about?"

Agent Stanford motioned toward a coffee shop across the street. "Why don't we get a cup of coffee and I'll fill you in?"

They sat at a small table outside the shop and since there were no other customers they felt free to talk without being overheard. Agent Stanford took a sip of his coffee and then leaned toward Mary and Carl, who sat across from him.

He began, "We, the agency that is, have been investigating the Senator for nearly a year now."

Carl interrupted, "Why would the FBI be interested in slum dwellings? There are dozens of them around Washington..."

Agent Stanford raised a hand to stop Carl. "While being a slum lord is a pretty despicable thing for a United States Senator to be, it is not a crime the FBI would get involved in."

The tone of the agent's voice told Mary he probably wouldn't vote for Senator Billings in the next election. She was beginning to like him. She leaned closer as the agent continued.

"We are more interested in the Senators dealing with, shall we say, less than desirable underworld figures..." Sanford raised his hand to let them know he expected their next question. "No, I am not saying that the good Senator is connected to the Mob, just that we have reason to believe that he could be. Now, I can't tell you any more now, but I promise you will get what I know when this is all done."

Carl was a bit skeptical." I don't want to sound ungrateful, but why would you give us the story? I mean what is in it for you, or should I say, the FBI?"

The FBI agent looked back with just a hint of a smile, "This may sound a little old-fashioned to you, but you see I am a patriot. I love this country and when someone in power, like a certain Senator we both know does something to disgrace their office I take it kind of personally. After all, I am part of the government myself."

Mary looked at Carl, who seemed to be deep in thought.

"Leroy," Carl began, using the man's first name to set a tone of intimacy. "I understand what you are saying and believe me when I say I don't think your patriotism is the slightest bit old-fashioned."

Carl stood and offered his hand first to one agent and then to the other. "I am sorry about that little thing back there in the parking lot. I am just a little jumpy right now. Just what is it that you want us to do? I'm not sure I could turn my files over to the FBI even if I decided to since they actually belong to the paper and not me."

Agent Stanford smiled; the kind of I know all about reporters and how they protect their information smile, "Don't worry Mr. Thompson, we aren't asking you or Ms. Lassiter to give us any of your files. We don't want you to tell us anything about what you have already discovered. I can guarantee you that we are aware of a lot more than you do at this point. What the Agency wants, is for you to let us know if anything is said or done to try and get you to back off, or even retract your story."

"But our paper is behind us one hundred percent and..." Mary objected.

"Oh, I am sure they are." Agent Stanford agreed, but then added, "right now anyway, but remember who we are dealing with here. A United States Senator, a senior Senator at that, who has many powerful friends. Some of those friends are willing to do some pretty dirty things, if need be, to protect the Senator and themselves. Look, most of this isn't news to you; either of you. All we are asking is that you be careful and let us know if you even think there is a problem."

Carl looked for a long time at both agents and then nodded slightly, "Agreed." He then turned to Mary with a questioning look and she nodded her agreement to Carl and the agents.

The two agents turned and started toward the door, but after a couple of steps, Agent Stanford stopped and turned to face Carl.

"Carl", the agent said, using his first name and sounding genuinely concerned. "What you did out there in the parking lot was impressive, but remember, we are your friends. There are certain people who would have just put a bullet between your eyes and then gone home and ordered pizza. I know what happened at that warehouse and admire you for what you did. Just be careful."

Carl gave a slight grin as he ran his hand through his hair. Mary frowned at him and punched him in the shoulder. Carl winced and then said, "Right, I understand. I am just a reporter, not a hero. I promise I'll be careful."

They watched the two men drive away in their government-issued black car. They were still hungry but decided to go ahead and get their food to go and eat it at Mary's place instead of the restaurant. Suddenly, being out on a dark night didn't seem comfortable.

Neither one of them said much until they were inside Mary's house with the deadbolt thrown.

As they dished out the food from the paper cartons Mary asked. "How did you know what to do? I mean...."

Carl smiled as he ladled pork fried rice onto their plates. "You mean the old grabbing the thumb thing? Well, several years ago I did a piece on a special training camp for a Green Berets unit. As part of the story, I went through part of the training."

Mary looked at Carl with surprise as she pulled her plate over. "Those are some pretty tough guys."

Carl said, taking a mouthful of the steaming rice, "Great guys too. They were training for search and rescue in Vietnam village areas. You know; disguises and all that stuff. I mean they even had one of the finest makeup artists from Hollywood teach them how to fool the natives. In any case, that's where I learned some self-defense techniques. Oh, and I am a pretty proficient shot too."

"You know, sometimes I don't think I know you at all," Mary said, shaking her head in wonder. "I mean, here I was working with a Green Beret and didn't even realize it."

"No, Mary, I am an open book to you," Carl laughed and held up his hands. "I am no John Wayne, believe me."

Mary laughed too, but then she put her fork down and asked seriously, "Do you think the Senator would hire someone to... I mean, you know..."

Carl gazed at Mary with his jaw clenched, then slowly shook his head.

"No, I don't. There are too many others who know what we have found. We both have copies of everything and so does Bodey."

Bodey Carson was their boss at the paper and a very close friend of both of them. "After all, would hearings even take place if there was much doubt about what was actually happening? No, Mary, I don't think the Senator would do anything to put more of the public spotlight on his dealings."

Carl stood, stretched, and said, "But remember, this is Washington. Once the Senator is back home, getting libraries named after him, there will be another power broker to take his place."

Mary began to clean the table, then she turned and said, "You sound so cynical."

"Well, if it weren't so there would be a lot less for us to do, wouldn't there?" Carl suddenly placed his hands on her shoulders and pulled her closer to him. Then he very softly kissed her on the forehead and then pushed her back to arm's length.

"But, Mary, if I didn't believe things could get better, I would find a job that was a lot easier and paid more to boot."

Mary pushed him toward the door. "No, you wouldn't. You would never be content reading the news when you could be writing it. Now, go home so I can get to bed. I am exhausted."

Carl reached for the door and then stopped. His voice took on a serious tone. "Are you sure you wouldn't rather I sleep on the sofa tonight?"

Mary laughed as she reached to undo the deadbolt. "No thanks, Carl, but I am a big girl and I have a first-class alarm system."

Carl often left his car at Mary's house and they rode to work together. Mary watched through a pulled-back corner of the curtain as he backed out of the driveway. Her hand unconsciously moved to her forehead, where Carl had kissed her, and she felt an emotion that took her a bit by surprise. She wasn't even sure what it was, but Mary was certain of one thing: something had changed in their relationship. Mary didn't know if she liked the idea of things changing right now. Too much had happened in a short period of time and Mary wasn't sure if she could trust her feelings.

She turned off the kitchen light and headed to the bedroom intent on a hot shower and bed. As she started to pass the living room Mary stopped and looked inside. Next to the sofa, sat the box of letters. The letters had suddenly changed everything she knew about her mother. She entered the room slowly and sat on the sofa. She reached down and picked up the box, setting it on her lap. She trailed her fingers across the lid.

"Oh, Mother, how many other secrets did you have?"

Chapter 8

The next morning dawned gray and dreary, with more than a hint of rain in the air. It seemed like the most appropriate thing for what Carl and Mary were planning.

Actually, things worked out better than either of them thought. They were both asked a few questions, and then they turned over the folders containing the information gathered during their investigation to the Grand Jury. There were over a hundred pages of interviews and summaries. Since the paper had sent the whole story to press that morning, there was little for them to hold back. In less than three hours they were thanked and led out of the chambers.

"Seems kind of anticlimactic," Mary said, with a hint of disappointment.

Carl took her arm and guided Mary toward a small coffee shop just down the street from the parking garage where Carl's Camaro was parked. When they were seated with two cups of spiced coffee Carl began to speak.

"Mary, I think you learned a lesson today." When Mary started to answer, he held up a hand to stop her. "I know you are a seasoned reporter and figure you know all the ins and outs, but this is different. This is the first expose' you have worked on involving politicians. They have a tendency to circle the wagons to protect their own or at least those in their own party. Before this is over, every one of them will have their holdings and friends sifted through a very fine screen. This will move slowly once the first public hearings begin."

Carl leaned back in his chair and slowly sipped his coffee.

Mary studied Carl closely and realized he was waiting for her to finish his thought. "So the rest of the scoundrels will have time to get themselves clean?"

Carl leaned forward and took her hand. "All of them aren't dirty Mary, but there are enough to slow down the process." He released her hand and fished for his wallet. "We have done our part, at least the first part. There will be a lot more print on this story and we will be expected to be the main contributors. For the time being, we can work on some other amazingly pertinent news items."

Carl laid money on the table, got up and went to Mary's chair, and waited for her to rise.

Mary stayed seated for a moment, in deep thought, and then looked over her shoulder at Carl. She had a concerned look on her face.

"Carl, things seem to be changing between us and I'm not sure if…." She began, but with a chuckle Carl interrupted.

"Mary, listen to me. You know how I feel about you. If our relationship starts to get in the way of our job then… well, we will work that out if it happens. But right now, what are your plans for the weekend?"

Mary smiled and then rose as he held her chair. She figured he had closed the discussion of their relationship, such as it was.

"I thought I would drive out to New Haven and see Grams tomorrow. I didn't get to visit her last weekend." Mary got that sad tone in her voice each time she talked about her grandmother.

"Great," Carl said as they left the coffee shop and headed toward his car. "The weather forecast for tomorrow is favorable for a drive in the convertible."

Mary touched Carl's arm and when he looked at her, she said, "Carl, I really appreciate the offer, but, this time, I would like to go by myself. I just need some time to think…"

"About Jack?" Carl asked.

"I am hoping Grams will know something about all this. Before you say anything, I know she probably won't remember," Mary said. Her grandmother's memory had begun to deteriorate more than a year ago and had only gotten worse.

Jack was about to respond when suddenly he stopped. Jack looked around quickly and then steered Mary between two cars and over to the side of the parking garage that faced the street. Before she could ask what he was doing, he said, "Get ready to scream and yell fire if anything happens."

"What?" Mary asked, but Carl was running toward his car, weaving between other parked vehicles. When he reached the Camaro he stopped to look down and then began scanning the area.

He jumped and spun around when Mary grabbed his arm and said, "What is going..." She didn't finish the question because she spotted the problem when she looked at the car. All four tires were flat, with long slashes in each sidewall.

"Well, I guess the Senators' friends aren't too happy with us after all. No big deal. I needed some new tires anyway." Carl said with a grin as he began to dial a number on his car phone.

Later, at Mary's house, they talked as Carl checked her security system to make sure everything was working. He had called their newly acquired FBI friend and filled him in on what had happened.

Mary sat on the sofa, the letter box beside her, as Carl talked to the FBI. He was assured they would be watching the moves of all the Senator's friends. When Carl got off the phone he strolled over and sat next to her, the box between them.

Mary cleared her throat and opened the lid of the box. She took out the Valentine's card that had been found earlier.

"I can't stop thinking about it, no matter what is going on. This simple card would have changed all our lives if it had been mailed: My mother's, Jack's, mine, and even yours. This man I didn't even know existed could have been my father. I wouldn't have grown up here. I would have had different friends, a different job, everything. Jack never knew my mother intended to marry him. He thinks she didn't care enough to answer his plea and she thought the same about him her whole life. If he is still alive, he has to know. I can't let him die thinking she didn't love him. I have to find Jack Young if I can. I have to give him this card so he will understand that it was a silly, unintentional mistake that kept them apart. It is something I need to do. Do you understand?"

Mary rushed through the words, expecting Carl to interrupt her with a protest. Surprising her, Carl sat and listened quietly. When she finished, he spoke with a steady even voice.

"Mary, I am not surprised by what you are saying. I have seen how it has affected you. Why don't you talk to Grams before you decide what to do? You have plenty of vacation time. To tell you the truth, after what happened with my tires, you being out of town for a while would make me feel a whole lot better."

Mary placed the card back in the box, set it on the floor, and slid close to him. To his total surprise, she put her arms around his neck and leaning forward, kissed him.

Mary pulled back, a little flushed, and asked. "Thanks, Carl. For caring so much for me, but what about you? What if they come after you?"

"As far as I know, the FBI is on top of it. He reassured her, "I don't expect anything more to happen."

Mary kissed him again, and then jumped up and began to pick up their coffee cups. She was full of feelings: feelings of joy, fear, and discovery all jumbled up in one package. One thing she knew for sure. Her life was changing, and for better or worse she committed herself to do her part to put things right.

Chapter 9

When the seat belt sign lit up, followed by a soft chime Mary closed her notebook and dutifully pulled the seat strap a little tighter. She didn't mind flying, but she wasn't fond of the takeoff and landings.

Peering out the window, she was still high enough to have a broad perspective of the landscape below her. She saw pine trees and huge ancient oaks covering the ground, which began changing to a seascape as the plane banked to come in for a landing. The blue water seemed to stretch forever, at least to the horizon. She could see the old town of Charleston as the plane began its descent. A forest of church steeples reached for the sky and made it evident why Charleston had once been dubbed the "Holy City".

She could make out the barrier islands that protected the coastline and she was pretty sure of where Folly was, in relation to the city. She had studied maps and the history of the area to prepare for her quest.

After she told Carl she intended to search for the man who had been in love with her mother so many years earlier, the following week was a blur. First, she had to get permission to take an unscheduled leave of absence, then she had to make sure all her commitments were covered.

She drove out to see her grandmother, but it was like visiting a stranger. Rebekah Lassiter had not even recognized her. Instead, she thanked her for taking the time to come visit her and told Mary it would be nice if her family would come and see her sometime.

It only made Mary more determined to find Jack. In some strange way, she felt finding him would somehow make up for the loss of her mother and now her grandmother.

Permission for her to take off for two weeks was granted with no problem and there was a surprise on top of that. The editor of the paper said that if she was willing to do an article on Folly Beach and Charleston, the paper would cover all expenses. Seems someone, Carl no doubt, had suggested to the Entertainment Section that since Charleston had once again been named as one of the top ten places in the world to visit an article on the city and surrounding area would be worthwhile reading.

One morning, when Carl came to take her to work he said he had a surprise for her. When she was seated at the kitchen table he pulled a newspaper clipping from his bag, laid it on the table, put his finger on the print, and asked. "Do you recognize this teenager?"

The picture was an old black-and-white image that was not very clear. Mary stared for a moment, trying to make out the features of a young girl standing with a group of boys. Then her hand flew to her mouth. "It's my mother! ... I can't believe it."

"And." Carl moved his finger to the middle of the picture. Mary leaned close to the photo and studied the face of the boy he was pointing at. She looked up at Carl with a questioning face. Carl leaned across the table and whispered in her ear, "Jack."

"What?" Mary asked as she stared intently at the clipping.

Carl pointed to the bottom of the group picture where a list of names was typed. Mary began to read the list.

"Bill Turner, Harry Phillips, Margaret Williams, Jack Young, Tom... JACK! It's Jack?"

"That's what it says," Carl answered.

In the photo, Jack stood next to Mary's mother, with his arm around her waist. Carl pushed his chair around the table and sat next to her. He looked at the boy again. The figure had dark hair and the kind of smile that was genuine and came easily. Carl thought he would have liked the boy right off, and Carl was a very sound judge of people.

"Well, what do you think? Not a shabby-looking couple," Carl said.

Mary regained her composure and set the picture on the table. "It is so difficult to believe, Carl. You just came across a picture of my mother and her lost love while looking at old newspapers?"

"If you think about it, Mary, it isn't really that difficult to believe. I contacted a reporter down in Charleston. Remember me mentioning Thomas Williams, a guy I met a couple of years ago at a conference? Look, Jack and your mother spent every summer together for years. Jack was a native of the island, which is pretty small. Everybody knows everybody else. It is only natural that they should show up in a picture together. Finding this article... what can I say? It almost seems like it was your destiny to find out about Jack and your mother." Carl said with conviction.

Mary leaned back in her chair and took a deep breath. She spent a few moments in deep thought and then grasped Carl's hand. She gave him a broad smile and picked up the clipping again. "You could be right, Carl. Maybe it is destiny. Maybe I discovered the letters because I was supposed to; like God had a plan for all this."

Carl took the picture from Mary and put it back in the envelope. "Mary, I don't know what you will discover. Think of it like a story you would cover for the paper. Find as much truth as you can. Once you have found all you need to find, put it away and move on to the next challenge. Whatever happens, I am here. I'll always be here when you need me."

Mary touched her hand to his cheek and looked into his eyes. What she saw was complete honesty and she realized that he really did love her.

"Carl, you are an amazing man and I am lucky to have you for a..." Mary began, but Carl held up a hand to stop her.

"I know we are friends, Mary. I know you are involved in something that is taking all your time and feelings right now. I can wait. I meant what I said, I am not going anywhere." Carl said.

Before Mary could answer Carl stood and took a note card from his pocket and handed it to her, as they headed to the front door.

"This is Thomas' number at the News and Courier in Charleston. Give him a call before you leave and let him know what you need." Carl said and kissed her lightly on the lips. He turned and quickly made his way down the steps.

Mary wanted to call him back, but at that moment the phone rang and he was gone when she returned in less than a minute.

When Mary contacted the Charleston News and Courier newspaper Thomas Williams said he would be more than pleased to help her out with background on an article. He also said he would continue to check archives for anything on Jack Young. She was glad to hear he would help because Carl, who was a fabulous researcher, had found out very little about Jack or his family.

Public records showed that Jack's mother was killed in a car wreck just a few months after her husband died. There was no evidence that Jack had any siblings and the house they had lived in changed owners just six months after Jack's mother died. That was all they had been able to discover. Nothing about where he was now or anything else about his life. Mary hoped the local paper would be able to turn up something else.

Carl had made her promise to call her each evening and let her know how things were progressing; calling immediately if something significant happened. They kissed again at the airport when Carl dropped her off. Mary realized that it seemed natural and that surprised her a little.

"Come back soon," Carl said to himself as she passed through the turnstile and made her way to the plane. Suddenly he felt strange, not really lonely, but like a part of him was now missing and would be until they were together again.

Chapter 10

On the walk to her rental car, Mary noticed the smell of salt in the air carried by a strong breeze from the direction of Old Charleston. As she headed for the Courier office Mary wished she could have just headed straight to Folly Beach. However, she knew a quick stop at the newspaper could save her time in the long run.

She hoped Thomas Williams, the reporter, would have some updated information for her. When she got to the newspaper office she found that Thomas was out interviewing a witness to a break-in in the most exclusive part of the Old Town.

Mary got the address of where Thomas would probably be, and after getting directions, she headed out to find him. She found herself gawking at the mansions that lined the street on the Battery, a seawall that formed the boundary between the city and the harbor.

A horse-drawn carriage slowed her to a crawl, the street being too narrow to pass. The weather was pleasant and she had her window down, allowing her to hear the driver as he gave his practiced spiel. By the time the carriage pulled off onto a side street, Mary had learned quite a bit about "South of Broad" as that part of the city was called. She made a mental note to include a carriage ride as a must in her travel article.

Mary saw the reporter's car as she made the left turn that would have taken her to Rainbow Row. A tall, slim man of about fifty stood just inside the gate of a magnificent old home.

Circling the block twice Mary was lucky to grab a spot as it was vacated. She was just a few yards past the house where she had spotted Thomas and he saw her as she crossed the street.

When she reached him, Thomas smiled and held out his hand.

"You have to be Mary. Carl said you would be the prettiest girl I saw today and he was right."

As Mary blushed, she took his hand and smiled.

"I take it you talked to Carl recently. I left a message for him when the plane landed; told him I was going to try and catch you before I headed over to Folly Beach."

"Talked to him just before I left the office a bit ago, and you can drop the Beach part of the name. Everyone around here just calls it Folly. I am assuming you are wondering if I have found anything else out about your Jack fellow." The reporter guessed, gesturing to an empty bench in the park across the street.

When they were seated Thomas pulled a small notebook from his breast pocket and flipped it open. It was the same gesture Carl had made a thousand times since she had known him and suddenly she missed him terribly.

Scanning the page, Thomas blew out a breath and responded, "I am afraid there isn't very much to tell. I have double-checked state records and unless Jack Young changed his name he is not living in South Carolina now or in the last number of years. Other than what I have already passed on, the only new thing I have is a record of the name change of a boat called the *LuLu* to the *Miss Margaret* and it was owned by one Jack Young. Carl said that wouldn't be a surprise to you, but I'll say I could find nothing to indicate the boat was ever sold or the name changed again. Now, don't get your hopes up too much."

Thomas warned, seeing her straighten a bit. "Shrimp boats travel all up and down the coast; they sink, burn up, and... well, all sorts of things. So all I can say for sure is there is no record here of anything changing."

Mary rose to her feet, disappointed, but not discouraged. Carl always said that confirmation of information was as good as a new lead because it answered a question. She thanked Thomas and he told her to check back with him in a few days and see if there was anything else he had uncovered. As she made to leave he asked.

"Are you staying on the island?"

"Yes, Carl found out that the house my mother lived in during the summers was still a rental. He was able to talk the manager into waiting to shut it up for the winter and let me rent it while I am here."

"That Carl is a resourceful guy. We had a couple of late-night talks when we were at the conference a few years ago and I was impressed."

"He is like a bulldog when he puts his mind to something." She thanked him again and started for her rental car.

"He is quite taken with you, Mary. You do know that, don't you? It is as obvious as it could be." Thomas asked after her.

Mary stopped and turned back to him and said, "Carl is very special to me, too."

"Just wanted to make sure you knew." The reporter said with a smile.

Getting out of the city and heading to her destination was not as easy as getting into the historic city. The positive was that she did get to see more of it.

Mary spotted a sign that said Folly Beach and headed in that direction. After a few minutes, she spotted a gas station and stopped. She wanted to call the nursing home and check on her grandmother as well as get directions.

It was reported to Mary that her grandmother was sleeping and had been sleeping most of the day.

When she asked the station attendant how to get to Folly he laughed and pointed to the road she had been on.

"Well, mam," he said with a heavy, slow accent. "That there is Folly Road. If you get back on it and keep driving, you will find Folly Beach at the end. You can't go any farther unless that car floats."

Ten miles later, at the foot of Folly bridge, Mary pulled over in the parking lot of a place called Andre's. They sold bait, fishing gear, live crabs, and fresh shrimp. She looked at her notes and saw that Andre's was the dock that the *LuLu*, the boat Jack's father owned, had usually tied up. She knew it was a slim chance, but she ventured inside and asked anyway.

The boy at the register was new and way too young to know anything that would help her. The man restocking chicken necks (Mary later found out they were for "crabbin'") said Andre himself might know, but he was out of town for several days.

As Mary crossed the bridge, lined with fishermen, and posted with a NO FISHING sign, butterflies fluttered in her stomach. She squeezed the steering wheel hard and wished again that Carl was with her.

Mary drove down Center Street and found that the one stoplight on the island was flashing orange so she continued another block until the road ended. Directly in front of her was a sign that said Welcome to Folly Beach Amusement Park.

The park was deserted and the buildings were closed with plywood over some of the windows. The Ferris Wheel and Carousel were still there, but most of the other rides were already packed up for the winter.

Mary's mind flashed back to the letters she had read from Jack to her mother. In several of them, he mentioned the time they had spent at this very place, riding the Ferris Wheel and driving bumper cars. In fact, it was while riding the carousel that Jack proposed marriage to her mother.

Mary pulled to the side of the road where she sat for a long time staring hard at the concrete Boardwalk. It was as if she expected to see her mother and Jack strolling along hand in hand or riding the horses on the Merry-Go-Round.

Mary had been to an amusement park not far from where she had lived many times when she was young and the carousel had always been her favorite ride. She could use a ride right now, thought Mary.

Following directions, Mary turned left at the Boardwalk onto E. Arctic Ave. On her right, she could see the ocean through the gaps in the sand dunes. She watched on her left for the house her mother had stayed at all those summers. Mary had memorized a photo from the box that had her grandmother and her mother standing in the yard. If it hadn't changed, she'd know the house when she saw it. The butterflies in her stomach increased as she drove slowly. When she got to the third block she slowed and watched carefully. Then she saw it. A pale yellow cottage built on stilts like most of the houses on the street. There was a big porch on the front and a little porch on top called a widow's walk. The house looked exactly as it had in the photo.

Mary pulled slowly into the drive and sat for a long time. She could hear the waves behind her and the gulls crying as they hunted for food. In her mind's eye, she was her mother, back for another summer, excited as she watched for Jack to come out of his house next door to greet her.

It still amazed her that she had known nothing about this part of her mother's life. Well, she was here now and Mary had a job to do.

Mary was jolted out of her thoughts by a rap on the roof of her car. She turned to see a middle-aged lady wearing a blue sundress smiling at her. She was a hair shorter than Mary and wore her brown hair in a bob. The grin on her face, joined by a Santa-like twinkle in her eyes quickly set Mary at ease and she opened the door to get out when the woman stepped back.

"Maebelle Barnette Bazzel is my name, but just call me Maebelle like everyone else. You must be Mary. I know your last name is Lassiter, but I'll just call you Mary. Here on the island, we don't use last names much, especially after the summer crowd is gone. That friend of yours, I'll just call him Carl, contacted me this morning and said you would be here this afternoon and here you are. Now, I am the caretaker of this house. We, my husband Milton and I; you can just call him Bubba like all our other friends do, live right next door."

She took Mary's arm and guided her toward the steps that led up to the front porch of the house.

"Listen to me rambling on and you haven't had a chance to say a word. I'll show you the house and then you can tell me why you are here. First, though, you need to take those shoes off. They will be full of sand in a minute. Lots of sand around here, 'cause it's a beach you know. You will have to get you some flip-flops. I am sure there are a couple of extra pairs around somewhere." Maebelle said.

Mary took her shoes off and let Maebelle lead her up the stairs and into the house. Maebelle took her from room to room pointing out different features. She told her that Carl had made sure the phone was on so she could call anytime she needed.

"That Carl seems like such a nice man, are you two..." Maebelle threw her head back and laughed heartily, "Bubba tells me God should have put a turn-off button on me. Sometimes I just get wound up and forget to stop."

Mary laughed with her. She already liked Maebelle, liked her a lot. She was what Carl would call a "real person". Someone you could always trust to be honest with their words and deeds.

"Carl and I work together, and yes, we are very good friends," Mary said.

Just friends? Maebelle asked with a cocked head.

"More, I think. Yes, more than friends." You had to be honest with "real people", and suddenly she didn't feel so alone.

"The sun is about to set. Let's go up to the widow's walk and watch it. I left a picture of iced tea up there for us. You can tell me all about yourself." Maebelle said, leading the way.

Chapter 11

The view from the widow's walk on the roof of the house was amazing. Mary could see the ocean right in front of her. When she looked to the west the sky was blazing red and a huge sun was sinking out of sight.

Maebelle turned out to be a very attentive listener. Her steady stream of chatter had stopped and she concentrated on everything Mary said as she gave a thumbnail sketch of her life. Maebelle asked occasional questions, but most of the time she just listened quietly. Mary continued on to her mother's death, finding the letters, and finally, her decision to come to Folly.

When the sun was down, the autumn sky was filled with bright stars and a cool breeze was coming from the ocean. Mary was glad that Maebelle had told her to grab a sweater on the way to the stairs that led to the roof. The other woman had left a windbreaker hanging over the railing for herself.

"Quite a story, young lady. You should write a book once this is over." Maebelle said as she finished her tea.

"I am not sure who would be interested in reading about my life, but I do hope to find Jack. Or at least find out what happened to him. I would like him to know that my mother really loved him and wanted to marry him. Jack should know that." Mary answered.

"I can see it is important to you, and I understand why." Maebelle leaned closer and said in a soft voice "Mary dear, I married the man I loved many years ago. I can't imagine what it must have been like for your mother and her Jack. They were in love and each thought the other had changed their minds about getting married." She sat back in her chair, was silent for a moment, and then asked.

"I have lived here most of my life, but didn't know this Jack and I never met your mother. We moved into this house ten years ago. " She pointed next door.

"We used to live on the West End. I am retired, but work part-time at the Library and know almost all of the islanders. That is what I call the people who live here year-round. I know you are a professional reporter and all, but would you like me to help you find some answers?" Maebelle asked.

Mary reached out and took both of Maebelle's hands in hers and gave a big smile.

"That is so sweet of you to offer and yes, of course, that would be wonderful."

"I have an idea," Maebelle said. "Today is Monday and on Wednesdays, we sometimes have potluck dinner at the church. Folly Beach Baptist Church, on the right as you cross the bridge, is where I attend church. Just so happens this Wednesday is one of those times. I could introduce you to a lot of the locals and we could get the word out about what you are doing. Someone may know someone that knows someone that might know something if you know what I mean."

"That would be great, but I, uh, I am Catholic. Would that be a problem?" Mary asked, a bit shyly.

Maebelle threw her head back and laughed. "As a newcomer to the island, you have a lot to learn. The Catholic church is right across the street from my church and the head deacon and his family were at our house for dinner last week."

Mary liked the fact that her neighbor laughed a lot. It was one of those laughs that infected others and made them feel like laughing too.

Maebelle started for the stairs saying, "Bubba is going to think I moved in over here if I don't get home and you need to call that Carl of yours. I am sure he wants to hear from you. I have to go to town early tomorrow so why don't you look around? Get to know the island a bit better and I'll catch up with you tomorrow evening."

When Mary got back to the house the first thing she did was call Carl. He must have been sitting by the phone because he answered halfway through the first ring.

The phone was near the front door and had a long cord so she stepped out onto the porch to sit in a rocker and talk. First, she said, yes, it had been a pleasant trip, and then she recounted her meeting with Thomas Williams. She told him about Andre's and her first impression of Folly as she crossed the bridge.

"Sounds like an interesting place," Carl said.

"It has the usual small town feel of not much traffic or people on the streets, but I am told that changes in the summer months."

Mary described the house and then her meeting with Maebelle, whom she really liked. She appreciated the neighbors' offer to help. Mary was sure Jack wasn't around Folly or Maebelle would have known it.

"She sounds just like I expected her to be after talking to her on the phone. I'm glad she is willing to help; it should open a lot of doors. By the way, how does it feel to be in the house your Mom stayed in all those years ago?" Carl asked.

"To tell you the truth, I haven't had time to take it all in yet. It is a very convenient location, within walking distance of the main street and right across the street from the ocean. You know, until I arrived here I had never been to the ocean," Mary said.

"Hmmm... "Maybe it brought back memories that your mother didn't want to stir up, so she never took you there," Carl speculated.

"Carl, it's so weird. This is a beautiful place and my mother must have had memorable times here and I knew nothing about it. It is like one of those movies where the wife finds out her husband has been a secret agent their entire marriage. She always thought he was traveling on business trips when he actually was in Russia stealing secrets."

Carl laughed, "A somewhat suspect analogy, but I do get the idea." He continued on, telling her any newsworthy things that had happened where he was, and asked again if she had everything she needed.

"Yes, my Carl, as Maebelle calls you, has taken care of everything," Mary answered.

"Your Carl, huh? I like the sound of that." He laughed and was delighted.

Mary was quiet for a second, and then she said softly, "Thank you, Carl. You are so kind to me."

"You are worth it, Mary," He replied emphatically.

They chatted for a while longer and then Mary said she thought she might go for a walk on the beach before retiring to bed. Carl said he was jealous and told her to be careful.

It was after nine o'clock, but the moon was so bright Mary didn't need the flashlight she retrieved from her glove box.

When she got back Mary felt hungry and was glad that Maebelle had been thoughtful enough to place a casserole in the fridge for her. She warmed it up in the oven and carried it from room to room as she ate.

She tried to imagine her mother walking these same floors, in love with the boy next door. When she walked into the back bedroom, the one her mother had always stayed in, she received a jolt.

As she looked out the bedroom window at the house next door, the one Jack had lived in, she saw that the window directly across from her had a light shining behind the drawn shade.

Mary knew from Jack's letters that his bedroom window faced her mother's window. They had sent each other good night messages by flicking their lights at each other.

Someone was moving around the room behind that shade. She was too old to believe in ghosts, but she was sure the house was empty. She hurried out on the porch and verified that there was no car parked in front of the house and there were no other lights on.

When she returned to the bedroom, the window next door was dark. Had she imagined it? Was she so wrapped up in this whole thing that she saw lights that weren't there?

Mary propped herself up with pillows so she could see the window from the bed, but no light reappeared and finally, she fell into a deep sleep.

Chapter 12

Mary was startled awake by the sound of a gunshot and sat up with a gasp. It took a moment for her to realize she was not back in DC. Who would be shooting at the house? A glance at the clock on the nightstand told her it was just past six in the morning.

Carefully edging to the window she peered out and saw that Jack's old house was dark inside, but there was light underneath. The house sat about ten feet off the ground. Half of the space under the house was taken up by an open concrete patio, while the other half was devoted to a storage area. She could see movement in the shadows cast by a weak light hanging from a cord under the house.

Mary hurried out to the porch after looking to see that Maebelle's lights were on in her house. Mary leaned over the railing and saw a figure squatting down, working on a motorcycle. The smell of unburned gas reeked in the salt-laden air. It hadn't been a gunshot, just a backfiring motorcycle.

"You stupid machine. I should just roll you out into the surf and let the sharks eat you." A voice hissed at the motorcycle.

Another male voice called in a hushed voice, "Charles Montgomery is that you?"

Mary saw a man coming from Maebelle's house and walking across the yard toward the figure, who stood scowling at the obstinate machine. She figured it must be Bubba and she began to relax. If Maebelle's husband knew the man it must be OK.

Mary got her second shock when the two figures met under the light and she could see them more clearly. If Charles Montgomery had been wearing sunglasses he would have looked just like Jack in one of the photos she had seen, of him and his father mending nets

The photo was a bit fuzzy and she had no idea what mending nets meant, but that is what it said on the back. In the photo, Jack wore some kind of heavy baggy canvas

work overalls, a stocking cap, rubber boots, and a tee shirt. The figure under the house was dressed the same way.

Mary stepped back from the railing and shook her head. What is she thinking? This wasn't Jack under the house and she wasn't her mother. Mary quietly stepped back to the rail and watched the two men. Bubba was laughing about something as Charles turned back to the motorcycle and began rolling it toward the open door of the storage area.

Bubba started back to his house, glanced up, and saw Mary on the deck. He waved, and then started climbing the stairs. When he topped the stairs and stepped onto the porch, Mary saw that he was a big man. He stuck out his hand and Mary took it.

"I am Maebelle's husband Bubba. Sorry 'bout the ruckus. Charles, also known as Chuck, needs a different mode of transportation. He spends more time threatening that thing than he does riding it.

"Oh, it's alright. I wasn't all the way asleep anyway. It takes me a couple of days to get into a routine when I am away from home." Mary answered. She wondered at the same time if anyone around the place besides Maebelle used their real name. Her clothes must have looked a mess at that moment because Mary realized she had fallen asleep in them.

"I better get a shower and eat breakfast. Is Maebelle still driving into town this morning?" Mary asked.

"She will be leaving in the next few minutes. She has to see her sister in North Charleston first," Bubba answered and then started to turn and head back down the stairs. He stopped and faced her again.

"Why don't you get a shower and come on over for breakfast? Chuck is coming and there will be plenty for all. I am planning to take him over to Andre's after we eat."

"I stopped by Andre's yesterday, but he wasn't there," Mary said, considering the offer. She didn't want to intrude, but breakfast did sound enticing.

"Maebelle told me about you and what you are doing. There are a lot of old timers that hang around the dock and most of them are probably already there. You could eat and then ride over when I take Chuck. We can introduce you to some of the regulars and maybe they might know something. Feel free to come on in when you are ready. I'll leave the door open," Bubba suggested.

Mary quickly agreed and headed straight to the shower while her host proceeded to mix up some pancake batter. When she was dressed in jeans and a light sweatshirt, Mary made her way to Maebelle's house. She stepped in through the screen door and followed the sounds of cooking and talking.

Mary found the sounds coming from a neat kitchen with a table spacious enough for four. There was an enormous pile of pancakes, scrambled eggs, and bacon in the middle of the table.

"Just in time. Are you ready to eat?" Bubba asked with a smile as he pulled out a chair for her. She sat down across from Chuck, who looked less like Jack close up and in bright light. He was still a good-looking man but he didn't have the size and build of Jack in the picture.

"I would have to be starving to even make a dent in this," Mary answered, pointing her fork at the abundance of food.

"Well, what we don't eat I am sure Chuck will polish off," Bubba assured her as he took a stack of steaming hotcakes from the serving plate and covered them with butter before soaking them in syrup.

He grinned at Mary and said. "Sugar-free syrup and low-fat butter. Orders from Maebelle. She said to tell you good morning and she would see you a bit later."

A pile of food soon appeared on her plate, and she found she was hungrier than she had thought. She ate and listened as Bubba and Chuck talked about the updated rules on how close the shrimp boats could come to shore in the winter. They also talked about why the price of shrimp was lower than last year. After a few minutes, she sat back in the chair with a groan. "I would have brought roomier jeans with me if I had known I was going to be eating like this."

Chuck took the last piece of bacon off the plate and crunched it down. "If you think this is good you should taste his bar-b-cue or jambalaya."

"I'm not sure what jambalaya is but if it is this delicious, I would be willing to try it," Mary said as she squelched a burp.

"Oh, it's good alright. You just have to keep a fire extinguisher or, at least, a pitcher of iced tea handy." Chuck said seriously.

"It isn't that hot Chuck," Bubba protested.

"Yeah, well all I know is you have to keep moving the serving bowl so it doesn't burn through the table."

They had a spirited laugh and then Mary cleared her throat and assumed her reporter's posture. She leaned slightly forward, just enough to let Chuck know she was very interested in the answer he would give to her question.

"Chunk, how long have you lived in Jack's... I mean in the house next to the one I am renting?"

"I guess...let's see...um...close to eight years or so I would say. My folks rent it and when they moved to Florida a few months ago they said I could just stay here if I wanted, for a while anyway."

"You didn't want to go with them?" Mary asked.

"They moved to Florida because my sister and her kids live there. They wanted to be near the grandkids. I had a good job as a striker on one of the boats, so I figured I would stay awhile."

"What is a striker?" Mary asked.

"Basically, the striker runs the boat while the captain sits in his chair, smoking a pipe and deciding where to drop the nets. Course now that I have my own boat and am the captain it is different." Chuck said, only half serious, and then broke into a laugh.

"What does 'drop the nets' mean?" Mary asked.

"I can see you are going to need a class in Shrimpin' 101." Bubba injected. "Let's hop into the truck and Chuck can lecture while we head over to Andres."

They cleared the table, rinsed the dishes, and put them in the dish rack to dry, then headed out to Bubba's truck.

"Carl would really like this truck," Mary said as she climbed into the cab between the two men. The Chevy was immaculate, had a lot of chrome, and sounded powerful.

"Who is Carl?" Chuck asked.

"That's her Carl." Bubba laughed as he started heading out of the driveway. "At least that's what Maebelle calls him."

Mary blushed and changed the subject by asking again about the nets. Chuck was a competent teacher and Mary knew a lot more than she had before when they pulled into Andre's a few minutes later.

Like the day before, the long refrigerated box that held bait was the center of attention. Bubba and Chuck traded hellos with several of the people getting their day's allotment of chicken necks, bait shrimp, and mullet. The three of them made their way to a table that sat in one corner of the store.

Around the table sat four old men, wrinkled by decades of salt water and sun. They all stood when Bubba introduced Mary to them. The oldest of them, Mary thought he must be in his late eighties, slid his chair in her direction and motioned for her to take a seat.

Mary took the seat with a smile. This Southern hospitality was taking some getting used to, certainly not the same as DC.

Bubba took the lead telling the others how Mary was staying in the house next to theirs for a couple of weeks. He didn't go into any details; just told them that Mary was a reporter for a newspaper and was doing research on something that happened around thirty years before. Mary took it from there.

"Did any of you know a young man named Jack Young?" Mary asked.

None of the men responded immediately so Mary continued.

"He ran or worked on a shrimp boat named the *LouLou* or maybe the *Miss Margaret*."

"*LouLou*? Didn't John Young used to have a boat by that name?" One of the men, a stout man with a thick head of white hair, asked his two friends.

Al, you are right. I believe this was a deep-rigged double. The man who gave Mary her seat answered.

Mary looked to Chuck for help, and he replied. "A double outrigger set up for dragging the nets in deeper water."

Mary remembered Chuck had explained how some of the shrimp boats used only one outrigger, the part of the boat that the nets were hooked to. However, most had two. She smiled and mouthed 'thank you'.

The third man said he had heard the name before but had never met the captain.

"His boy did work with him, but I recollect he was John Jr," Al said.

"Sometimes people use Jack as a nickname for John, you know, like John Kennedy. I don't know what Jack's father's name was, but John could have been it." Mary said, excitement welling up inside her.

"Yep, the daddy was named John and their son could be this Jack you are looking for then." One of the men said.

They talked for several more minutes, and two of them remembered when John Young had died. None of them had any idea what had happened to Jack after his father's death or where the boat might be.

Somewhat disappointed, Mary thanked them and Bubba said he would take her back to the house. As they stood to leave Al snapped his fingers and said.

"You know Frenchie is down at the railway working on his boat right now. He travels all up and down the east coast and the Gulf. If anyone might have seen either one of them boats it would probably be him."

"Great idea," Chuck agreed." Franchie helped me set my nets for the winter. He knows more shrimpers than anyone. The railway is just down the end of the road past the dock. We can walk there pretty quickly."

"His real name is Louis Lasne, but we have always called him Frenchie." Mary was not surprised to hear Bubba say. Then he added apologetically, "I have a Water Commission meeting this morning."

"No problem, Bubba. I'll walk Mary down to talk to Frenchie. One of these guys can give her a ride back to her place later. Right?" Chuck asked, looking in the general direction of the table where a game of dominoes was starting.

"Sure thing."

"Gotcha."

"Right."

The chorus of answers from the men made her smile. Amazingly, the thought of getting in a car with someone she hadn't met but a few minutes before didn't even make her nervous. This place was certainly different from any other she had been to before.

Bubba left with a promise from Mary that she would stop by the house and let him know if she had discovered anything new.

The sun was fully up and warming everything nicely. As they left the store they headed down to the railway, which Chuck explained was a contraption that allowed people to get their boats completely out of the water. This allowed them to be worked on.

Chuck asked. "Have you ever seen an alligator up close?"

"Alligator?" Mary asked, looking around nervously.

"Yeah, he is a big one. You don't have to worry. He is in a cage over there," Chuck said, pointing to a large wire enclosure with a tin roof.

Mary was interested, but not really sure just how close she wanted to be to a real alligator. Chuck strolled over to the enclosure and motioned for her to join him.

Inside was an alligator, at least eight feet long. He or she, Mary wasn't sure how you determined the gender of an alligator, seemed to be dozing. When she leaned a few inches closer to the screen the reptile suddenly whipped his head around, opened his mouth wide, and gave a loud hissing sound.

Mary let out a shrill screech and jumped back. She would have ended up on the ground had Chuck not grabbed her around the waist and steadied her.

"Don't worry," Chuck said as he suppressed a laugh. "He can't get out and besides, he likes you. See the smile he has on his cute face."

"Hardly cute," Mary said, gaining her composure. Mary had seen a lot of things in her job and wasn't about to be intimidated by a lizard, no matter how big.

Mary stepped back to the cage as Chuck took a fish from a bucket next to the enclosure and tossed it into the open mouth of the reptile. The creature closed its mouth with a snap and appeared to return to its nap.

"Are there many of these things around here?"

"Some, but not that many. You spot one every now and then, but this guy here came all the way from Florida."

Chuck answered as they turned and continued their way toward the dock and railway. The crushed oyster shells that made up the bed of the road crunched under their feet.

"How did it get all the way from Florida to here? Swim?"

"Nope," Chuck said with a grin. "Came by car."

Mary knew he was kidding her so she played along. "Did he drive or hitchhike?"

"I guess you could say he was kidnapped. You see, there was a time when you could buy baby alligators on the side of the road in Florida. Sometimes for a buck." Chuck said, serious now. "The Blanton family lives four blocks east of where you are staying. Mr. Preston Blanton is a biology teacher at James Island High. He brought a couple of gators and turtles back from Florida one time. Built a pond in the back yard with a fence around it and put them inside."

"In his backyard?" Mary asked, not sure if Chuck was kidding.

"You might find it difficult to believe, but if you knew him it wouldn't surprise you at all. I had him for biology and he was the smartest guy I ever met. I mean he is like a walking set of encyclopedias." Chuck said, admiration in his voice.

"Sounds like an interesting character."

"Sometimes we would ask him a really tough question and he would just say, I don't know, but I know how to find out. The next class period he would have a whole lesson on the question we had asked."

"But, how did Buster get from his backyard to here?" Mary asked, nodding toward the enclosure behind them.

"Buster?"

"I always name animals in the stories I write if they don't already have one. I named that one Buster," Mary gestured behind her.

"Well, the story goes like this." Chuck stopped walking and looked at the ground in thought. "When the gators, there were two of them, got around five or six feet long they got out of their cage. Seems there was a dog across the street that would come over all the time and bark at them. One morning, one of the gators had enough so he ripped a hole in the wire and the two of them went looking for the dog."

Mary's reporter instincts took over and she was mesmerized by the story, listening to each detail and seeing the events in her mind's eye.

Chuck continued, "They crossed the street and chased the dog, who was probably thinking about then that he should have stayed on his side of the road, under the house. One of them ate him. The man living in the house heard all the ruckus, came out, and saw Buster and his friend coming out from under his house. He ran inside and called the police. They came and shot one of the gators, but Buster got in the canal next to the house and got away. Years later a guy caught him, sold him to Andre and this is where he lives now." Chuck explained.

"They knew it was one of Mr. Blanton's because he had tagged them," Chuck added, knowing the question would be asked.

As they passed the dock Chuck pointed out his boat and they continued for just a couple minutes before they came in view of the railway. A shrimp boat, looking huge out of the water, sat in a cradle attached to an oversized dolly. The dolly sat on train tracks that disappeared into the river. A heavy cable had pulled the dolly and boat out of the water and onto dry land.

A man had his back turned to them and a cloud of smoke hung over his head.

"Frenchie!" Chuck called as they approached. "Got someone here who wants to talk to you."

When the man turned Mary was, for the second time that day, hurled into the past.

Chapter 13

Mary's mind flashed back to the photo of Jack and his father working together. Frenchie fit the picture exactly. He was no taller than her with broad shoulders and muscles hardened by decades of manual labor. A captain's hat sat crooked on his head and a pipe was clamped in one corner of his mouth.

With a genuine grin and a sparkle in his eyes, Frenchie set down the bucket of paint. As he reached out for her hand, he took it in his calloused hand. When he spoke, he did so with a distinct accent. It was obvious that the name Frenchie was a perfect fit.

"What can I do to help you, young lady?" Frenchie asked as he propped his foot on a small nail barrel.

Mary gave the same thumbnail sketch she had given the men at the store and asked if he had ever seen the *Miss Margaret* or Jack.

Frenchie gazed across the river to Folly and beyond. Finally, he shook his head slightly and said. "Sorry, but I haven't seen a *Miss Margaret* or this Jack of yours. Now, I did know John Young a long time ago. I remember his boy worked with him, but I am afraid that is it. I was making port in Key West when John died and by the time I moved back he was long buried. I heard his boy took over the boat, but that is about it." When he saw the disappointment on her face Frenchie added, "But, I am heading out in the morning to take this boat down to Miami. I'll be stopping for fuel and talking to other boats on the radio. I'll ask around and if the *Miss Margaret* is out there I bet we might find her."

Mary smiled and gave him a hug. She stepped back, shocked at what she had done. This place and the people were changing her and Mary hadn't been there for but a day.

"Guess I have to find this Jack fellow now." Frenchie laughed and turned back to his work.

As Mary and Chuck walked back to Andre's, she said, "Frenchie seems like a very kind man."

"He is. He is also a legend in the shrimping world."

"Legend?"

"Yes, there are guys that bring their boats hundreds of miles to have him set up their nets, and he gave me my first job on a shrimp boat," Chuck said, and then realized Mary didn't have a clue what he was talking about.

"Why don't we stop at my boat and I'll show you? By the way, have you ever seen a shrimp boat up close?"

"Actually, not too long ago, Carl and I ate lunch on one."

Mary laughed when she saw the puzzled look on Chuck's face. Then she told him about Captain Hap and the restaurant.

"That Carl of yours is quite a guy." Chuck mused out loud. Before Mary could respond, he pointed toward the dock where several boats were tied. "There she is The Jenny Lou. All fifty-five feet of her."

Chuck's boat looked a lot like the one she and Carl had eaten on. However, it also had a few more cables, ropes, and other items she had no idea what they were for. There was also a very strong fishy smell and here and there she could see dried blood and parts of sea animals stuck to the railing and deck.

"Sorry about the mess. Some of it is just how real working shrimp boats are. However, now that I have the pump working, I'll clean a bit more." Chuck apologized. Then he proceeded to describe the purpose of much of what she saw on the boat.

"Sounds pretty complicated," she said with a sweeping motion across the deck.

"I have a guy that usually goes out with me, but he is down with the flu or something, so I am taking a few days to get some things done that I haven't had time for. Hey, here's an idea. I need to take the boat out for an hour or so and check out some repairs. We won't be too far from shore if you would like to take a ride."

Having never been out on a big boat before, Mary wasn't too sure at first. After all, she would probably never get the chance again so she said yes. Besides, it would be something exciting to tell Carl, since she didn't have much else to report.

In ten minutes Chuck had the engine running and was untied from the dock. Slowly at first, he cleared the dock and made his way out into the middle of the river while Mary stood just outside the cabin watching his movements. She was impressed at how fluidly Chuck moved, moving through each step like it was second nature.

In one of the letters from Jack, he had mentioned taking her mother out on his boat one time. This made her feel a connection to her mother's past as the shrimp boat rumbled its way down the river toward the inlet that led to the ocean.

Chuck shouted over the noise, "Step up to the bow and watch down by the water."

Mary looked puzzled at first, but then followed the instructions and carefully moved as far forward as she could and sat on a large coil of rope. Holding on to the rail, she leaned over and was alarmed to see a huge fish swimming along with the boat only inches from the bow.

She looked back at Chuck, who smiled and hollered, "Just a porpoise. They do it all the time."

Mary turned back and watched with fascination as the porpoise matched the speed of the boat easily by surfing the bow wave. She was unaware of Chuck studying her while she did the same with the porpoise. Mary was unlike any other girl he had ever met. She was self-assured and smart, not the kind of girl he was usually attracted to, but he was fascinated by her. Coming down here to Folly to look for her mother's lost love seemed a touch strange, but he was glad she had come. Chuck knew she really liked this Carl guy, but he was way up in DC and she was down here. The summer crowd was gone and there weren't too many year-round girls he was interested in and...

"Wow, that was something," Mary said excitedly. Chuck had been lost in thought and had not seen her come back to the cabin.

He told her about some of the things he had seen and caught in the ocean and Mary seemed interested in it all.

Chuck took the boat close to the beach and pointed out Maebelle's house. On the way back an hour later he asked Mary if she would like to steer the boat. She was nervous at first but warmed up quickly. Chuck stood close behind her catching a whiff of her perfume and the clean smell of her hair. He thought she was very pretty, and he would like to know her better.

Chuck was a little disappointed when Mary exclaimed, "Carl is going to be so jealous when I talk to him this evening!" But he also hoped that maybe Carl had something to be jealous of.

When they docked Chuck asked one of the men on the dock if Andre had gotten back in town yet. Upon hearing the news, they headed to the store.

As it turned out there was nothing he could offer other than to say he would ask anyone that showed up for fuel or ice if they had seen the *Miss Margaret*. He remembered the boat and Jack's father but hadn't really paid much attention to Jack himself.

Chuck explained that most of the time the boats left the dock long before sunrise and sometimes stayed out for days at a time. They often came and went with little notice.

Al and one of the other men, Billy, got up from the table where they had been playing dominoes and ambled over to Chuck and Mary.

"Billy and I are going to run across the bridge for a bit. Would you two like a ride back to the house?" Al asked.

When they were dropped off Maebelle's car was once again in the driveway. She headed over to see her and Chuck went to work on his motorcycle.

"Thanks, Chuck, for everything. Hopefully, Frenchie will be able to find Jack, and the boat ride was excellent. I even liked meeting the alligator," Mary said over her shoulder.

Chuck waved and said to himself. "Yes! Score one for me. Watch out Carl, I am on the move."

Maebelle, who had gotten home earlier than expected, opened the door when Mary reached the porch and announced that lunch was almost ready. Mary followed the other woman to the kitchen and told her everything that had happened that day.

"Sounds like you have had a busy morning. It is fantastic that you met Frenchie. If anyone can help it would be him. And a shrimp boat ride, I bet you liked that."

"Jack took my mother out on the boat too. It was like I was following in her footsteps." Mary said as she helped set the table.

I'llbelle's voice sounded a tad hesitant when she said. "Mary, I don't want to be out of line. Chuck is... well... Chuck is a bit of a lady's man. Don't get me wrong, he is a nice kid and all but well... it really isn't any of my business."

Mary set a plate of cold chicken on the table and looked at her new friend with a slight smile. "I had a good time today, but I'm not forgetting why I am here. Chuck was really helpful today. He helped me a lot and I'm grateful. That's all."

"I just can't help giving advice. Just be.... oh, I think Bubba is home." Maebelle brushed her hair into place with her hands and headed to greet her husband.

Mary retold her story to Bubba as they ate chicken and potato salad. When they had cleaned up Mary said she needed to call Carl and check on a couple of the stories they had been working on. She also wanted to write up some notes for the Folly and Charleston piece her boss was expecting when she got back.

Maebelle invited Mary to join her and Bubba for dinner and an evening beach walk after it got dark. Mary said she would love that and left to call Carl. As she climbed the stairs Mary could hear Chuck whistling as he worked on his motorcycle. She stopped for a moment and watched as he worked. Mary couldn't help but wonder if her mother had done the same thing many times when she first met Jack.

Shaking her head and clearing her mind Mary headed inside, gathered her notes from her briefcase, and called Carl. As the phone rang, Chuck's whistling carried through the screen door.

Chapter 14

Before Mary could say anything Carl asked excitedly, "Have you seen the news? Senator Billings is stepping down! Can you believe it? We might even get a raise out of this."

"I didn't know. There is no TV in the house and I have been busy, but that is wonderful. What about his slum buildings?" Mary asked.

"That is even better news. He is selling them to a co-op of owner-tenants. The plan is to convert them into condos. They have gotten a state and a federal grant to purchase their own homes and fix them up."

"Then it was all worth it, all those hours of research and looking over our shoulders," Mary said with conviction.

"This is it, Mary. This is why I love this job. I am so proud of you."

"Me?" Mary questioned.

"Yes, you! You were the one that pushed until the paper decided the only way to shut you up was to investigate," Carl said with pride in his voice.

They talked about the news for a while and then Carl said, "Enough with the minor stuff, what is going on down there?"

"Let's see. I met a huge alligator that I named Buster and I got to ride on a shrimp boat," She explained.

"Tell me more."

For over an hour Mary talked about all that had happened the night before and that day.

"Sounds like everyone down there is willing to help. It is kind of crazy if you think about it. You are staying in the house your mother stayed in, and right next door is a guy that runs a shrimp boat just like Jack did. Like a Twilight Zone episode or something," Carl laughed, thinking about how that was one of his and Mary's favorite shows.

"There is something about this place. I don't know, it's different. I mean, different in a pleasant way. I am not sure how to explain it. After a couple of days, it is like I have known these people for a long time. I wish Mom had shared stories of her summers down here," Mary said, a little bit of sadness in her voice.

"But you are on Jack's trail, right? Before long you will be on your way back home. I really miss you, Mary. You know this is the first time in over two years we haven't seen each other nearly every day?" Then he added in a serious tone, "I'm not much good without you Mary. I need to see you, hear your voice..."

"Carl, you are hearing my voice now," Mary laughed, although she was touched by his words.

"Not the same, Mary, it's not the same at all." After a pause, he asked, "You are coming home soon right? I mean you aren't going to stay there, marry that Chuck guy, and work on a shrimp boat the rest of your life are you?"

"Carl you are such a drama queen. Besides, shrimp boats smell terrible, and the salt air makes my hair frizzy all the time," Mary sighed.

"But you are beautiful when you have frizzy hair. Oh, got to run. The boss is waving me to the office. Love you."

Great with frizzy hair, Mary thought as she heard the phone click. I doubt it.

As Mary placed the phone back on the receiver she still heard whistling. She walked out onto the porch and leaned over the railing. Chuck had finished working on his motorcycle and was cleaning his hands with a rag. He sensed Mary watching him and looked up.

"Hi, how was your phone call? How about a ride? Have you ever been on a bike before? I can take you on a tour of the island," Chuck said with a big grin.

"I am eating dinner with Maebelle and Bubba this evening," she replied.

Chuck glanced at his watch. "Folly isn't that big and I'll have you back in plenty of time. Besides "Molly" and I can show you places you won't see from your car."

"Molly, huh? Not exactly a manly name for a motorcycle," Mary said. She and Carl had done a piece on DC bikers and Mary had ridden behind Carl several times during their research. He had even taught her how to ride by herself, although Mary had left the kick-starting to him.

"Well, if you knew the Molly she was named after you would think differently," Chuck laughed.

Mary was interested in seeing everything her mother had seen when she spent the summers on the island. After a moment's thought, she said yes and headed inside to slip on a sweatshirt and a pair of sneakers.

They drove up and down most of the streets. Chuck stopped several times pointing out things like the two log cabins that were on the island and the house with a totem pole in the front yard. He rode all the way down to the west end of the island. Instead of stopping at the end of the road he just climbed a dune and kept going.

"Are you allowed to ride on the beach?" Mary shouted in his ear.

"No, but hey, what's the fun of only doing things you are supposed to do?" Chuck gunned the bike and they flew through the air as they topped the sand dune. Mary tightened her grip around his waist. She couldn't see the grin on Chuck's face.

As Chuck made a turn and headed back toward the road he called over his shoulder, "Better get you back or Maebelle will be waiting supper for you."

Back at the house, Mary handed Chuck the helmet she had been wearing and made her way up the stairs to wash up and change. "Thanks, that was fun."

"Tomorrow I'll take you down to the other end of the island and show you the lighthouse," He answered.

"I'm going to church tomorrow with Maebelle and Bubba. Are you going?" she asked as she reached the top of the stairs.

"Not much into the church thing. I would rather do things that are fun, ya know."

"I'll let you know about the ride tomorrow if you are around." Mary looked at him seriously and added. "And Chuck, I enjoy church and I don't really go there to have fun. I go to worship God. Actually, now that I think of it, that is fun." She thanked him again for the tour and stepped inside.

Chuck thought about following her, but when he saw Maebelle open the door to come outside, he thought better of it. He quickly rolled the bike to its place under the house.

"One battle at a time, my friend, one battle at a time," he said to himself. He liked Maebelle and she was friendly with him. However, he also knew she had taken Mary under her wind, and getting on her bad side was not something he wanted to do.

After a quick shower and brushing through her hair, Mary dressed in 'walking on the beach' clothes and strolled next door. Maebelle called for her to come in before she even got to the door.

Mary thought Maebelle must have some kind of secret power because she always seemed to know when someone was coming.

"Ever had shrimp and grits?" Maebelle asked when Mary entered the kitchen, where Bubba was stirring a big pot on the stove. Mary gave the other woman a quick hug and looked inside the pot.

"Smells good," Mary commented as she took a deep whiff of the brew.

"It tastes even better than it smells," Bubba said and motioned to a skillet that simmered next to the pot. "Stir the shrimp and onions. Just enough to keep them from overcooking."

"Mary, please come on in from now on. No need to be invited. Down here by the third visit you are just treated like family," Maebelle added as she started pouring iced tea into tall glasses full of ice.

Mary smiled and concentrated on stirring the shrimp. It felt good having a family again, even if it was for just a short while.

The phone rang three times that evening, but Mary never heard it because it was after midnight when she got back from her beach walk. She did hear it the next morning when it rang again at seven o'clock.

Chapter 15

"Mary, Christopher Hagen here. I wanted you to know that Carl is in the hospital. He didn't want to call you because he didn't want you to be upset, but I knew you would want to know. Now, Carl isn't seriously injured; he's just a little banged up. The doctor just wanted him to stay the night for observation."

Mary's heart was pounding and she felt dizzy. Why would the editor of their paper, The Washington Times, call with this news? "Chris, what happened, and how serious is it really?"

As I said, he is not in any danger, so don't worry about it. Carl was leaving the gym last night around nine and two guys jumped him in the parking lot."

Mary knew that Carl often went to one of the local gyms, sometimes late in the evening, when he needed to work off stress. She figured it was less dangerous than the way he sometimes drove his car. Maybe she was wrong.

"Does this have anything to do with the paper?" Mary asked, figuring it did and that was why the editor of the paper was calling her.

"The police and the FBI believe it has something to do with the Billings thing. One of the guys isn't talking, but they are hoping when the other one gets out of surgery he might."

"Chris, please tell me everything," Mary asked in a soft voice laced with worry.

"Carl was parked away from the other cars in the lot and when he reached to open the door one of the men, the one in surgery, grabbed him around the neck and the other guy pulled out a knife..."

"A knife!"

"Was Carl stab..." Mary started, but Christopher interrupted.

"No, nothing like that. Carl somehow got loose and spun the guy around in front of him and the other creep stabbed his own buddy. Anyway, Carl slipped when he spun the guy around and fell. The one that wasn't stabbed kicked Carl in the head and tried to run away. This two-hundred-fifty-pound weightlifter was coming out of the gym and saw it all. He clothes-lined the guy that was trying to get away."

"Carl was kicked in the head?" Mary said, shaking and imagining the worse. "I am getting the first flight out."

"No, wait! Carl said you would do that and would be really mad just knowing I called you. He is in room 212 at St. Mary's. Call him yourself and you will see he is going to be fine." Christopher pleaded.

"OK, Chris. I'll call him right now. Thanks for calling. I mean it, Chris, thanks a lot," Mary said, and as soon as Christopher hung up she dialed the hospital number from memory.

It only took Carl a few minutes to calm Mary down. He explained that the guy that had kicked him had mostly gotten his shoulder and he only had a small cut on his chin.

"Mary, remember last year I decided to try skydiving and write a story about the experience?"

"You mean when you landed in the tree and they had to get a fire truck to get you down?" Mary laughed.

"I was twice as hurt then. Really, it is nothing to worry about. The cops are planning to put a squad car on me and the FBI is really mad. I guarantee they are going to crack these guys. Besides, you have church dinner tomorrow, and there's no telling what you might discover about Jack. I really want you to come back soon, but not until you are ready. This is important to you, so it is important to me. OK?"

Mary sighed deeply and finally agreed to stay provided he called her as soon as he got home the next day. She gave him Maebelle's number in case she happened to be at her house.

"I don't want any more calls from Christopher Hagen or anyone else telling me you are hurt," she said firmly and finally breathed normally again.

"I'm fine Mary," Carl assured her.

An hour later she was recounting everything Carl had told her while eating breakfast with Maebelle and Bubba.

"Never knew reporting was such a dangerous job," Bubba mused.

"Actually, there is a lot of paperwork and other boring stuff most of the time. When you are doing a story on crooks or politicians you are never quite sure just what might happen," Mary said between bites of bacon.

"Not much difference most of the time," Bubba laughed.

"I told Carl to call me as soon as he got home. Is it alright if I told him to try here if I wasn't at the house?" Mary asked.

"Of course dear," Maebelle answered.

"I am tempted to call him on his car phone now, but I don't want to distract him," Mary said.

"He has a phone in his car? I didn't know you could do that." Bubba was really interested now.

"They are a new thing. The paper got them installed in some of the reporters' cars so that they could get hold of us when we were on the road. They don't always work right, but it is easier than stopping and calling in every hour," Mary explained.

They talked a little longer about the incident and then Mary asked about the church dinner that night.

"We have a program every Wednesday night. There is a thing called Training Union for the young folks and Bible study for the rest of us. Tonight is a bit different. We are having dinner on the grounds as it is called. Everyone is bringing food and Mr. Porter and some of his boys are out getting oysters right now and they will be steaming them," Maebelle explained.

"Never had steamed oysters before," Mary admitted.

"There will be at least five bushels and that is plenty even for Bubba here," Maebelle joked.

"Right," Bubba agreed, "Three of four bushels for me and some for the rest of y'all."

"That sounds like a lot of oysters. How many boys does this Mr. Porter have?" Mary asked.

"Technically just two of his own, but, at least, ten or more at the church. Believe me, those boys love him, probably as much as his sons do," Bubba explained.

"Must be quite a guy," Mary said.

"Oh, yes, he is. An amazing man with an inspirational story. You will meet him tonight," Maebelle informed her.

Carl called right after noon. "I'll never go to the hospital again."

"I think you said that the last two times you ended up there," Mary reminded him.

"Yeah, but I didn't have to stay overnight. Don't get me wrong. The people are very kind, but they won't even let you order pizza delivery."

"Imagine them being so callous. Whatever were they thinking?" Then Mary asked seriously, "Carl, are you OK? I don't want the answer you give so I won't be worried, the truth."

"Yes, Mary, I promise I am fine. Chris said I had to work from home today, but there wasn't really any reason," Carl answered.

"Good for him. When I call you this evening after church I expect an answer on the first ring," Mary instructed firmly.

"OK, OK. Now tell me again about tonight. Some kind of cookout right?"

Mary repeated what Maebelle had told her and they talked for another half hour.

"Carl, I want you to know. This morning when I got the call from Chris I was so afraid...afraid of losing you. Please be careful. Promise me," Mary demanded.

Carl understood all that Mary had suffered through in the last year: losing her mother and now her grandmother's memory problems were catching up with her. He knew it was part of the reason she was so adamant about finding Jack. She was afraid of losing her family and being alone. It was irrational. Carl was sure Mary knew that but if finding Jack would help, he was all for it.

"Mary I told you I would always be there for you no matter what and I meant it. You will find Jack and you will always have me," Jack said forcefully, wishing he could hold her and tell her in person instead of over the phone.

"I know you want to be there for me, but if you get killed you can't be. Now, if you promise me you will be careful, I'll feel a lot better," Mary said softly.

"Mary, I promise. Call me this evening and let me know if anyone at the church was able to help. I better write something up for the paper about my current problem," Carl said reluctantly.

After the call, Mary ventured outside and saw Chuck talking to a long-legged blonde at the beach access directly across from her house. She was laughing at something he was saying to her and Chuck had a big grin on his face. He happened to see Mary out of the corner of his eye and suddenly ushered the girl across the dune and out of sight.

A moment later Chuck reappeared and waved at her and flashed a broad smile. He jogged across the street and up to the steps of her porch.

"Hi there, beautiful. Ready for that ride now?" He asked.

"Wouldn't you rather take the blonde with you? You both seemed to be having a good time."

"Oh, I just met her. Her name is Abigail and she was just asking if there was anywhere to get fresh seafood on the island. You know, we should go get something to eat this evening ourselves," He suggested.

I appreciate the offer, but don't you remember that we have the cookout at the church? I am sure you would be welcome to come," Mary suggested.

"Oh yeah, I forgot. But that is hours away, we still have plenty of time. The view of the Morris Island lighthouse is great from the end of the island."

"I am planning to stick close to the house today and get some writing done. I want to be here if Carl calls again," Mary declined.

"Oh, you can write anytime. Isn't Carl that guy you work with? You can talk to him anytime," Chuck said.

"Writing is what I do for a living. The paper is paying for most of my trip and Carl is much more than "that guy I work with". He is my very best friend and was jumped by two thugs last night and could have been killed," Mary informed him with a touch of anger.

"Yeah, well OK. If you change your mind, let me know. Maybe you can come to the storm party later this week. It will be cool?" With that, Chuck jogged away toward the beach and Mary had a pretty clear idea she knew where he was headed.

Chapter 16

After loading food and folding chairs into the trunk of Maebelle's car the three of them drove the short distance to the church.

"Chuck said something about a 'storm party'. What is that all about?" Mary asked as they turned on Center Street.

"Chuck and a storm party, why am I not surprised? There is a small hurricane that is moving fast toward Florida. Most of the weathermen think it will come up the coast. Now, don't worry. As I said, it is only a small one right now and it shouldn't get too close. I mean we might get some pretty strong gusts and a lot of rain for a day or so. It isn't near the full moon so probably no flooding," Bubba explained.

"And so Chuck is having a party, for what, to celebrate a storm?" Mary asked a little confused.

Maebelle laughed and told her that some people looked at a storm as a suitable reason to party. For example, like 'I ain't scared of any storm, just pass me the beer'.

"But if it did get serious, wouldn't there be a lot of damage? I mean I have reported on what has happened when there is a big snowstorm and a hurricane is surely much more dangerous," Mary said, somewhat confused.

"Chuck is young and he doesn't take a lot of things seriously. He is a pretty decent kid, just a tad immature. I am sure he will grow out of it," Maebelle said.

"Assuming he lives that long," Bubba added.

Just then they reached the church and Mary could see people were already there and tables were loaded with casseroles and other yummy foods.

"Carl would love this. He is a real people person and he loves to write about local characters," Mary said.

She had called and checked on Carl before leaving and he was already stir-crazy, but he was staying put and had ordered pizza. He had told her to eat some of everything for him and made her promise to call and give him the scoop on everything that happened.

"Well, there are plenty of characters on Folly, for sure. Carl will just have to come down here and find out for himself sometime, but he will have to bring you along," Maebelle said.

"I promise I'll come back no matter what happens," Mary said, with conviction in her voice.

Bubba laughed long and deeply. "Well, young lady, I can see you have already contracted Folly Fever. I have to warn you that there is no cure."

"Bubba. Maebelle. Glad to see you, and who is this young lady?" A tall, somewhat thin man with a sparkling smile asked.

"This is Miss Mary Lassiter. She is staying next door for a couple of weeks," Bubba said and then introduced the man. "Mary, this is Preston Blanton, Jr. He is probably the smartest man on Folly."

"The alligator man?" Mary blurted and blushed "Sorry."

"I see you have been over to Andres and met my decamped reptilian ward." He leaned over and said in Mary's ear, "When I talk that way Bubba thinks I am really smart."

Mary immediately liked this man and sensed he was indeed an intellectual as well as a humble man. Without being asked, Mary told him why she had come to the island.

Preston's eyes never left her as she spoke and she felt he would have patiently listened to her for as long as she wanted to speak.

Without a pause, when she had finished, he said, "I have an idea of how I might help you find this Jack fellow. I have a ham radio setup and I can spread the word up and down the coast as well as the Gulf. With a couple of hundred extra pairs of eyes and ears, we might get lucky."

"That is great Mr. Blanton! Between you and Frenchie I can't help but find Jack."

"So you met Louis, my brother-in-law. He left for a trip down to the Keys this morning, so he is probably already looking," Preston said.

"Chuck didn't say anything about Frenchie being married to your sister yesterday," Mary said.

"Charles Montgomery? He was one of my students about ten years ago. Let's see, not really big on being serious. Likes the girls and is a bit of a smooth talker. Am I close?" Preston asked, smiling.

"You are amazing! You had him in your class ten years ago and you remember all that?" Mary seemed amazed.

"They are all more than just students to me." Mary believed that and figured that any kid lucky enough to get assigned to Preston Blanton's class was getting more than just a teacher.

"Anyway, I'll keep in touch with Louis on the radio and I'll call Maebelle if I hear anything," Preston stated as Maebelle walked up with another man in tow.

The man with Maebelle was about her height with hair that had been turning gray for a while. His fluid movements and the bounce in his step made it nearly impossible to guess his age. He had been in a horrific accident in the past. His left hand was missing above the wrist and his right was missing most of his thumb and all of his forefinger. His face bore numerous scars and part of one ear was missing.

Instead of being repelled by his disfigurement Mary found herself drawn forward and took his offered hand in both of hers.

"Mary, I would like you to meet Jesse Porter."

Despite his injuries, it was obvious to Mary that Mr. Porter had been a very good-looking man. Even as he was there was a magnetism about him that Mary could feel.

"You are supplying the oysters this evening I understand," Mary said with a smile.

"I provided the boat, but my boys did the work," He said with a grin and then added, "Maebelle filled me in on your search for Jack Young. I am sorry to say I never met him. I do know pretty much everyone on the island and see quite a few of them off and on so I'll ask around for you."

A boy of about twelve came up and told Jesse that they needed help getting the bushels of oysters out of the back of his truck. He excused himself and followed the boy across the churchyard.

Two other boys had a large basket of oysters between them as they struggled to get it to where they were to be steamed. She watched as Jesse reached inside the truck and with his one hand pulled another overflowing basket out like it was empty.

"Strongest man I ever knew," Bubba stated from her side, where he had appeared. That was saying something because Bubba was a big man and obviously very strong himself.

"Jesse can do more work with one hand than two people can do with four," He added, with a tone of respect in his voice.

Mary would like to know more about Jesse Porter. As a reporter, she knew there was a story there. As she followed Maebelle, who wanted to introduce her to the pastor, Mary saw that Jesse had a kid under each arm in a headlock. He was spinning them around.

The pastor, Reverend Joshua Philips, was a kindly gentleman with a quick smile and a warm hand. Maebelle had already told him Mary's story and he asked if there was anything new. She told him about Frenchie and Preston. "

"The Blanton and the Lasne families have been members here for a long time. Preston sometimes fills in for me on Sundays," The Pastor said right before Bubba banged a serving spoon on a bucket to let everyone know it was time to eat.

Reverend Philips thanked God for the beautiful day, the great turnout, the delicious food, and the visitors that had come.

"I would like to take a moment and introduce a special guest who is with us this evening all the way from the nation's capital," He said, motioning toward Mary who sheepishly waved when everyone clapped.

He continued on to explain that Mary was doing a special newspaper piece on the area. In addition, she had been trying to locate a friend of her mother's from years ago when she came to stay the summers on the island. He named the Young family and the boat the *Miss Margaret*. He requested anyone who might know something to talk to Mary.

Mary ate her fill of potato salad, and a half dozen steamed oysters. Mr. Porter even talked her into trying a raw oyster on the half shell. She told him it tasted a lot better than it looked and she would get her friend Carl to try them when she got back home.

"I talked to your Carl before you came down here. I kind of run the water department for the island and was over visiting Bubba one day when he called about the house. Bubba was busy so I took the call. Worked out because he was calling to make sure the water and electricity would be on when you got here." Jesse explained.

Carl had been a busy guy getting everything ready for her visit. It was nice, she thought, to have someone looking out for her. She thought Carl would fit in just perfectly down here.

"Mary, I have told you three times I am fine. You don't need to worry about me. Now tell me everything." Carl insisted when Mary called that evening.

It was a long conversation and Mary ended by saying it was a memorable time and that dozens of people had wished her luck. Unfortunately, no one had anything relevant to add to her search for Jack. Mary said she wasn't discouraged, though.

"Maebelle has a couple of new ideas and Mr. Blanton told me he was getting on his radio for a while when he got home and would start putting out the word."

"What about the storm? It could get pretty windy down that way near the weekend, according to Percy." Percy Rogers was the weatherman for one of the local TV stations. He was also a friend of Carl's.

Mary assured him that it would be fine. All the locals had been through quite a few storms and even hurricanes. They knew what to do. She had seen Chuck ride up with a case of beer strapped to the back of his bike so she figured everyone was ready. Finally, after a couple of suppressed yawns, Mary said she had to get some sleep.

"Goodnight, my Carl," Mary said with a laugh and hung up before he could respond.

Chapter 17

Even though the day dawned bright and sunny Mary could feel something different in the air. The bedside radio, which she hadn't had on since arriving, delivered the news that there was indeed a hurricane on the way up the coast. It was still small and wandering.

Mary realized that she had almost cut herself off from all outside news as she searched for her mother's elusive love. Strange thing for a reporter to do she thought.

Before joining Maebelle and Bubba for breakfast, Mary decided to take a walk on the beach. The wind had gotten stronger and the air was brisk, so she put on one of Carl's old sweatshirts and her jeans. A couple of people were walking along the water line looking for shells and shark teeth, but for the most part, the beach was empty.

Mary watched several shrimp boats bobbing in the roughening water and wondered out loud. "Mother, did you stand in this very spot and watch the boats? Did you plan the life you expected to have with Jack? Did you ever miss all this and wish you could come back?"

"Hey, who are you talking to?" A voice asked from behind her and when she turned Chuck was standing there grinning.

"Oh, hi Chuck. I was just thinking out loud. It looks like the hurricane is really headed this way."

"I hope so, 'cause man I have an awesome party planned. You gonna come?" Chuck asked as he stepped up to her.

"I don't know Chuck, maybe I could stop over for a few minutes."

"Cool. I gotta run and get some more beer. Wouldn't want to run out halfway through the storm. That would be a bummer." Chuck said with a big grin. Then, before she could move Chuck grabbed her by the shoulders, gave her a quick kiss, turned, and ran back toward his house.

Mary stood stunned for a moment, watching his receding figure. She touched her fingers to her lips and looked around to see if anyone had seen what had just happened.

Mary had not dated much. There had been a couple of short-lived relationships in college, but before they got serious they had ended. She wasn't willing to go beyond holding hands and light petting and the guys always seemed to want more. As for Mary, she never showed impatience, and she would never have kissed a near stranger like that.

When Mary landed her job at the paper things had moved so fast. The late hours and busy schedule left her with little time for socializing, except for the time she spent with Carl.

The differences between Chuck and Carl couldn't have been more extreme. Where Chuck seemed flighty Carl always had a plan for what was next. Carl was confident but always considered his actions, whereas Chuck was impetuous. Not that Carl wasn't adventurous, the skydiving and Green Beret stuff was just a few of the things he had tried. And he certainly wasn't a wimp. The fact that he had taken on two thugs in a dark parking lot was proof of that. If anything, Carl was maybe a little too fearless.

In all their time together he had never been anything but a gentleman. Mary knew Carl thought he loved her. He also wanted more than just a working relationship, but not once had he ever pressured her beyond letting her know how he felt.

Still, Mary thought Chuck was good-looking and fun to be around. Mary heard Chuck's bike roar as he took off down the road toward Center Street. This whole experience had been so unreal. Finding the letters and coming down to Folly in search of Jack, meeting all the people that lived on the magical small island, and riding on the beach behind Chuck on his motorcycle; it was almost too much to take in.

Shaking her head, Mary started back to the house. As Mary looked up, she saw Maebelle standing on her porch waving at her. She waved back and hurried to breakfast.

Throughout the meal, Mary wondered if Maebelle had seen Chuck kiss her on the beach. If she had would she think there was something going on between them? Mary didn't know what to do the next time she talked to Carl. Should she tell him? It wasn't a real kiss since she hadn't kissed Chuck back. Mary reasoned that there was nothing to tell Carl. Mary suddenly realized that all conversation had stopped and the other two were looking at her as if they expected an answer to something.

"I'm sorry. My mind was wandering. Did you ask me something?" Mary apologized.

"I was saying," Maebelle said with a knowing smile and Mary knew she had seen what had happened on the beach. "There is a place called Shem Creek across the Cooper River on the other side of the harbor from Charleston. A lot of shrimp boats have docked there at one time or another. It is possible that when Jack left here he might have ended up here. Here, let me show you."

Maebelle got up and opened the kitchen drawer. She pulled out a map of the Charleston area and laid it on the table. "Now here is Folly and there is Charleston Harbor. Shem Creek is right here. You can almost see it from the end of Folly. There are plenty of seafood restaurants there and they buy the shrimp and fish right off the boat and cook it up."

Mary studied the map for a moment, drawing a line with her finger from the end of Folly Beach to the mouth of the inlet.

"Looks like it would be easier to get there by water than to drive all the way around." Mary surmised.

"That's exactly what we will do. If you want to go." Maebelle announced.

"Do you have a boat?" Mary asked.

"We used to but not anymore. Jesse Porter does and since this was his idea, he said he would be glad to ferry us over. I figure a close-up view of the water around here would be suitable for your article."

"What about the storm?" Mary asked, concerned about being out on the water.

"It will be alright," Bubba replied. "Y'all should be home before anything really starts to change. Most of the time these things come and go in a day or two and this is a small one."

"In that case, let's do it," Mary said and began clearing the table. She realized that she had assimilated into the household of these two people. Mary didn't knock before coming into the house. She just announced her arrival, and helping with the dishes and meals just came naturally. It was nice to have a family again. For the first time, Mary realized she wasn't anxious to return to DC, although she did miss Carl a great deal.

An hour later Maebelle and Mary met Jesse Porter at the boat landing. Mary had expected to take to the water in a fancy speedboat like the ones she had seen speeding up and down the Folly River. Her water chariot, however, was not like that. The boat was nothing fancy at all. There was no cabin or even a steering wheel. Instead, Jesse sat in front of a big outboard motor in the stern on three wooden planks.

Jesse stood and offered Mary a hand as she attempted to get in the boat without ending up in the water. Maebelle just jumped in and took a seat on the middle plank. She motioned for Mary to sit beside her.

"This seat will be the smoothest ride and we shouldn't get wet here."

"You ladies ready?" Jesse asked and then began motoring down the river. Mary liked the wind and salt spray as they skimmed across the water. Pulling her jacket closer, Mary watched Folly Beach pass her on the right. It looked very different from the river.

She looked over her shoulder and Mr. Porter gave her one of his impish smiles.

After returning the night before from the church supper, Bubba had told her the story of Jesse Porter.

"Eleven or so years ago Jesse was out fishing with his sons, James and Brian; fishing with dynamite."

"Dynamite!" Mary exclaimed.

"It kind of got started during the Depression. People would do that sometimes when they were trying to catch a lot of fish quickly. The dynamite stuns the fish and they float to the surface. It was a way of getting a load of fish quickly to sell them so they could buy other things they needed. Several people used to do that around here. Anyway, the dynamite blew up in his hand and it was something awful. What you see now is only a small part of it. Jesse's son James saved his life, although both of them would say it was the Lord and they are right. I have no doubt. Some of his bones punched holes in the bottom of the boat. He had two shotgun shells in his pocket and they both fired off. James says you could see his lungs through the hole they blasted in his chest. The zipper of his coat was blown through his intestines and lodged in his spine," Bubba explained.

Mary had one hand over her mouth. She shuddered at the thought of what Mr. Porter had been through. Bubba gave her a second to recoup and then continued.

"The only thing that kept him from bleeding to death on the spot was the fact that the heat from the explosion cauterized some of the arteries. Even at that by the time he got to the hospital, he had lost over twenty percent of his blood. The doctor said his heart should not even be beating at that point. They gave him about five or ten percent chance of living."

"Mr. Porter must be an incredibly tough individual," Mary stated.

"They don't make them any tougher," Bubba agreed. "He walked from the police station to the ambulance when they came for him."

Mary just shook her head in disbelief. Carl had to meet this amazing man, she thought.

Bubba continued, "When he was in the hospital, Jesse told me he had promised the Lord that if he lived, he would be a better husband, dad, and Christian. Now, a lot of people would probably say that I am sure. Others would become bitter men, drunks, and probably recluses. I believe Jesse is proud to wear his injuries as a witness to the miracles the Lord can do with body and soul."

"Amen to that, Bubba, amen to that," Maebelle whispered and Mary silently agreed.

Chapter 18

Maebelle pointed out things of interest as they motored by. First was the Coast Guard Station at the end of the island, then the long abandoned Morris Island Lighthouse. Mary saw Fort Sumter, Fort Moultrie, and Castle Pinckney. They passed the Battery, where Mary had met Thomas Williams when she had first arrived. Mary couldn't believe it had only been a few days ago. Time seemed to stretch and twist around her as the past and present intertwined.

Mr. Porter ferried them expertly across Charleston Harbor and soon they were entering Shem Creek. The creek, which wasn't all that wide, was packed to overflow with shrimp boats. Some were tied three or four across.

Mary just stared, amazed. At Andre's she had never seen more than a couple boats tied up at the same time, but here at Shem Creek, there were dozens. Men clamored across the decks, sometimes jumping from boat to boat. Boxes, of what she assumed to be shrimp, were passed hand to hand until they reached the dock. Mary decided it was a form of organized chaos.

Mary pulled a small camera from her bag and took some photos. The editor had offered to let her use one of the professional cameras that the paper owned but it was big and bulky. Besides, she had decided that for her article she wanted the same kind of pictures that a normal visitor would take if they were there on vacation.

Mr. Porter threaded the narrow passage between the boats. Mary wondered how in the world a boat could leave the dock unless all the ones in front of it moved first.

At that moment, she saw one of the shrimp boats pulling away from one of the docks about fifty feet in front of their small boat. She looked back at Mr. Porter wondering if he had seen it too. He just smiled and somehow maneuvered their much smaller craft into a gap between two of the much larger boats.

As the boat passed slowly by, Mary reached out and touched the side. She watched as it slipped between the rows of other boats with less than a foot on each side.

Carl was proud of how he could maneuver his car into just barely big enough parking spaces. He was really going to be impressed with this she thought as she snapped several pictures.

Once the shrimp boat had passed Mr. Porter eased forward and pulled into a spot designated for smaller boats to dock. Cutting the engine, he jumped out and offered his hand to the women. Mary felt like she was holding a piece of solid steel as he lifted her from the boat. She had no doubt that Mr. Porter was every bit as strong as Bubba had said he was.

"Ladies, I am heading down the dock to find the *Miss Isabelle*. Capt. Rick is an old friend of mine. When you are ready, that's where you will find me. If anyone has seen Jack in the last few years, he should know about it," Mr. Porter informed them.

"Mary and I'll make our way to The Trawler Restaurant and check with the manager. They buy more seafood from the boats than almost anyone else." Maebelle said and they headed in opposite directions.

Seagulls dove, shrill voices sounding, for the scraps that were tossed over the side as the decks were scrubbed. There seemed to be plenty for the birds to eat, but still, they vied for the biggest pieces like they were starving.

The two women reached the restaurant, just before the bridge that crossed Shem Creek. Mary's head was practically swimming with the sights and sounds surrounding her.

"Why don't we order some lunch and while we wait for the food we can ask the manager if he has ever done business with Jack?" Maebelle suggested.

Mary agreed and they were led up the stairs to a rooftop dining area. They picked a table right by the railing overlooking the creek. The wind had died down to a breeze and the sun was shining. Maebelle said it was just one of nature's tricks. The proverbial calm before the storm.

They decided to split the seafood sampler and after ordering, Maebelle asked the waitress if they could speak to the manager. Five minutes later a man dressed in jeans, a lightweight turtleneck sweater, and wearing a stocking cap came up to their table.

"Ladies, I am Jeffery Hopkins, the manager of The Trawler. I hope there isn't a problem."

"No, nothing like that." Maebelle, not one to stand on formalities, reached over and pulled one of the other chairs out. "If you have a minute we would like to ask you a couple of questions."

With a smile, the manager took the offered seat. "I'll do my best to answer any questions you might have."

"Thank you, I am Maebelle and this is my friend Mary. We came over by boat from Folly and we are looking for a man."

"Well, Maebelle I am afraid I am already taken, but..." With a big grin, the man offered back.

Maebelle gave her signature laugh, "Good one, Jeffery. I have my hands full with Bubba and Mary has her Carl."

Maebelle motioned to Mary and she picked up from there, giving him an abridged version of why she was there instead of Washington DC.

"A reporter from a nation's capital, that's impressive. I am afraid, though, that I have nothing I can give you that would help. I have been manager here for just a couple of years and during that time I haven't met any Jack Young or seen a boat named the *Miss Margaret*. I don't know if you might have thought of this, but sometimes a captain will change the name of his boat. They may believe the name has become unlucky when they go a while without getting a substantial load of shrimp. Last year one of the men changed the name of his trawler from The Mary Black, his girlfriend's name, to The Black Witch when they broke up," Jeffery laughed.

"Believe me, Jack would not change the name of his boat and if he got another, he would name it the *Miss Margaret*," Maebelle assured Mary.

"Well, I wish I could have helped. It was very enjoyable meeting both of you." The manager said as he slid his chair back and started to leave. The waitress had arrived with the food and he thought he should let them eat.

He stopped mid-stride and turned back to them. "I almost forgot about Billy, our head chef. He has been around Shem Creek his whole life, most of it spent right here at the docks. Listen, go ahead and eat while your food is hot and I'll send him up here in, say a half hour," He told them.

Mary thought she was too excited to eat. Finally, someone might actually have met Jack. After one bite of crab cake, she decided maybe she could eat just a little.

"I am glad you suggested we split a plate. I am so full." Mary declared and then added with a thought, "But shouldn't we have saved something for Mr. Porter?"

"I'll get him a Flounder Po Boy to take home, but I imagine he has already eaten twice by now. Shrimpers are exemplary hosts," Maebelle informed her.

They could hear someone on the stairs heading their way. A short, thin man with snow-white hair finished his climb and Mary felt guilty that this man had come to them instead of the other way around. She figured he had to be at least eighty years old and was wheezing a bit from the effort.

"You must be Billy. We are sorry you had to come all the way up here," Maebelle apologized.

"Don't even give it a second thought," Billy said as he reached the table. "Believe it or not, I try to make the climb at least twice each day for exercise and to get out of the kitchen."

Taking the seat that had been vacated by his boss earlier, the old man squirmed until he found a comfortable position. After a round of introductions, Mary asked Billy if he had ever met Jack or seen his boat.

"Both," He replied, and then added, "I knowed a John Young and his son Jack. The boat was originally called the *LuLu*, until the boy changed it to the *Miss Margaret*. But you know that was a long time ago."

Mary sat and stared at the boats tethered to the dock below her for a long pause and then asked almost in a whisper. "Can you tell me about Jack? I mean what he was like and what happened to him?"

"Jack and his father were both kinda quiet. I never did hear them argue about nothing. They would tie up here at Shem Creek a couple of times a year fer a week or two. Course they comed over at least once a month too. Lots of the captains did that cause they kin get nets and stuff right heya."

"Was it always Jack and his father on the boat?" Mary asked.

"Mostly but towards the end, John weren't up to shrimping much so Jack would have a kid by the name of Butch helping. I recollect a couple times he brought that little girlfriend of his along. She were a pretty thing and real nice like too."

"That would have been Margaret," Maebelle surmised.

"That's right. I only talked to her a couple of time but them two was fun to watch, all lovey-like an all. They would always be holding hands and whispering back and forth like. It's a shame what happened and all." Billy said.

"What did happen, Billy?" Mary was balanced on the edge of her chair, leaning toward the old man.

"Ain't too sure zackly, but I am eighty-four and I kin tell you I never seed two people more in love. Jack told me that he was gonna give up shrimpin' and move to where his girl was alivin. But then his daddy got real sick and they needed all the money Jack could make."

"What happened then?" Mary asked even though she knew the old man wouldn't know about the Valentine's card.

"Well, I didn't see hide nor hair of Jack for a couple months. I knowed his daddy had died and all so I figured he musta sold the boat and gone after his girl. One day I had come down to the boats to see ifin they had any xspecialy good fish what had got caught in the net along with the shrimp."

Billy glanced at his watch and realized he had been away from his kitchen for some time.

"Please carry on. I'll tell your boss we delayed you," Mary pleaded.

"Anyway, as I was asayin, I was looking for some of the captains I usually dealt with and tied up right in front of this place I seen the *LuLu*. There was Jack apaintin right over the name. When he had finished it was *Miss Margaret*. I asked him if his girl had come back down here and he said she weren't his girl no longer so I kinda thought puttin' her name on the boat was strange."

"Is that the last time you ever saw him?" Maebelle asked.

"He told me he was gonna be gone for a good while and the next morning about six there was the *Miss Margaret* halfway down the creek headed for open water. That were the last time I seen Jack or his boat."

Maebelle and Mary both thanked him, then found Jeffery Hopkins and did the same.

About a half hour later Mr. Porter guided his boat through the creek and they made for home.

"You all ready for the storm?" Carl asked when Mary called him that evening.

"It is clear tonight and not very windy," Mary said, giving her weather report from the porch.

"Yeah, I know. Percy told me that is the way it can be and then suddenly the storm is right on top of you."

"I bet he also told you to stop calling him every hour for an update." Mary laughed. "Carl, you are a strange man."

"What do you mean by that?"

"You almost get stabbed, end up in the hospital after being kicked in the head, and have FBI agents protecting you. You tell me 'Oh, it is nothing, don't worry' and yet you are a mother hen about a storm coming through down here." She explained.

"That's different."

"And just how, may I ask?"

It isn't that difficult to explain. You see the difference is, you are more important to me than I am," Carl stated matter-of-factly.

"You are impossible," Mary sighed, "Now, would you like to hear how things went down here today?"

Mary spent an hour giving Carl all the details of her trip to Shem Creek and what she had found out about Jack. The whole time she talked Mary toyed with her Valentine, the one that had brought her to Folly.

Carl injected comments like 'I would have liked to see that' and 'that sounds so cool' and Mary knew he would love this place she had discovered.

"The boss, remember Body Carson, wanted me to ask when you were planning on coming back?" Carl asked, only half kidding.

"I have only been away for four days Carl, not four weeks." Mary chided.

"Is that all? Seems longer. Anyway, I hate having to get my own coffee and donuts," Carl said.

"You don't eat donuts. Remember you told me you were the only reporter in the world that didn't drink a pot of coffee and eat a box of donuts before the sun was up?" Mary reminded him.

"I forgot, see, that just proves my point. I am a wreck without you. I can't even remember I don't eat donuts. Oh, by the way, I am guest lecturing at your Alma Mater tomorrow evening. No pressure or anything, but there will be young women there who would love to have your job."

"I'll keep that in mind while I walk on the beach in the morning and watch the sunrise," Mary said with a drowsy yawn.

"OK, now that hurts. I guess you should get some rest for your walk in the morning. Be careful Mary and remember that..."

"I know." Mary interrupted.

"That you love me."

"Did I say that?" Carl asked.

"A couple of times."

"Then it must be true."

Chapter 19

Mary met Maebelle coming out of her house with two big cups of coffee. Mary accepted hers gratefully and they made their way to the beach crossing through the sand dunes.

"Did Chuck's hurricane party bother you last night?" Maebelle asked.

"Sounded like they were having a grand old time, but no, DC is a lot noisier than his party most of the time. He invited me to come over again when I got home last night," Mary said.

"And..." Maebelle held the 'and' like a question mark.

"I told him I wanted to call Carl and that our trip to Shem Creek turned up some helpful information. He kind of looked at me like he had no idea what I was talking about and then left," Mary said.

"Chuck is just a tad shallow and more than a touch impulsive, but you know that."

Mary blushed and knew Maebelle was referring to the kiss Chuck had given her before.

"Does it seem warm to you this morning? I thought with the storm and all it would be cooler."

"Mary, I'm not saying anything you did was wrong. After all, you aren't engaged to your Carl. Are you?"

"I guess the old 'change the subject' thing doesn't work on you, huh?" Mary sighed and sipped her coffee.

"Just ask Bubba, and yes, it is a little warmer this morning. The storms pulling all the warm air towards her. It helps gather strength," Maebelle laughed and then took Mary's arm as they headed to the Pavilion.

"I didn't kiss Chuck, he kissed me. He caught me by surprise or I would never have let him. But you needn't worry Maebelle, I don't have any romantic plans for Chuck. "Carl has asked me to marry him, but I'm not ready yet," Mary replied.

As they walked Maebelle told Mary she had talked to Preston Blanton the night before. Preston said the word had been spread via his shortwave radio. He added that a dozen other operators had joined in the hunt all up and down the east coast and the Gulf of Mexico. Several boat captains had said they would keep an eye out.

Frenchie had checked in and was talking to every boat he encountered, but had not gotten any leads. He had told his brother-in-law that most of the boats were at the dock due to the storm so he had a chance to talk to quite a few of the crews.

Maebelle could see that Mary was disappointed, so she reminded her it had only been two days since the two men had taken on the task of locating Jack.

"They are taking the seats off the Ferris Wheel. Guess they are trying to beat the storm." Maebelle said as she pointed toward the Pavilion. Mary had seen the amusement park at the end of Center Street when she arrived.

Mary watched as men swarmed over the big ride, loosening bolts and lowering the seats with ropes. Since she wanted a picture, they walked faster and soon reached the concrete boardwalk.

They watched for several minutes as the men worked and then Maebelle suggested they walk out onto the pier.

"Bubba and I have danced many an hour away right here," Maebelle said as they crossed the dance floor. "Tommy and Jimmy Dorsey, Benny Goodman, The Ink Spots, and even Hank Williams have performed here in the past. The Tams, The Drifters, Otis Redding; they all played here."

Mary was impressed. "I went dancing with Carl several times, but neither of us had good moves."

"Dancing isn't about being good at it. Lots of folks around here dance every chance they get because it makes them happy. That's what it's really about. You know, if you are still around next weekend, the Volunteer Fireman's Ball will happen right here."

Before Mary could reply Maebelle added, "You don't need a date to come. All you need is a volunteer fireman to invite you and Bubba has been one for years, so you are invited."

Mary met Maebelle coming out of her house with two big cups of coffee. Mary accepted hers gratefully and they made their way to the beach crossing through the sand dunes.

"Did Chuck's hurricane party bother you last night?" Maebelle asked.

"Sounded like they were having a grand old time, but no, DC is a lot noisier than his party most of the time. He invited me to come over again when I got home last night," Mary said.

"And..." Maebelle held the 'and' like a question mark.

"I told him I wanted to call Carl and that our trip to Shem Creek turned up some helpful information. He kind of looked at me like he had no idea what I was talking about and then left," Mary said.

"Chuck is just a tad shallow and more than a touch impulsive, but you know that."

Mary blushed and knew Maebelle was referring to the kiss Chuck had given her before.

"Does it seem warm to you this morning? I thought with the storm and all it would be cooler."

"Mary, I'm not saying anything you did was wrong. After all, you aren't engaged to your Carl. Are you?"

"I guess the old 'change the subject' thing doesn't work on you, huh?" Mary sighed and sipped her coffee.

"Just ask Bubba, and yes, it is a little warmer this morning. The storms pulling all the warm air towards her. It helps gather strength," Maebelle laughed and then took Mary's arm as they headed to the Pavilion.

"I didn't kiss Chuck, he kissed me. He caught me by surprise or I would never have let him. But you needn't worry Maebelle, I don't have any romantic plans for Chuck. "Carl has asked me to marry him, but I'm not ready yet," Mary replied.

As they walked Maebelle told Mary she had talked to Preston Blanton the night before. Preston said the word had been spread via his shortwave radio. He added that a dozen other operators had joined in the hunt all up and down the east coast and the Gulf of Mexico. Several boat captains had said they would keep an eye out.

Frenchie had checked in and was talking to every boat he encountered, but had not gotten any leads. He had told his brother-in-law that most of the boats were at the dock due to the storm so he had a chance to talk to quite a few of the crews.

Maebelle could see that Mary was disappointed, so she reminded her it had only been two days since the two men had taken on the task of locating Jack.

"They are taking the seats off the Ferris Wheel. Guess they are trying to beat the storm." Maebelle said as she pointed toward the Pavilion. Mary had seen the amusement park at the end of Center Street when she arrived.

Mary watched as men swarmed over the big ride, loosening bolts and lowering the seats with ropes. Since she wanted a picture, they walked faster and soon reached the concrete boardwalk.

They watched for several minutes as the men worked and then Maebelle suggested they walk out onto the pier.

"Bubba and I have danced many an hour away right here," Maebelle said as they crossed the dance floor. "Tommy and Jimmy Dorsey, Benny Goodman, The Ink Spots, and even Hank Williams have performed here in the past. The Tams, The Drifters, Otis Redding; they all played here."

Mary was impressed. "I went dancing with Carl several times, but neither of us had good moves."

"Dancing isn't about being good at it. Lots of folks around here dance every chance they get because it makes them happy. That's what it's really about. You know, if you are still around next weekend, the Volunteer Fireman's Ball will happen right here."

Before Mary could reply Maebelle added, "You don't need a date to come. All you need is a volunteer fireman to invite you and Bubba has been one for years, so you are invited."

Folly Beach Pier - 1969

Chapter 20

The decision to stay the night at Maebelle's house had been a wise one for Mary. For hours, they had stayed up listening to the howling wind and feeling the rocking of the house on its tall pilings. A couple of times Mary was sure it would fall over. It was pitch black outside and the rain pelted the protective shutters, which sounded like hands full of gravel being slung at the house by a giant.

Carl had called three times to make sure everything was alright and she had assured him she was fine. Or rather she had been fine until the lights suddenly went out and plunged them into total darkness. Bubba quickly lit a lantern and added to the light from the fireplace it was almost cozy.

When an errant trashcan slammed into the side of the house Mary let out a small cry and Maebelle moved over to sit beside her on the sofa. She put an arm around the younger girl and said. "Not to worry, my dear, it sounds a lot more serious than it is."

"I'm sorry," Mary apologized. "I am not usually this jumpy."

"We have been through more than a few of these things so we don't get too worked up. This is your first time, so be as skittish as you want. Nothing to apologize for," Bubba said, and then he got up and sat on her other side.

In the warmth of two bodies, Mary felt safe and the wind and rain became less threatening. When she awoke a couple of hours later, her head was on Bubba's shoulder. He snored softly and she heard Maebelle in the kitchen rattling pots and pans.

Light streamed through the shutters and the wind had diminished to a stiff breeze. The electricity was still out and when Mary quietly got up and checked the phone it too was dead.

Peering out the window, Mary saw a lot of debris scattered around the yard, but there didn't seem to be any major damage. She tiptoed past the still-sleeping Bubba and headed into the kitchen.

Maebelle was cooking on a portable camp stove as if it was something she did every day.

"Good morning," she called over her shoulder to Mary as she entered the room.

"Well, that was fun," Mary said as she stretched and yawned loudly.

"Was it as terrible as you thought it would be?" Maebelle asked as she whipped eggs in a bowl.

"Let's see. The part before the lights went out and I thought I might die and my body washed out to sea wasn't too bad." She joked and then started getting plates down from the cupboard. Then she turned to Maebelle and said seriously, "Thanks for letting me stay here last night. It would have been pretty scary by myself."

"It was Bubba's idea. He is kind of old school, you know. He would have been a heroic Knight of the Round Table; rescuing maidens in distress and fighting the dragon to protect the town. Kind of like your Carl. If you hadn't come over, Bubba would have stayed up all night watching your place and making sure you were okay."

"I know he would do anything for you. I look at you two and I want what you have. The way he looks at you, worries about you, takes care of you." Mary admitted.

Maebelle set aside her cooking and sat in one of the chairs, motioning for Mary to take the one across from her.

"Mary, let me tell you a story. When Bubba and I were first married, I got a terrible cold that turned into pneumonia. I coughed and coughed and couldn't sleep. Finally, at about two o'clock in the morning, Bubba said he was off to James Island, to wake the doctor up and get me some medicine. Of course, I said he didn't have to do that, but he did it anyway. It was similar to last night, pouring rain and windy when he left."

"Well, he was away for almost two hours and when he got back, he saw, through the window, that I had fallen asleep on the sofa. When I woke up later that morning Bubba was asleep on the porch. He had pulled a chair up to the window and his ear was pressed against the window pane. He had a terrible crick in his neck for days."

Mary smiled as she got the picture of the story in her mind.

"Bubba didn't want to wake me up so he didn't come into the house. He kept his ear to the window so that if I woke up and started coughing again he would know. That was when I realized what an amazing man I had married."

Maebelle leaned back in her chair, crossed her arms, and looked at Mary.

Mary hesitated for a moment and then spoke slowly and softly like she was revealing a secret.

"When my mother died suddenly, I was an emotional wreck. The house seemed so big and lonely. Carl came over and for a few nights, he would just sit in a chair while I cried myself to sleep on the sofa. When I woke up in the morning he would either be fixing breakfast or sitting at the table drinking coffee."

"I felt so guilty because it was obvious he was getting a lot less sleep than I was but he just kept showing up every night. Finally, one night I insisted I was OK and was ready to get back to living a normal life. I told him it was time for him to sleep at his house and not in my chair. He resisted, but they finally agreed when I promised to call him as soon as I woke up in the morning."

"When he left, he handed me a slip of paper. It was the number of the car phone he had just gotten installed the day before. He told me to use that number to call because his house phone wasn't working right."

"So what happened?" Maebelle asked.

"I did sleep pretty well that night because it felt like Carl was still there watching over me. On the way to the kitchen in the morning, I glanced out the window and there was Carl's car sitting in the driveway. I was startled at first because I could see him in the light from the porch, asleep with his head on the steering wheel."

"I was just about to go out when I saw him wake up. He let the car coast down the driveway and then carefully drove off. I grabbed the phone to call him, but before I dialed I understood what he had done. Carl had driven away the night before and then came back after the lights were off and parked in front of my house," Mary said.

"He wanted to be right there for you in case you called and said you needed him to come over. The reason you felt like he was there watching over you was because he was," Maebelle finished the story for her.

"Yes. I knew then that I could always depend on him. That when he said he would always be there for me, he would." Mary said in a quiet voice.

"And you never said anything?"

"No. It didn't seem like the right thing to do. Like it would somehow cheapen what he had done for me if I knew about it." Mary answered.

"And maybe you were just a little afraid. Afraid of your relationship becoming something you weren't ready for?"

"I don't know. Probably. Yes." Mary admitted sheepishly.

"What is your favorite food?" Maebelle asked, catching Mary off guard.

"Uh, Chinese," Mary answered.

"Carl's?"

"Pizza with lots of meat and mushrooms."

"When you go out to eat where do you usually go?"

"Leus Chinese Bistro."

"And when you go to the movies..." Maebelle left the rest of the question blank.

Mary didn't need to answer the question. They went to see the movie she wanted to see because Carl always insisted he had wanted to see it for a long time.

Maebelle reached across the table and patted Mary's hand. "It has been a rough time for you; your mother's death, grandmother's decline, and now all this with Jack. You said you wanted what Bubba and I have. You can stop looking, Mary. You already have it. You have had it for a while now. Let Carl know how you feel about him. You have your Bubba if you really want him."

Just then Maebelle's husband came into the kitchen. His usual perfectly combed hair was scattered across his head and he scratched his belly with one hand as he tried to pat his errant locks down with the other.

The two women looked at each other and burst out laughing.

"What?" Bubba asked, mystified. "What is so funny?"

Before they had finished eating the phone rang, once again in service, and Maebelle said to Mary, "Go ahead and answer it. I'm sure it's your Carl."

Mary stepped into her temporary bedroom and picked up the phone.

"Are you OK?" Carl asked before she could even say hello. "I tried a bunch of times at your place and Maebelle's but the phone was out."

"It's all right Carl, we are all fine. I stayed here last night and it was a little scary. Both the power and the phone went out. I have never experienced anything like it. No real damage that I can see, and we just ate breakfast on a camp stove," Mary rushed to assure him.

"That's terrific. Tell me what it was like," he insisted.

Mary did her darnedest to describe the night before, knowing she couldn't really describe what it was like. "...and so Bubba says we are heading out to check on the rest of the people this morning. To help if anyone needs anything." Mary ended the story and said she would give him an update later in the day.

"Just be really careful," Carl requested.

"I'll be careful..." Mary paused for a long moment and added. "Thank you, Carl, for everything. I love you."

Mary listened for a moment and wondered if the phone had gone out again when Carl didn't answer. Then he asked, "What brought that on? I mean I am happy to hear you say it and all..."

"Chinese," Mary answered.

"Chinese?" Carl asked, confused.

"I'll explain later," Mary said with a lighthearted laugh and hung up the phone. It was nearly impossible for her to understand how uttering those three words had made her feel. Mary felt truly happy and it was a nice feeling.

When she returned to the kitchen, Bubba was already outside loading the truck with tools and tarps. Maebelle had finished the dishes and was hanging her apron on a hook. When she saw the smile on Mary's face, she just nodded knowingly.

Chapter 21

Everyone was out and about checking for damage to their homes and cars. A few trees were down and, unfortunately, a couple of them had fallen on houses. Bubba pulled into the yard of one of the rental properties where half a dozen men were working to get a large oak tree off the front porch.

"Need any more help?" Bubba called from his truck.

"We got it covered Bubba, but the Baxter place has a tree through the roof. You got any tarps?"

"Right in the back. I'll get over that way right now." Maebelle and Mary finished handing out cups of coffee from an oversize thermos and then climbed back in the truck.

Bubba drove a couple of streets over and a block east of where they were and pulled into the yard of the Baxter house. An older couple, in their seventies, Mary figured, stood in the front yard and looked up at their roof.

A man was on the roof examining the large tree limb that perforated the roof and Mary saw that it was Mr. Porter. Bubba pulled a couple of large tarps from the bed of his truck along with a chainsaw. He tied a rope to the big saw and carried it over to the house.

"Jesse, here catch this rope. I'll be right up," Bubba called and tossed the end of the rope high into the air. Jesse swiped it out of the air and tied it to the limb. Bubba scurried up the ladder that was against the house and crossed over to where Jesse was hauling the saw up.

As they watched the men on the roof, Maebelle introduced Mary to the Baxters. Working together, they made short work of cutting the intrusive limb apart and tossing the pieces into the yard. Then they spread one of the tarps over the hole, secured it in place, and climbed down.

They talked about the storm and agreed that it had not done much damage overall. Jesse headed over to the water department building while Bubba, Maebelle, and Mary drove around the island checking for any more house damage. Bubba cut a tree off a car and used another tarp to cover the broken back window. They didn't spot anything else until Mary asked.

"What are all those cars doing over there?" A small concrete block building was surrounded by cars. A tall antenna pole was strapped to one corner of the building.

"Preston's radio building," Maebelle informed her as they joined the other vehicles. Mr. Blanton stepped out of the building and began talking to one of the men waiting outside near his car.

Preston saw Bubba and the women and walked over to the truck.

"Some of the phones are still down and these folks want their families to know they are safe. Got a couple of people patching calls through. There isn't much room inside so they have to come in one at a time."

Preston looked over at the building and saw a man and woman come out. "Better get back to work. Oh, Mary, I was going to call Maebelle today and tell her to pass a message along. We might have a lead on Jack Young. Louis talked to one of the boats he passed on the way to Florida. The captain said he thought he had seen a boat named *Miss Margaret* down in Freeport, Texas about three months ago. I got a guy on the radio in Galveston, which is right over from Freeport and he is planning to check with the dockmaster and get back to me. I'll let you know when I hear anything."

Before Mary even knew what she was doing, she jumped out of the truck and gave Preston a hug.

"Thank you so much," Mary exclaimed.

Preston blushed and said, "I was glad to do it and it is no big deal."

"It is for me. More than you could imagine," Mary disagreed as Preston hurried back to the waiting neighbors. She got back in the truck, her spirits soaring. Three months ago was a long time, but a lot less than thirty years.

Mary excitedly told Maebelle and Bubba what Preston had said and their response was positive.

"See, I told you. The people on this island won't let you down. We help our own," Maebelle said.

"But I'm not from here. I'm not..." Mary started and Maebelle stopped her.

"Now, Mary, you have to understand something. Folly isn't just a place at the end of the road. It is much more than that. It is a frame of mind. It is... well... it..." Maebelle paused for a moment, trying to find the right words and then Bubba said.

"Mary you came here looking for answers to some questions. A big part of your mother's youth was spent here on this piece of sand. She walked the beach, smelled the sea air, drifted off to sleep, and woke up to the sound of the waves. She even fell in love here. Mary, you have only been here for a few days. Do you think you will remember Folly ten or twenty years from now?"

"Of course, I'll never forget this place," she replied with conviction.

"My guess is that your mother never stopped thinking about her time here, even though it ended the way it did. Maybe all of the places along the coast are the same, but I doubt it. When you cross that bridge, things are different," Maebelle said thoughtfully.

"That my dear Mary is why you are one of us. It came to you through your mother at first and you didn't even know it. Now that you are here, looking for your mother's Jack, you have become part of this place. And you always will be. Someone once said, "You can never wash all the sand out of your hair once you have been here."

Bubba started his truck and backed out As they drove away, he waved at two women that were coming from the house across the street. One of them was a pretty lady about Preston's age and a small older woman. The younger of the two carried a tray of steaming coffee cups and the other a carton of Coke in each hand.

Bubba waved heartily and the women smiled and nodded at him.

"That is Preston's wife Verna and his mother Lottie. Preston Senior was a dentist and he moved to the island with Lottie a long time ago. Like a lot of people who live here, this was a retreat that became their home. Senior died a while back and Verna and Buddy, some of us call him that, live with Lottie now." Maebelle explained as they headed to Center Street.

"Thought we would stop by Wienges and see if anything else is going on that we don't know about," Bubba said.

"What is Wienges?" Mary asked.

"Tommy and Kitty Wienges own the *News Stand* on Center Street. Many of the locals just refer to it as Wienges. Nearly everyone stops by there at least once a day for something. They have newspapers from all over, tasty food, comic books for the kids to read, and rocking chairs on the porch. It is probably the main hangout on the island, especially after summer is over," Maebelle explained.

"I remember now. On the left, after you pass the Catholic Church right before the Post Office?" Mary recalled.

"Very good. You are exactly right. And now that you mention it, maybe we will drop by Our Lady of Good Counsel and see if Father Williams is there today. He doesn't stay on the island, but he might be here today because of the storm," Maebelle suggested.

"I would like to meet him and find out when Mass is held," Mary replied, adding that she and Carl always attend Mass together.

"Well, let's just see what we can do about that," Maebelle said in the tone that Mary had learned meant she would find a way to make it happen.

A number of people were standing on the porch when Bubba pulled up in front of the News Stand.

"How do things look out there?" Tommy Wienges asked as they climbed the steps to the porch.

Mary recognized some of the folks from the church cookout and several of the ladies came up to ask how her search was going. They seemed genuinely happy about the news she had received earlier from Preston.

Bubba filled everyone in on what they had done and seen and they all agreed that the island had gotten through pretty well. Mr. Wienges invited them all inside for some coffee and donuts.

As they entered Mary saw several young boys sitting on the floor and in rocking chairs around a revolving stand of comic books. They handled them carefully and placed them back in the rack when they had finished.

Bubba had told her that he didn't know if the News Stand actually sold very many comic books, but he stocked all the favorites. He said the owner sometimes put forth an exterior of gruffness but was a genuinely caring man. He often fed the island kids hamburgers and told them he would put it on their account. The 'on account' part was a joke on account of the fact that he never wrote it down.

"During the off-season, the News Stand gives the kids a place to hang out with their friends," Maebelle had told her.

Mary liked what she saw in the News Stand owner and his wife. As people came and departed, it was apparent that the store was indeed the hub of everything that happened on the island.

Maebelle suggested to Mary that they walk down to the Catholic Church and see if Father Williams was there.

She told Bubba they would be back in a while and left the others to discuss the storm and solve all of the world's problems.

It was a short walk and Maebelle spotted the Father's car as they approached the building. They circled around the side and knocked on the door labeled Office. After a moment, the door was opened by a middle-aged man, fit and trim, wearing his clerical collar.

"Well, hello Maebelle how are you today? Did you make out alright in the storm?"

"Yes, Father, we did just fine. Are all your parishioners OK? We covered most of the island and didn't see a great deal of damage. I just wanted to stop by and introduce you to a friend of mine, Miss Mary Lassiter. She is staying in the house next door to us for a short while. She is Catholic herself and wanted to meet you," Maebelle said explaining their visit.

"Then you must be the young lady looking for a fellow named Jack Young. I know the fine folks of Folly are being a lot of help. By the way, how were the oysters at the cookout? I was invited, but unfortunately already had other plans." Father Williams took Mary's hand and shook it warmly.

"Small island," Maebelle laughed at Mary's surprised look. She hadn't expected the man to know about her visit.

Mary and Maebelle took turns telling Father Williams everything that had happened since Mary discovered the Valentine meant for Jack. He listened closely and only interrupted occasionally if he needed clarification on something.

"Well, Mary that is quite a story. I wish there was something I could do to help with this, but I am fairly new to the parish," The Priest explained.

"Thank you for taking the time to listen and I would like to attend Mass at least once before I leave. Carl and I go several times a week back in DC," Mary said.

"I am glad to hear that and would love to have you attend Mass with us here. In fact, our early Sunday Mass finishes just in time for you to cross the street to the Baptist church where you can join your friends. A double dose of God's word never hurt anyone," The Priest said with a chuckle and handed Mary a bulletin that gave the times of services.

"We better get moving or Bubba is liable to think I have converted," Maebelle laughed and hugged Father Williams goodbye, after reminding him he had a standing invitation for lunch any time he was on the island during the week. As they left the building Bubba drove up and they jumped in the truck.

"Figured we might as well run over to Andre's and see how things are at the dock," Bubba said as he headed to the bridge.

The only problem was that one of the crab boats had gotten its bow under the dock and when the tide came in it had sunk. The boat was about eighteen feet long and was open with a shallow side so the crab traps could be hoisted over and emptied. Everything seemed under control so Bubba headed back home to eat lunch.

As they drove up Chuck was staggering down the front stairs of his place with a giant trash bag full of after-party leftovers. He put it down next to several other bags that had been placed under the porch and walked over to the truck.

Looking at Mary, he said, "You guys missed a really fun party. We had a blast even if the storm kind of fizzled out."

"Well, I am glad it did Chuck. The rest of the people that live here don't need the expense of repairs after a severe hurricane," Maebelle replied sharply. Chuck had to move back when she flung the truck door open and headed into the house.

"Whoa, is Maebelle mad about something?" Chuck asked as he ruffled his shaggy hair.

Bubba had gotten out of the truck and walked over to the other side. He stood towering over the younger man as he placed a hand on his shoulder.

"Chuck, it's about time to grow up. Life is more than parties and chasing girls," he said, shaking his head and following his wife into the house.

"All I said was it was a cool party and all," Chuck called after Bubba as he closed the screen door. Then he turned his attention back to Mary. When he reached out to touch her arm, she took a step back out of his reach.

"Man, everyone is mad at me today."

"No one is mad at you, Chuck. I think Bubba and Maebelle are just disappointed you didn't think about your neighbors. While you were cleaning up after your party Bubba and Mr. Porter were on a roof with a chainsaw." Mary explained.

"Listen, I need to help Maebelle fix lunch," Mary said as she turned toward the house.

"Wanna go for a ride on the bike later? We could go back down to the west end again. Ya know, jump some dunes and stuff."

Mary looked at Chuck and thought he seemed so young and immature. It dawned on her that she was always comparing other men to Carl and they always came up short. Suddenly she really wanted to hear Carl's voice.

"I don't think so Chuck, but thanks for asking. Maybe Abigail would like to go for a ride," Mary suggested and hurried away.

Chuck fished into his jeans pocket and found a piece of paper. He uncrumpled it and sighed, "Good thing I got her number."

Chapter 22

While Maebelle was fixing lunch Mary stepped into the spare bedroom and called Carl, but there was no answer either on his car phone or at his house. She was disappointed but figured she would catch him later. There were a lot of areas where the car phone didn't work.

Like she did every day Mary called to check on her grandmother's condition, but nothing had changed. She missed her visits with her but knew most of the time her mother didn't know who Mary was.

After lunch she tried Carl again, but still no answer. Mary decided if she couldn't reach him during the day she would just call him when he should be at home.

When she came back into the kitchen Maebelle said, "Mary, I want to go down to the library for a while. Nothing exciting, just need to check on a few things and shelve some books."

"Well, I should work on my draft of the newspaper article unless you need me to assist with something," Mary said.

"Oh, no. I don't have that much to do. If you decide you need more pictures you should go on down to the east end of the island. You can get some pretty shots of the old

Morris Island lighthouse from there and there should be some surfers out too." Maebelle suggested.

Mary caught a glimpse of the lighthouse when Mr. Porter had taken them over to Shem Creek, but it had been too rough to get suitable photos. She helped Maebelle pick up in the kitchen and then returned to her house. Mary spent the better part of an hour banging away at her typewriter. She told how it felt to go through a hurricane (even if it was a small one) and how the islanders had worked together to help each other.

Mary tried Carl again after she had finished writing. Getting no answer, she grabbed her camera and headed out the door. Mary wasn't really worried about Carl. If anything had happened to him someone would have contacted her. Still, Mary wanted something to occupy her mind while she waited for more news on Jack and until she could talk to Carl again.

Mary drove slowly, stopping several times to take pictures. Many of the year-round occupants were out cleaning up debris left behind after the storm. Some of them saw her as she drove slowly by and waved as they worked. Mary stopped and helped an elderly man tape a piece of cardboard over a broken window.

Mary realized just how at home she felt in this place and wondered if it had been the same for her mother. As Mary continued on E. Ashley, she saw a woman standing in the yard near the street and thought she recognized her. As she stopped and saw the address on the house she realized it was the front of the Blanton house where Preston lived. Mary got out and walked over to the woman.

"Excuse me, I don't mean to bother you, but are you Preston's mother? I think I saw you and Verna Blanton yesterday as we were driving away."

The woman was small and somewhat frail-looking, but Mary saw a deep-seated strength in her.

"My name is Lottie and yes, Preston Jr. is my son," she answered.

Lottie Blanton studied Mary's face intently for a moment and then shocked Mary by adding, "You look a lot like Margaret, your mother."

"You knew my mother?" Mary asked, stumbling over her words.

"Oh, yes, I remember her quite well. Preston told me all about you and your attempt to find your mother's old beau. Would you like to sit for a moment or two and I'll tell you what I remember?" Lottie asked.

Without waiting for an answer, she led Mary up the steps and onto the screened-in porch that faced the dunes.

Lottie motioned toward one of the rocking chairs and disappeared into the house, only to return a moment later carrying two bottles of Coke. She handed one to Mary and then sat next to her.

"Perhaps you'd also like to know how I came to know your mother," Lottie said as she took a sip of her drink.

"Yes, please. You are the only one so far on Folly that says they actually knew her."

"Your mother came to Folly every summer when she was a young girl. She had a bright blue bicycle she would ride all over the island. Margaret would get up at dawn and ride for hours." Lottie rocked and sipped as she told the story. Mary listened intently.

"It was early in the morning when Margaret walked past the house pushing her bicycle. The chain had come off and she was walking home. I was sitting on this same porch and I called for her to come up. She told me her name was Margaret and I told her I had a daughter by that same name. My husband Preston Sr. fixed her bicycle for her. He was a dentist and was always adept with his hands. In fact, he helped build the house that my daughter Joyce and her husband Louis lived in after he came back from the war."

"Preston told me Louis, Frenchie, was his brother-in-law," Mary said.

"True and I understand he is helping you find Jack," Lottie answered.

"Yes, both of them are helping. Did you ever see my mother again?" Mary asked, wanting to hear everything Lottie knew about her mother and Jack.

"Oh yes, many times. She rode that bike until she could drive and Margaret always came by the house when she rode this way. We would sit and drink cokes or hot tea and she would tell me everything that was transpiring in her life. In fact, I probably knew about the blossoming romance between your mother and Jack before anyone else," Lottie said with a smile. Mary was sure the woman was reliving those visits with her mother in her memory.

"Did you ever meet Jack?" Mary asked, excited about this new information about her mother. Another part of her mother's secretive past was being revealed to her.

"Just once, when your mother was probably...let's see, around eighteen. She didn't visit much after she traded that bike in for a car. Teenage stuff you know. No time to just sit and talk," Lottie said with a hint of regret in her voice.

"Margaret drove up in her fancy brand-new car, ran up the steps, and gave me a big hug. She announced that she and Jack were in love and were planning to get married someday. Then Margaret said she wanted me to meet him."

Lottie finished her Coke and set it on the floor next to her chair. Mary realized she had been so intent on listening to the story that she hadn't taken a drink of her own.

"I hadn't noticed anyone else was in the car until Margaret ran down the stairs and brought a young man back with her. It was Jack, of course. He was a nice-looking boy, tall and somewhat shy."

Mary wanted more and Lottie gave it to her.

"They sat for a while and we talked some more. Well, Margaret did most of the talking. She told me about all the things that had happened since the last time I saw her. Margaret told me she had tried blond hair, but the friend that had helped didn't really know what she was doing. Margaret ended up with cotton candy-colored hair."

Mary laughed as she imagined her mother with pink hair and was reminded just how little she knew about her mother's younger years. Now Mary was trying to piece together a puzzle, like the one Carl had talked about. Each new thing she discovered was a piece that she hoped would help her to see the whole picture in time. Mary realized that Lottie had stopped talking and apologized for her wandering mind.

Lottie wasn't the least bit perturbed, instead, she just continued on. "I can tell you this, there was this thing between them that was... You could say that it was so intense that you could feel it in the air. Jack's eyes never left her face. It was like if he looked away, he might miss something she said or a gesture she might make."

"Young love," Mary said more to herself than to Lottie.

"They were teenagers, that is true. But Mary, young love can be just as powerful as any other. I was pretty young when I married. There was never a moment that I didn't love my husband. He died of a heart attack much too young. It was a while ago now, but the love is as strong as ever. That is the kind of love I felt between those two, your mother and Jack. That's why I remember it so vividly," Lottie insisted with passion in her voice.

"But it didn't last," Mary sighed and felt a heaviness in her heart.

Lottie reached for Mary's hands. She held them in her hands and looked into her eyes.

"You might think it just didn't work out, but I don't believe that. For some reason, they were destined to be apart. But the love they had for each other...that kind of love doesn't just go away. Maybe you think I am just a nutty old woman, but when you do find Jack I believe you will see I am right."

Somehow that thought lifted Mary's spirits. She smiled at Lottie and gave her a hug. Mary had never been a big hugger, but since arriving on Folly that had changed. "Thank you for sharing all this with me. It helps me understand things better."

"Mary, somehow, in some way, God is using what happened to change your life. Just keep an open mind and heart. You will figure it out," Lottie assured her.

Driving away a few minutes later, Mary could picture her mother riding her bike. A carefree young girl, spending her summers on Folly Beach and falling in love with a young man named Jack.

Mary drove east until she was stopped by a gate. The road did continue on down to the Coast Guard Station, but the public was not allowed any further. Taking her camera, Mary walked the beach until she rounded the curve of the island and spotted the old lighthouse sitting in the middle of the water.

Mary knew from her reading that the lighthouse had been constructed in 1876 and had originally been nearly a quarter mile from the water. Decades of erosion had separated the structure from Morris Island by many yards of open water at high tide.

Bubba had told her that at low tide you could wade across to the abandoned structure if you knew the way to go. The tide was in and the hundred-and-forty-foot tower looked lonely standing there all by itself. Mary took numerous shots with the camera and then made her way back to the car.

Down the beach, some distance away, she could see several people out in the water with surfboards. The waves seemed bigger than what she had seen so far and she figured it was probably the aftermath of the storm. When she reached the wooden groin that disappeared into the rough water, she sat and waited to take some action shots.

Mary didn't have to wait long to use her camera. A young man started paddling, on his knees, and then quickly stood as a wave caught up with him. He rode the wave all the way to shore, where he simply stepped off the surfboard.

Grabbing the fiberglass board quickly under one arm, he began making his way back out past the breaking waves.

Mary stayed a long time, watching more than photographing, and only when she began to shiver with cold did the spell break. Realizing she had stayed longer than planned, Mary returned to the rental car and headed back to the house.

It was nearly dark when Mary pulled up to the house. Maebelle came out on her porch and called to her. "We were wondering if you had gotten lost. Come on over and tell us how your day turned out."

Mary joined Bubba and Maebelle in their living room.

"I have spent more time over here than in the rental house," Mary joked.

"Well, I do suppose you could have saved a little money by just staying here with us to start out with. Next time, when you come back, just plan on doing that. I like your help in the kitchen," Maebelle suggested. Mary knew it wasn't just polite talk and took notice that it was 'when' and not 'if' Maebelle had said.

"This time, the paper is paying for it, but next time that would suit me just fine. It is a comfortable place next door, but roomy for just one person." Mary said, knowing that regardless of the outcome of this trip she would be back.

"How did things work out at the library?" Mary asked, taking a peppermint from the dish that sat on the coffee table.

"Everything is fine. Our library is about the size of this room. We do have books, of course, but our biggest business is getting our orders in for the Bookmobile. It comes once a week and we usually have a pretty big order to fill. Now, what about your day?"

"I talked to Lottie Blanton today. She knew my mother and even met Jack one time." Mary recounted the conversation and said she really liked Lottie.

"I am sure you did. Lottie is quite a lady. Her family comes from the Richmond area and she travels to visit them several times a year. She will just hop in that yellow Studebaker of hers and take off without a thought. A real independent lady that one," Bubba said as he put down the newspaper and joined the conversation.

Mary told about taking photos of the lighthouse and watching the surfers. She said surfing was something she bet Carl would like to try.

"In fact, if it is okay, I'll call and see if Carl is home," Mary said, really hoping he was there. She wanted to tell him about her day.

"You know where the phone is dear. Go call your Carl and then you can help me with supper," Maebelle directed.

Mary entered the bedroom, sat on the bed, and set the phone on her lap. She was so anxious to talk to Carl that she dialed the wrong number the first time. As she hung up Mary heard a knock on the front door and thought maybe Chuck had come over to make amends and mooch a meal. Dialing the right number, she only got Carl's answering machine. She was about to leave a message when Maebelle called from the other room.

"Mary, can you come out here for a minute?" Maebelle's voice sounded a little strange, so Mary quickly hung up and hurried into the living room.

Maebelle stood beside the front door and Bubba held the screen door partially open. In the darkness, Mary could just see a figure on the porch holding a box.

"Did you order some Chinese food, Mary?" Maebelle asked stone-faced.

"What? I mean, no I didn't order anything," Mary stuttered, confused by the question.

"Well, this here fella says you did?" Bubba said and opened the door the rest of the way. The man stepped into the room and she could see it was...

"Carl!" Mary shouted as she raced across the room. Carl barely had time to pass the box he was holding to Bubba before Mary almost knocked him back out onto the porch. She threw her arms around his neck, hugged him hard, and then kissed him eagerly. Suddenly aware that she was in someone else's living room, kissing a man they didn't know right in front of them Mary stepped back, blushing.

"Well, that was worth a nine-hour drive," Carl laughed and pulled Mary to him again.

"What are you doing here?" Mary asked when they had separated again.

"You said you wanted Chinese food and Leus Chinese Bistro has the finest there is," Carl said, matter-of-factly.

"When did I say...?" Mary was still puzzled for a second and then she remembered their earlier conversation. "Because I said love you and Chinese food in the same sentence?" Mary asked with a laugh.

"Exactly," Carl said. "And so I ordered two of everything and got down here as soon as I could. I am starving, by the way. Do you know what it is like driving for nine hours smelling Chinese food and not being able to eat it?"

"Too bad you didn't mention a new car and love at the same time," Bubba laughed.

Carl and Mary strolled over to where Bubba stood with his arm around Maebelle, who beamed with joy.

"It is great to finally meet you, Carl," Maebelle said, giving him a big hug and then with her usual efficiency added, "Mary, help me set the table while Bubba and Carl get acquainted."

Chapter 23

"Carl must really love you, Mary. He really did bring two of everything on the entire menu," Maebelle laughed.

Bubba agreed by groaning and pushing away from the table, "That's it. One more bite and I'll explode. That place makes some really tasty food. Thanks for the supper, Carl."

"I may never eat Chinese again. Well, maybe for a couple of weeks anyway. Carl, what possessed you to drive all the way from DC?" Mary asked.

"Don't tell me it was because I said I love Chinese food and you."

"That sounds like reason enough to me," Maebelle said, as she too pushed her plate toward the middle of the table.

"True, but also it seemed like Mary was having all the fun and I decided to come and see Folly Beach for myself. I heard the waves were high after a storm and thought I would come down and get some surfing in." Carl said with a smile.

"You never told me you could surf. When did you learn to do that?" Mary asked.

"Well, I haven't yet. But I thought I would give it a try. Anyway, it is a free trip so why not come? Didn't want you to forget me," Carl teased.

"Not much chance of that," Bubba said, rolling his eyes. "It has been Carl this and Carl that ever since she got here."

Maebelle kicked her husband under the table and he made a big deal of pulling up his pant leg to check for bruises.

"It wasn't quite that bad," Maebelle laughed.

Mary blushed and tried to steer the conversation to less embarrassing grounds. "What do you mean by 'free trip'?"

Carl pushed back from the table and crossed his legs before answering. "Our piece on the honorable Senator has gotten a lot of print around the country and a couple of University Journalism Departments have contacted me about speaking and one of the schools was the College of Charleston. They want us to give a couple of lectures on Tuesday. I told them you were already down here and that you were the one that spearheaded the investigation, but for some reason, they want me too. Anyway, they said the school would cover expenses so I took a week off, grabbed Chinese, and headed this way."

"That is just great, Carl. There will be more co-eds swooning over you and trying to get my job," Mary said in mock disappointment.

"I have eyes only for you, Mary, only you," Carl promised as he leaned forward and took her hands in his. He lifted both to his lips and kissed them gently.

Mary remembered what Lottie Blanton had said about Jack watching her mother talk and she shivered a bit. Carl sat back in his chair and covered his mouth as he yawned.

"We are all excited you are here Carl," Maebelle said as she saw Mary's reaction to Carl's words. She stood and took charge in her usual Maebelle fashion.

"I believe you will both be attending an early Mass tomorrow before coming over to our church. Everyone will be so happy to meet Mary's Carl. Now, the second bedroom next door has clean sheets and there are extra towels in the bath. Let's get your luggage up to the house so you can get some sleep."

Mary took Carl's arm and led him toward the front door, sharing her story of meeting the Priest and indicating she would attend tomorrow's service.

"Two churches in one day. I'll really be set for a whole week," Carl joked as they all made their way down the steps.

Chuck was standing next to the Camaro admiring the sporty car. "Wow! Cool car."

"1967 Camaro RS/SS with a 396. Pumps out over 400hp." Carl said with pride.

Mary introduced the two men and saw that a contest of strength took place as they shook hands. Although she thought the male macho thing was silly, Mary was still glad it was a contest Carl won easily.

Inside Mary showed Carl where the bedroom was and checked to see that there were fresh towels for his shower. She was excited that Carl was there and even though he had spent numerous nights sleeping on her sofa and in the overstuffed chair, this time, it was different. Mary chided herself for acting like a silly teenager and entered her room for a shower.

While washing her hair, Mary wondered if one day she and Carl would live together as a married couple. Mary didn't know if she was ready to think about it now. She still had Jack to find and after that, Mary didn't quite understand exactly what she wanted. She just knew things would never be quite the same again. Too much had happened.

When she had finished Mary slipped into a comfortable jogging outfit and headed to check on Carl. Listening at the door for the sounds of the other shower, she heard nothing. She tapped softly on the door and got no answer. After a moment, she knocked harder and still got no answer. Mary opened the door a crack and peeked in. She was about to call Carl's name but didn't when she saw him asleep on the bed. He had showered, slipped on a robe, and was probably waiting for her to finish when he had fallen asleep.

Mary closed the door softly and returned to her room, leaving the door open so she could hear if Carl woke. She worked on her article for a while and then curled up with a book. Without being aware of it, Mary's eyes closed and she fell asleep.

The squeak of the screen door woke Mary a couple of hours later. Slipping into her shoes, Mary stepped to the window overlooking the porch and looked outside. Carl sat in one of the rocking chairs drinking a cup of coffee.

Mary walked into the kitchen and poured herself a cup from the pot he had made, wrapped an Afghan around her shoulders, and ventured out onto the porch.

Carl looked up and smiled at her as Mary took the chair next to his.

"Not too romantic, huh? Falling asleep without even a goodnight kiss," Carl apologized.

"Driving all the way down here to bring me Chinese is pretty romantic I would say," Mary answered as she reached over and took his hand.

"Carl, I want you to understand why I said I loved you. It isn't..."

"It's okay Mary. I won't hold you to it as much as I like hearing it." Carl interrupted.

"No, Carl. You have it wrong. I have been falling in love with you for a long time, but in my usual cautious way didn't want to admit it." Mary turned in her chair until she was staring into his eyes.

"The other night Maebelle and I were talking and I told her a relationship like she and Bubba have is what I want. I said I wanted to be needed, protected, and loved more than anyone should have the right to be. Maebelle just laughed and pointed out that I already had those things...in you." Mary shivered and pulled her cover closer.

"This last week has been... I am not even sure what the word is, maybe unbelievable is the right one. I have met amazing people, people willing to help me find Jack. I mean really going out of their way to help. This place..." Mary made a sweeping motion with her arm, "is like no place I have ever been and it has changed me somehow."

Carl brushed her cheek with the back of his hand and said, "I like the change, Mary. I heard it in your voice when we talked on the phone. That is one of the reasons I had to come down here, to see for myself. We don't know what the future holds for us, but I'm willing to wait and see. In the meantime, you have Jack to find. I am here to help, for as long as it takes."

Mary got up, moved to sit on his lap, and then curled up against his strong chest. Carl rocked the chair and hummed a tune as he pulled her closer to him.

"You are always so warm," Mary muttered in his ear.

"Side benefit of sitting in my lap."

"Mmmmm," Mary muttered and they stayed that way for a long time. Suddenly Mary sat up and said, "Let's get dressed and go for a walk on the beach."

Reluctantly, Carl released his prize and said, "Great idea. I can't sleep anymore right now anyway."

Ten minutes later, dressed in warm clothes they strolled across the dunes hand in hand. The sky was clear and the moon lit the white sand with a soft glow. They set a comfortable pace and headed toward the boardwalk.

They encountered no one on the beach, although there were a couple of young couples strolling along the boardwalk.

"Not exactly a Saturday night hot spot," Carl remarked.

"The locals like it that way, but I understand it is a different story during the tourist season," Mary said and told him what Maebelle had said about summers on Folly.

"Yeah, I read some about the history of the island. As I understand it, this place put the roar into the Roaring 20s back then, and it keeps doing so every summer. Kind of neat having it both ways, I guess."

A while later they were climbing the stairs to the house and both of them were finally ready to sleep again.

"One o'clock," Carl said, glancing at the clock on the wall of the kitchen. He pulled Mary close and gave her a long kiss, before holding her at arm's length and pointing Mary to her room. "Better get along. Maebelle is probably watching right now to make sure I don't misbehave," Carl said, only half kidding.

Chapter 24

Sunday morning dawned sunny and clear. The weather was just right for a walk and that's what Carl and Mary decided to do. She popped in and told Maebelle they would see her and Bubba at church later. They walked quickly and soon passed the *News Stand*. A small group of people stood outside on the porch and as Mary and Carl passed by

one of the women called out.

"Hi, Mary. Is that your Carl with you?"

"Yes Kati, this is my Carl. We are on the way to church. How are you today?" Mary answered back.

Carl laughed and waved at everyone. "Boy, the word travels fast around here."

"How do you like being known as my Carl?" Mary asked and squeezed his arm.

"Actually, very much. I like it very much," Carl replied and patted her hand.

When they reached Our Lady of Good Counsel, Father Williams was standing out front greeting the parishioners as they arrived.

"Father Williams, this is my Carl," Mary said and then blushed when she realized what she had said. "I mean this is Carl Thompson, my friend…"

The Priest laughed and took Carl's hand shaking it warmly, "Oh yes, the word of your arrival has been bigger news than the hurricane."

"I would guess there are few secrets on Folly Beach Father and I am indeed Mary's Carl." He took Mary's hand and they followed the Priest into the church.

After the service, Carl and Mary spent a few minutes chatting with the members of the congregation before heading across the street to the Baptist Church. When they entered the building Maebelle waved from one of the front pews where she had saved them seats.

Following the first song, the Pastor welcomed the visitors. It seemed everyone in the church wanted to shake Carl's hand and welcome him to the island.

"Are you sure you didn't tell everyone I was a movie star or something?" Carl laughed.

"It does seem like you are quite a celebrity," Mary said with a smile.

"I think they just wanted to see if I was good enough for you. Chuck is a local boy after all," Carl whispered as the music started again. He received an elbow to the ribs for an answer.

When the service was over a crowd gathered around them outside in front of the church, where more hands were shaken and questions asked. After a while, Maebelle and Bubba extricated them and led them over to where Jesse Porter and Preston Blanton were talking.

As he talked with the two men Carl understood why Mary had been so impressed with both of them. They were completely different, with Preston being two heads taller than Jesse and a scholar; and yet alike because they were both impressive men. They were the kind of people Carl had met a couple of times in his life. He knew he would learn something new and worthwhile if he spent time with them.

The churchyard seemed to hold others of the same ilk; Bubba and Maebelle, Preston's wife Verna, who played the piano for the church, Mr. Porter's best friend Mr. Kennedy, and Joyce Lasne, Frenchies wife. Carl was sure there were many more he hadn't met.

As Carl looked around him he knew there was a book full of interesting people if someone chose to write it down.

As the congregation began to thin Verna came over and invited Carl and Mary to have lunch with them. Mary wanted Carl to meet Lottie Blanton. Maebelle had told her that she and Bubba were invited to their daughter's house for the Sunday meal so she quickly accepted.

Mary helped in the kitchen while Preston took Carl over to see his radio setup. Preston was able to contact

Frenchie and he said that he had a lead on Jack and would be checking it out the next day. Preston touched base with several other shortwave radio enthusiasts. They had been busy talking to boats and had gathered a couple of possible sightings but nothing certain.

Back at the house, Carl had time to see Preston's sea shell, stamp, and coin collection. With his shortwave connections, Preston was able to gather material from around the world.

After dinner and the dishes, Mary found Carl and Lottie in rocking chairs on the porch. They were drinking Cokes and listening to a Whispering Bill Anderson country record. Mary didn't want to intrude so she sat with Verna on the sofa and looked through a family photo album.

"Did you know that Preston rode a horse from here all the way to Tennessee and back when he was only eighteen?" Carl asked later that evening as they took a walk on the beach. "And that yellow '53 Studebaker belongs to Lottie and she has put over 250,000 miles on it. Frenchie was in the Free French Navy and spent four years in combat zones and had three ships sunk from under him."

Mary squeezed his hand and said, "Welcome to Folly Beach. Believe me, you have just scratched the surface."

They walked in silence for a few more minutes and then turned to go back down the beach. A breeze had whipped up and chilled them. Suddenly they were startled by a scream.

"Help! He's drowning! My boyfriend is drowning!" In the moonlight, about thirty yards down the beach they could make out the form of a woman standing knee-deep in the water. She was frantically waving with one hand and pointing at the breaking waves with the other.

In an instant, Carl was running at full speed in her direction. Halfway to her, he spotted movement in the water. A collapsing wave drove someone under the water as they splashed around way over their heads.

Carl's eyes never left the spot where he had seen the person go under the water as he entered the surf at a diagonal full sprint. He felt the tug of the current as it swept toward the boardwalk. He dove into the water and swam hard, aiming for the spot where he had last seen the person disappear.

Mary hurried to the woman and on reaching her saw that she was a young girl of about seventeen. She was frantically searching the surf for her boyfriend, but neither he nor Carl could be seen in the foaming turbulence.

"Billy is going to die!" The distraught girl screamed when she saw Mary. "It's my fault! I dared him to go out and ride a wave!"

"Come on!" Mary ordered and taking the girl's arm started running to where she had seen Carl go into the water. Once she thought she saw a head bob up and then dive back under the water. Mary had no way of knowing if it was Carl or the younger man.

In just a few seconds, Mary kicked off her shoes, tossed her jacket onto the sand, and stepped into the cold water. She intended on trying to swim out and help in some way. She was not a strong swimmer, but she was determined to try. Before she reached the depth of her knees the girl yelled.

"I see someone!"

Mary looked to where the girl was pointing and saw a figure heading back to shore, but it was too dark to tell who it was. As the swimmer drew closer she let out a breath she didn't even know she was holding. It was Carl. He was swimming on his side, pulling a body with him.

When he reached shallow water, Carl was able to get to his feet. Mary and the girl rushed out into waist-deep water and helped him pull the unmoving boy onto the sand. Carl laid him on his stomach and turned the teenager's head to the side. Carl began trying to get his lungs free of water so he could breathe.

Mary was aware of several people running toward them from the entrance to the beach but kept her attention on the task at hand. With a heave, the once-drowned man vomited water and groaned loudly. Carl sank back onto his heels in relief as Mary and the girl helped the boyfriend into a sitting position.

"What happened? Is everything alright here?" A large man in a uniform asked as he shined a flashlight over the group sitting on the wet sand.

"Billy almost drowned. He would have died if this guy hadn't saved him." The girl pointed at Carl as she hugged her boyfriend, trying to warm him. He was shaking hard and his teeth were rattling uncontrollably. Mary couldn't even imagine how cold he must be since she had only gotten waist deep and she was freezing. A blanket suddenly fell over the man's shoulders and when Mary looked up, she saw Chuck had been the benefactor. He was also holding Carl's shoes and the jacket that had been discarded before Carl took to the water. Chuck moved over to Carl and draped the jacket over his shoulders.

Then there were two more that joined the group on the beach. Mary was flooded with relief when Maebelle took charge.

"Chief Burch, we have wet people here and they need to get off this cold beach and warm up. You should take this young lady and her friend to the fire station and have them checked out. Carl and Mary are coming with me to their place."

"Maebelle, I need to get statements from everyone about what happened here..." The Chief of Police started and was cut off by a stern look from Maebelle.

"I can get their statements," He nodded in the direction of the two young people, "at the station. I'll need one from him tomorrow." The Chief said, pointing to Carl.

"That won't be a problem. Now get these young folks into a warm place," Maebelle agreed and motioned for Carl and Mary to follow her. Carl was grateful when Bubba wrapped a heavy blanket around him.

When they reached the house, Maebelle sprang into action. She followed Mary to her room and Bubba stayed with Carl. They got them out of their wet clothes and into a hot shower and then headed into the kitchen to make hot coffee.

Maebelle had steaming cups sitting on the coffee table when Carl emerged from his room. Bubba had a roaring fire blazing in the fireplace. Carl's skin was red from the hot water he had streamed over his frozen body. With thanks, he grabbed his cup and headed straight to the chair that Bubba had moved in front of the fire.

"Well, that was different," Carl said jokingly, his eyes never leaving the door to Mary's room.

"I'll say this," Bubba said, "You certainly know how to make a splash when you arrive in town."

They all laughed at Bubba's play on words, including Mary, who came out of her room toweling her hair.

"That's my Carl for you," Mary said, as she took her coffee and sat on the arm of Carl's chair. "Never one to just blend in."

"How did you know what was going on?" Carl asked of Bubba, as he sipped the hot brew carefully.

"Chuck was outside working on his motorcycle again and heard the woman scream for help. He ran over and told us to call the rescue squad. Maebelle tossed him the blanket off the sofa and he took off for the beach. We called the police, grabbed another blanket, and headed over ourselves," Bubba explained.

"It is a good thing for those two young people that you and Mary were out on the beach. The way the wind and current are running tonight that poor boy's body would have passed Kiawah by now. The Lord was looking out for the both of you," Maebelle said and took Carl's cup for a refill.

"Where did you learn to swim so well?" Mary asked Carl as she sat on the arm of his chair next to him.

"I was a lifeguard at a summer camp for a couple of years when I was in college. We would race across the river and back every morning and evening. We even did a couple of midnight races, so I kind of got used to swimming in the dark," Carl explained.

"Well, I would say all that practice paid off tonight. And don't worry about the paperwork at the station tomorrow. This kind of thing happens more times than you would imagine every year," Bubba informed them and then standing, offered his hand to Maebelle, "Come on dear. Let's leave these two lovebirds alone."

As they watched Maebelle and Bubba cross the yard Mary turned to Carl and asked, "Are we really love birds? It seems kind of strange to me."

"Works for me," Carl replied casually. "I'll be Big Eagle and you can be Little Sparrow."

"You do know those are Indian names, right?" Mary laughed and shoved him back into the house.

"My great-great-grandmother was an Indian," Carl disclosed.

"Oh well, that changes everything," Mary said, rolling her eyes.

Carl added wood to the fire and opened the window a crack. Now that he was warm again, he wanted the fire for the ambiance more than the heat. They pulled the sofa closer to the fire and Mary curled up next to Carl holding his right hand in both of hers.

"I was scared out there. What if you hadn't been such a skilled swimmer? What if..."

Carl placed a finger over her lips to silence her and said "All of life is a what-if, Mary."

Mary laid her head on his chest and could hear his heart beating. She knew that Carl always did what he thought was the right thing and that was one of the reasons she had come to love him. She closed her eyes and immersed herself in the sound of his heartbeat and the warmth of the fire on her face.

When Mary woke the next morning she found herself lying on top of her bed covered with a spread. Sometime during the night, Carl carried her to her room and put her to bed.

Mary could hear Carl in the kitchen rattling around. He met her at the door with a cup of coffee and some toast and they ventured outside to catch the sunrise.

After a while, Chuck came outside and began working on his motorcycle again. Carl stepped inside, got another cup of coffee, and carried it down to Chuck.

"Thanks, man," Carl said, offering Chuck coffee. "Glad you heard the ruckus out on the beach and got help."

"No sweat. That was a pretty brave thing you did out there last night," Chuck said, accepting the coffee and taking a swig.

"I am sure if you had been on the beach at the time you would have done the same. Anyway, thanks again." Carl repeated and turned back to join Mary on the porch.

"That was kind of you," Mary said with a smile and handed him a fresh cup of coffee.

"Yeah, well, I hope the Chief of Police is nice to me and I don't have to spend the whole day filling out paperwork," Carl muttered as he leaned back in the chair. He held Mary's hand as they watched the sun rise in the east.

Chapter 25

As it turned out Carl was only at the station for less than an hour on Monday morning. The Chief had him write out his version of what had happened and sign it. The paper was filed in a cabinet full of accounts similar to the one Carl had given. However, the outcome wasn't as good as some of the others.

"Is this the hero?" A smallish man of forty or so, who had come through the door to the adjoining fire department, asked as he came across the room and offered his hand to Carl. "Names William Hitchkins. People call me Willie. I am the de facto fire chief and head of the rescue squad. You have already proven yourself with the rescue last night. Have you ever put out a fire?"

Carl thought for a moment and answered. "I put out a dumpster fire in the alley behind the newspaper office once."

"Well done, you are fully qualified," Willie announced. He pulled a Folly Beach Auxiliary Fireman's badge from his pocket and handed it to Carl.

"This is an honor, but I don't live here. Mary and I'll be going back to DC after she makes things right with

Jack," Carl said and attempted to hand the badge back to the man.

"Just keep it. You will be back. Everyone comes back to Folly. Besides, it does come with some perks. If you get stopped for speeding on Folly Road just show the officer your badge and he will probably let you off with a warning."

"I get it. When he asks "Are you going to a fire?" I just show him this and say "I think there might be one?" Carl laughed.

"You got it," Willie said.

"In that case, I'll accept the honor," Carl said as he dropped the badge into his shirt pocket.

When Carl had finished with his civic duty he walked the couple blocks to the Boardwalk where Mary waited for him. After filling her in on the events at the station, he showed her the badge he had received from Willie.

"My hero!" Mary said as she took his arm and guided him down the steps to the beach.

As they walked back toward the house Mary told him that she was confused about how she felt.

"Confused?"

"I know it has really only been a little over a week and everyone has been wonderful, but I want an ending to this quest," Mary said, kicking at the sand.

"According to what I understand Jack is close to being located. A lot of people are looking for him and I'll bet you that in another week you will be seeing or, at least, talking to him. Then you will be able to tell him what happened and get on with your life," Carl said.

"I know this is liable to sound stupid, but I don't know what that means; the getting on with my life thing. A month ago I could have told you exactly what I wanted to do with the rest of my life, step by step. One part of me wants to find Jack tomorrow and the other part wants the search to go on so I have a reason to stay. I can't understand what has happened to me. I look in the mirror and hardly recognize myself," Mary confessed.

"Well, like you said your hair is a lot more frizzy down here on the coast," Carl quipped.

"Oh good, one more thing to worry about," Mary laughed and pushed Carl so that the incoming water lapped across his shoes.

"Hey. I like it. It really looks pretty like that." Carl said, as he balanced on one foot and emptied the water from his shoe. Then he took Mary's hand and turned her toward him. He looked into her eyes and said seriously. "Whatever happens, whatever the outcome, you have done the right thing. Two people's lives were changed by one small event: an unmailed Valentine's card. It is unfinished business, and I know you, Mary. You don't leave things unfinished. The Senator found that out the difficult way. You will figure all this out in time."

Mary took his face in both her hands and kissed him softly on the lips. "I love you, Carl. I know that at least."

When they crossed the dunes and came into view of the house they saw a group of people in the front yard. Several cars lined the road in front of the houses.

Maebelle approached them quickly as they crossed the road. Before either Mary or Carl could ask if something was wrong, she blurted out, "They found Jack! He is coming home!"

Mary stood in the middle of the road too shocked to speak for a moment and then she stepped into the other woman's embrace. "Thank you Maebelle, thank you."

Mary felt Carl's hand on her shoulder and she turned toward him and saw the beaming grin he had on his face. He enfolded her in his arms and kissed the top of her head. They stayed that way for a long time until they realized a car was waiting for them to move. There was no honking horn from an impatient driver, just a nod, and a smile as Carl waved apologetically and guided Mary out of the street.

Preston Blanton and Jesse Porter stood talking to Bubba while Chuck quietly listened from where he was sitting on the steps of Maebelle's house. They all turned and watched as Mary approached.

"I guess you heard from Maebelle that we finally located Jack Young. Louis tracked him down offshore of Miami. He was on the way to Key West when he heard that people were looking for him all up and down the coast," Preston told her.

"Preston was home from school today and out in his radio shack when Frenchie called him on the shortwave with the news that he was tied up next to the *Miss Margaret* at a small dock in Florida." Bubba took up the story he had just been told.

"What did he say about me looking for him?" Mary asked, shaking with excitement.

"When Louis told him that Margaret's daughter was trying to find him, he just said I guess it's time to get back to Folly then, fueled up his boat, and is currently on the way back right now. He should arrive Thursday or Friday at the latest," Preston concluded.

"This is so difficult to believe. How can I ever thank you, all of you, for everything you have done? I would have never found Jack without you."

"What else would we do? That's just the way it is here on the island," Maebelle surmised.

"And your boyfriend **is** a member of the Rescue Squad and the Auxiliary Fire Department," Mr. Porter added.

Carl gave a laugh. "I got my badge less than an hour ago. There is some grapevine on this island."

Mary noticed just then that someone was sitting in Preston's station wagon that was parked in Chuck's yard. She saw it was Lottie Blanton and walked over to say hello.

"Mrs. Blanton…"

"Lottie please, Mary. I am happy that things are working out for you. Buddy was glad to get that radio call this morning. He couldn't wait to get over here and tell you."

"I owe him a lot… and you too."

Lottie laughed. "Me, what for?" she asked.

"The things you told me about my mother helped me understand what kind of girl she was back when she came for the summer. And the way you described how you knew she and Jack were in love, well, it helped me see something in myself." Mary explained.

Lottie patted her hand and then handed her a folded piece of paper. "My daughter Margaret and her husband Keith Samuels live over toward Charleston. When I told her your story she said she would like to meet you and your young man since she and your mother share the same name. Here is her address and phone number."

Mary took the paper, leaned in through the window, and gave Lottie a hug. Preston walked up just then and opened the driver's door to get in. "If I hear anything else I'll be sure and let you know. Right now I need to get Mom over to the store. She is running low on Coke and tea bags."

Lottie leaned out the window as the car began to move and said, "I am truly glad you have found both of your men."

Mary waved and smiled as the car drove toward Center Street. Jesse Porter was right. There are very few secrets on the island.

"So now we wait for Jack to arrive. We need something to help us pass the time. What do you say we head to Charleston for the day? I only caught a glimpse on the way here and I would like to touch base with Thomas on a couple of things. I have the car phone if anyone needs to get hold of us in a hurry. It works fine down here," Carl suggested to Mary after the group in the yard had dispersed.

"It is still early and if we are going to speak at the college tomorrow I would like to check it out. Just let me try and call Grams again while you let Maebelle know our plans." Mary agreed, knowing it would make the waiting easier if she had something constructive to do.

Chapter 26

"You are mighty quiet. Everything OK?" Carl asked as they drove the ten miles from Folly to Charleston.

"Yes and no," Mary admitted, "I am not sure I ever really expected to find Mother's old fiancé, and now that it has happened what if it was the wrong thing to do?"

"Go on," Carl encouraged.

"Maybe Jack doesn't even remember my mother? What if he put her down as a mistake he made and moved on with his life?"

"Well, let's see; Jack is on his shrimp boat hundreds of miles away, he hears someone is looking for him, Frenchie tells him that Margaret Lassiter's daughter wants to see him, Jack turns his boat around and heads, full steam, back to Folly Beach. Does that sound like someone who has forgotten the love of his youth?"

"You're right, I know, but I am really nervous about meeting him. What do I say to someone that wanted to marry my mother over thirty years ago and thinks she dumped him?"

"Mary you have faced down gang members, crooks, and even a senator. A shrimp boat captain doesn't stand a chance against you. I know you. You will plan a dozen different things to say to Jack when you meet him. However, as you always do, you will say what you feel in your heart when the time comes. That, my dear Mary, would be the right thing to do. Just let it happen," Carl replied as he squeezed Mary's hand.

As they crossed the Ashley River they could see the many church spires in the old city pointing to Heaven. Carl passed the Citadel Military College and Hampton Park on his way to the newspaper office. Thomas was waiting for them in the lobby when they arrived and took them to meet the editor and owner of the paper.

"I was impressed with the Senator Billings piece. That was impressive", Gary Jackson, the editor said.

"Actually, it was Mary's idea and she did most of the hard work," Carl alleged.

"Carl keeps saying that, but we both put in a lot of time on the story. Carl even had his tires slashed and someone tried to kill him after the whole thing was made public," Mary said with a shudder. She remembered the call she had received about Carl's ambush and his hospital stay.

"However that might be, I understand the two of you are down here for a different reason. Mind filling me in?" Mr. Jackson said as he took a chair behind his desk and motioned for them to sit in the other empty seats. For the next hour, Mary told her story, from the beginning to her sitting in the newspaper office.

"That is quite a story, and to think that after all these years you and this Jack fellow are going to meet. What do you think his reaction will be when he finds out what happened?" Mr. Jackson asked.

"I would like to think it will bring him comfort to know that my mother was deeply in love with him and that it was all just an accident, the way it happened," Mary explained.

"I guess in a few days we will know how it turns out. I am sure there will be a lot of second guesses about what might have been, but I have a positive feeling about it all," Carl added.

"Whatever happens, I did learn a lot about my mother that I didn't know and met some amazingly kind people too," Mary surmised.

"I think it is safe to say that both of you found something else too." The editor said with a wry grin, "And I understand that y'all will be lecturing at the college tomorrow. Your names are pretty well known across the country right now. Channel 4 called me this morning and asked if I could persuade you to give a short interview about the story. I imagine you will hear from many others. Now, what are your plans for today?"

"We are intending to play tourist today for a while and then check out the facilities at the College of Charleston for tomorrow's program," Carl explained.

"I have a meeting with the mayor in less than an hour. Y'all have fun today. Here is the number for Channel 4 if you want to call them." The editor wished Mary the best of luck in her meeting with Jack. She thanked them both for coming by.

As they wound through the newsroom Carl suggested that Mary look around while he spoke with Thomas about something. Mary readily agreed, curious to see how this newspaper operated in comparison to the one where she currently worked. Mary found the people friendly and the equipment modern and of top quality.

About forty-five minutes later, Carl joined her in the proofing room and apologized for being so long. "Sorry, Thomas and I got to talking about the conference where we met. He suggested a place for lunch. I'm ready to eat, how about you?"

They ate lunch on the rooftop of an old warehouse turned B&B overlooking Charleston Harbor. Only one other couple was there and the staff had placed them on the far side to give each couple more privacy.

"This is lovely Carl. The view and food are wonderful, so why are there just four of us eating?" Mary asked as she watched a large Navy ship navigate the channel.

"Actually, Thomas said the guy that owns this place is a friend of his and he often recommends this B&B to visitors when they ask where they should stay. The restaurant is usually open only to guests, but they make exceptions for people Thomas sends over," Carl explained.

After eating, they spent two hours walking around the city, Mary taking pictures while Carl read from a guidebook. They loved the architecture, the narrow side streets, some paved with cobblestones, and the feel of history.

"I could spend days walking around this city," Mary said as she put in yet another roll of film.

"Maybe someday we can. According to the map in this book, we haven't touched the surface yet. We had better head on over to the college and check it out. We can cut across George St. if we stay a few more blocks on Meeting." Carl disclosed as he traced a route with his finger on the map.

"Lead the way Big Eagle, Little Sparrow will flutter along behind you," Mary said. She knew she could trust Carl's map reading and sense of direction. He always seemed to know the right direction to take.

"I think I am going to regret the bird names," Carl muttered and set off in the direction they needed to go.

"The College of Charleston was founded in 1770 and chartered in 1785, which makes it one of the oldest in the country. Several signers of the Declaration of Independence and the Constitution were founders," Mary informed Carl from the tourist guide as they drew close to the college.

"Thomas told me it was a great school, one of the finest. His daughter attends there so he may be a little biased," Carl said, taking Mary's arm as they climbed the stairs of the Administration Building.

Inside they were directed to the Calhoun Lecture Hall, where they were told things were being prepared for their program the next evening. As they entered the large room they saw a beehive of labor taking place. A ten-foot blowup of the front page of a newspaper with their story was the backdrop. The article had been published with Carl's photo on the top left, and Mary's top right. U.S. SENATOR FACES POSSIBLE CHARGES was the headline at the top. Senator Billings could be seen leaving the Capital Building, trying to hide his face from the cameras with his hat.

Instead of a podium, a microphone had been positioned between two stools on a stand. The seating was stadium style and in a half-moon shape, which meant everyone could see the stage and those on the stage would be close to the audience.

"I like this. Very nice," Carl said approvingly as he looked around the room.

A very scholarly-looking older man strode across the stage toward them with a tall, lanky redheaded youth right on his heels.

"Mr. Thompson and Ms. Lassiter, welcome to our school. We are honored to have you come and speak to our students and staff."

He offered a firm and enthusiastic handshake to Carl and the traditional southern finger shake and bow to Mary. "This is my assistant Mr. Jerry Jacobs and I am Professor Robert Kingsberry."

Carl liked the way the man introduced his assistant first and then himself. It showed that the professor was confident in his position as well as polite. In DC, so many of the people he had met were always protecting their territory. They often ignored those who helped them succeed in their job.

"Please, let's make it Mary and Carl," Carl said with a smile and swept the room with a wave of his arm. "This is a very impressive setup you have here. We are looking forward to tomorrow afternoon. Is it still on at four o'clock?

"We will probably start around four-thirty if that is alright with you both. There has been much interest and we will probably be setting up chairs along the side to accommodate everyone." The Professor said with obvious satisfaction.

Carl leaned over and said to Mary, "Probably when all the guys saw your picture the demand for seats doubled."

Mary came back with, "You told me the other day my job was in danger because all the coeds wanted to work with you."

When they looked back at the Professor he had a broad grin on his face and was rubbing his hands together. "This is going to be fun. By the way, most of the students just call me Professor Bob."

They spent the next several minutes discussing how the professor envisioned the program structure. He would introduce Carl and Mary after giving a brief overview of the slumlord pieces they had written about the Senator.

After hearing that there had been much discussion in the department about the articles, Carl suggested that they dive directly into questions from the audience. After agreeing that they would be willing to go as long as they felt there was interest, the professor said he had a class to teach. However, Jerry would be happy to take them over to the Journalism building if they would like to see how the school newspaper was run. Both Mary and Carl nodded in agreement, much to the delight of the young man. Carl smiled as he quickly became the third wheel in the small group. Jerry pointed everything out to Mary and introduced her to everyone they met.

"He was a very pleasant young man don't you think?" Mary asked as they walked back to where Carl's car was parked.

"A young man infatuated with him, I would say. A beautiful reporter from the nation's capital who brought one of the most powerful men on the Hill to his knees with the help of her trusty assistant. Who wouldn't have been in awe?" Carl joked.

"You can take solace in the fact that you are a very competent assistant Mr. Thompson. If you can behave tomorrow I just may keep you on," Mary said using her most serious speaking manner. Carl's laughter almost caused a student on a bicycle to run into a parked car as he looked back to see what was so funny.

They drove slowly along the South Battery admiring the old stately mansions and the small sailboats in the harbor. After stopping at the small Charleston Museum, which Carl thoroughly enjoyed, they made their way back to Folly.

"You are liable to think I have turned totally nuts, but when I cross this bridge I feel like I am coming home. How can that be in such a short period of time?" Mary asked as they passed the Welcome to Folly Beach sign at the foot of Folly Bridge.

"I can feel it myself. It is sort of like a movie about an enchanted forest. You know once you enter it you are always drawn back no matter how far away you go." Carl ruminated as he turned onto East Ashley. Mary had wanted him to see the lighthouse from the end of the beach.

Carl slowed as they passed the Blanton house, but no one was in the yard or on the porch. A few surfers were still in the water even though it was near sunset. They watched for a few minutes, but the waves were small and choppy so not much was happening.

Holding hands, they walked around the end of the island and saw the lighthouse, glowing red in the setting sun. The reflection from the glass at the top made it look as if the lamp was still burning, guiding ships safely through the harbor to the city.

"Imagine the view from the top of that thing. I am going to have to go up there sometime." Carl said as he gazed at the striped structure sitting in the water. Waves broke around the concrete base.

"Jesse Porter says you can climb to the top although some of the steps are getting kind of rusty. He has taken 'his boys' up there a couple of times," Mary told him.

It was quickly getting dark, so they made their way back to Carl's car and drove back to the house. When they arrived, Bubba was unloading some things from the back of his truck.

"Need help?" Carl asked as they got out of the car.

"Last load, but you can come on over and tell us about your day. Maebelle just finished frosting a chocolate cake."

They followed Bubba into the house where they could hear Maebelle working in the kitchen.

"The kids are here," Bubba called out as they entered the living area. Maebelle appeared, wiping her hands on a dish towel.

"Good, I want to hear all about what you two did today. But first, come into the kitchen and have some cake and iced tea."

Carl and Mary gave an account of their day in town as they ate. They finished with their trip to the east end of the island to see the lighthouse.

"Bubba and I climbed to the top many years ago. It is quite a view from up there. I remember there were lots of dead birds inside the area where the lamp used to be." Maebelle said.

"They flew in through one of the windows or the door, got to the top, and couldn't figure out how to get out. They would just keep flying into the glass until they killed themselves," Bubba explained.

"Tough way to go," Carl observed.

"Did you tell Carl about the dance this Saturday? It would be a great way to celebrate finding Jack," Maebelle said.

"And on top of that now that Carl has a fireman's badge you have to come. After all, it is the Fireman's Ball," Bubba explained.

"I am so nervous about meeting Jack I'm not sure what condition I would be in for a dance," Mary said with trepidation.

"Now Mary, the Almighty Lord has worked everything out so far. No reason to think things will change now. Besides, most everyone will be there and if you have to go back to DC it will give everyone a chance to say goodbye," Maebelle insisted. She gathered the plates to take them back to the kitchen.

"A dance sounds good to me," Carl said and then added, "We can pick you up a new dress in town tomorrow when we finish the program at the college."

Chapter 27

Tuesday morning was an idyllic early fall morning. There was just the right amount of chill in the air and the sky was a deep blue. Mary and Carl carried their coffee with them to the beach, perched on one of the groins, and watched the huge red ball rise from the ocean.

"Carl," Mary broke the silence and turned to look into Carl's face. "Have you ever thought about living somewhere other than DC?"

"Occasionally, I think a fresh start somewhere else might be fun. Things are running so well right now that it would be difficult to start from scratch," Carl answered honestly.

Mary looked deeply into his eyes for a long moment and turned back to watch the sun as it continued its journey. She started to say something else but changed her mind. Mary didn't see Carl, as he watched her intently.

Maebelle and Bubba had driven to North Charleston for the day. Mary wanted to check with Mr. Blanton to see if he had heard anything new about Jack but knew he was at the high school.

"We have some time to kill before we have to head over to the college so what do you think about some exploring around the island?" Carl asked.

"It is a small island and Chuck took me to see most of it already," Mary informed him.

"That's right, I forgot you were Chuck's biker babe," Carl said with a wide grin. "But I have an idea Chuck didn't take you to where I had planned."

"What place is this we are going to see?" Mary asked.

"Bubba told me about a couple of really old graves he saw years ago down in the woods at the end of West Indian Avenue. He said that if he remembered right the names on the graves were Scottish or Irish. Said he wondered who the people were that were buried there. So I thought maybe we could take a couple of hours and see if we could find them."

Mary's interest was piqued and her reporter mode was activated. She was always ready to solve a mystery or pursue a clue no matter how small or ragged.

"Let me change from these flip-flops into sneakers," Mary said excitedly as she headed toward the bedroom for shoes. She knew Carl always kept spare clothes and shoes in the trunk of his car and when she came out on the porch, he was sitting on the steps pulling on a pair of well-worn hiking boots.

"Ready to go do some exploring?" Mary asked as she came down the stairs.

"Yup, little lady. Let's go find us some graves," Carl said as he doffed a pretend hat.

"Good, lead the way Giant Eagle."

"Big Eagle, my dear Tiny Dove," Carl answered with a laugh as they walked to the car.

"A dove is a step up from a sparrow," Mary countered.

Carl drove his car slowly down a rutted dirt road. He took care not to scratch the paint on the limbs that seemed to stretch out for the car as it passed. The rental car Mary had rented had been returned the day before, or Carl might have driven it.

When he spotted a place he could turn off the main road into an area of clear ground Carl turned in. Shutting off the engine, Carl walked around and opened the door for Mary.

"This island is full of surprises. Less than five minutes ago we were crossing Center Street and now we are in the middle of the woods," Mary said. She looked around her at the moss-covered oaks.

"Bubba said some of the kids come squirrel hunting here."

At that moment, a chattering came from the branch above their heads. They both looked up to see a fat gray squirrel scolding them for being on his land.

They began walking on the old road, which shortly turned into a one-lane path until it entered the woods and became a barely discernible trail.

"Bubba said when this ends we should be almost to the river. Then we head west until we see a big oak that has been split by lightning." Carl instructed. He pointed off to his left to indicate which direction was west. "Then we go south for about a hundred feet. There should be a small grove of trees in the middle of a clearing, and that is where the graves should be."

"Lead on, I am right behind you," Mary instructed.

They found the split tree easily enough, but the grove of trees was another thing. The clearing Bubba remembered had long since been replaced with trees and large bushes. They tried several different search patterns but to no avail.

Carl looked at his watch and told Mary they had better call it quits or they would be late for their lecture. When she didn't answer, he looked around but didn't see her.

"Mary!" Carl called through cupped hands.

"Over here!" Mary called back and then popped up from behind a large bush about fifty feet away. "I think I have found it!"

Carl trotted over to where Mary stood and she parted the bushes so he could see. At first, all he saw were two depressions in the ground and then he spotted the headstones. A small tree had pushed them face down on the ground. With each other's help, they managed to lean against the very tree that had pushed them over, allowing the stones to stand up again.

"Great job Mary," Carl said as he brushed the loose dirt from the weathered stone, and then using a bandanna rubbed most of the rest away.

Mary straddled one of the graves and took several close-up photos of the words etched into the stones. "This one says Mary McLeod, born seventeen-seventy-something. I can't tell for sure what the death date is. The other says William McLeod I believe. It is in worse shape than the other one."

"We can stop by the paper after the program to have the film developed and some large prints made. Right now, though, we need to get moving," Carl insisted as he helped Mary out of the bush.

They drove back, showered and changed quickly, and then made their way to the college to start their program.

At the entrance of the lecture hall, they were impressed to see it packed to overflow even though it was still twenty minutes before they were to start.

Mary pulled Carl down and whispered in his ear, "I have never done anything like this before, remember?"

"You will do great," Carl encouraged as he led her up to the stage where Professor Kingsberry waited for them with a smile. He greeted them and then stepped up to the microphone Carl was to use and with a raised hand quieted the room and began his introductions.

"Thank you all for coming this afternoon. From the turnout, I would say that there is much interest in hearing our guest speakers today. As you are all aware Mr. Carl Thompson and Miss Mary Lassiter are reporters at the DC Times in our Nation's Capital." The Professor indicated Mary and Carl where they sat on their stools.

"Now, as I explained in the bulletin that was posted about the event today, this program is not for rehashing the recent events involving a certain Senator and his, hmmm, problems. Rather our guests will be taking questions about their chosen field of journalism and aspects of reporting the news."

Carl could see that the Professor was much respected in his school and had no doubt that the students would be on their finest behavior during the program. He smiled and nodded at Mary who smiled back and relaxed.

"I think everyone is ready so let's begin. First question, please."

Thirty hands shot up at once and Carl searched the audience for a moment before pointing at a young lady seated in one of the chairs along the wall.

"In the pink sweater," Carl instructed.

As the girl rose to ask her question, Carl knew what it would be. He had done this same thing several times in the past and the first question was the same every time.

"Mr. Thompson, why did you decide to become a reporter? Was it because you wanted to change the world?"

Carl pondered the question for a moment as if it was the first time he had ever had it asked of him.

"I have always been an avid reader and reading the newspaper each day was one of the things I did. One day I decided that reporting on the news would be pretty cool. After all, if I enjoyed reading what others wrote maybe someone would want to read what I had to say. Writing for a newspaper seemed a great way to accomplish that in my young mind. It seemed exciting and maybe even a little dangerous. The answer to your second question may surprise you, but I never set out to change the world. As a reporter, I feel my job is to report the news, not to make it. If I wanted to express my opinion, I would write an editorial column."

The girl sat down somewhat surprised by the answer Carl had given her. Quickly a hand shot up from another female student in the front row. Carl made eye contact and nodded permission for her to ask her question.

"Sir, I know we aren't supposed to ask questions about Senator Billings, but weren't you trying to change the lives of the people that he was hurting by being a slumlord?"

"I think Mary should answer that since she is the one that is responsible for the whole sordid mess coming to light," Carl suggested as he motioned for Mary to give the answer.

Taking her cue, Mary pulled her microphone closer and spoke.

"I may be a touch more emotional about the stories I cover and write about than Mr. Thompson. I'll call him Carl since we work on a first-name basis every day, but my goal is simply to inform the public of the truth. My journalistic integrity, which I learned from Carl, by the way, requires that I don't try to convince the reader to feel the way I do about a story. That being said, I truly believe that the truth will always point the reader in the right direction. In this case, yes, lives were improved. But that doesn't always happen."

Mary pointed to a young man in the back that had raised both hands to get attention.

"All that research stuff sounds kind of boring. What about the action stuff? You know, like you see on TV, do you ever have any of that?"

Mary smiled as she thought about some of the close calls both she and Carl had faced over the last several years.

"There have been a few of those if you consider being caught in the middle of a gunfight between rival gangs, Carl having his tires slashed and someone trying to stab him, and catching an arsonist red-handed as action," Mary explained.

For the better part of an hour, they continued, taking turns answering questions. Professor Kingsberry stepped back on stage and announced that they had time for just a couple more questions. Carl called on the Professor's assistant, who sat in the front row listening intently to everything that had been asked and answered.

"What is the most valuable advice you can give to someone that wants to be a journalist?" The young man addressed his question to Mary.

"Several years ago I was sitting in the front row of an auditorium just like you are today and I asked the same question. A very smart man answered my question and I have followed his advice and it has proven invaluable." Mary looked at Carl with a smile and then continued.

"Respect everyone and treat them as equals. Assume the people you are interviewing know much more than you do and most importantly, don't ask stupid questions like *your house just burned down, how do you feel?*"

Everyone in the room laughed and applauded her answer. Carl gave her the thumbs-up sign and they both stood to signal that they were finished.

As the students and other guests filed out of the room the Professor joined the two reporters on the stage and congratulated them for a wonderful program.

"One of the largest turnouts we have ever had. I must say you have educated all of us on the fine points of journalism. I do hope we can repeat this some time in the future. In fact, Carl, if you have a moment before you leave I have something else to discuss with you. It won't take too long. Do you mind Mary?"

"Not at all, Professor," Mary said agreeably and then asked, "Is there a public phone I could use? I would like to call my Grandmother."

"Use the phone in my office. The school would be more than happy to cover the cost of a long-distance call after what you both have done for us today."

The Professor led her to his office and closed the door to offer her privacy. Carl and he took a stroll through one of the many small gardens on the campus.

Twenty minutes later, Carl and Mary were headed back to his car. They talked about how well the program seemed to have gone and how pretty the school grounds were. Mary was buoyant because her grandmother had known who she was, even if she talked about things that had happened years before. As they approached Carl's Camaro he spotted a red light flashing on the dash.

"It's the phone," Carl said and jogged to his car. When he yanked the door open Mary could hear the beeping sound the car phone made instead of a normal ring.

As Mary approached, she saw a smile on Carl's face as he had a conversation with someone on the other end of the line. He stood with the passenger door open and his foot propped on the door sill.

"Here she is, why don't you tell her yourself?" Carl suggested and motioned for Mary to take the phone from him. Cart mouthed 'Preston Blanton'.

Her heart quickened as she took the receiver. "Hello, this is Mary."

"Mary this is Preston Blanton and I wanted to let you know I just finished talking to Jack on the radio. The moment I got home from school, I contacted him. I wanted to let you know he should be in port, at Andres, sometime early Friday morning. Louis is on the boat with him, so they are making good time."

"That is wonderful news! How did Frenchie get on Jack's boat? I thought he was headed in the other direction?" Mary asked.

"Louis dropped the boat off he was delivering and took a bus to St. Augustine. He was there when Jack stopped for fuel and is coming back with him. He hates buses, by the way, so it is to his liking. Anyway, Maebelle gave me this number and I figured you would want to know the latest news," Preston explained.

Mary thanked him profusely and then handed the phone back to Carl. "Friday. The day after tomorrow, I can hardly believe it."

Carl replaced the phone in its cradle and turned back to Mary, who gave him a tight hug.

"Thank you, Carl, for everything," Mary said.

Carl gently placed a finger under Mary's chin and tilted her head back to look into her eyes. "For what? You did it, not me."

"For understanding, for caring, for driving all the way from DC to bring me Chinese, for being here… and for loving me," Mary said with a faint smile.

Carl stroked her hair and kissed the top of her head. "That was easy, Mary. Loving you just seems to come naturally to me."

Taking her shoulders, Carl held her at arm's length and announced. "You have a dress to buy! We have a real reason to dance now."

"Let's go find me a dancing dress," Mary said as she kissed him quickly and slid under his arm and into the car.

Mary made Carl wait in the car while she shopped.

"I want it to be a surprise," Mary explained.

Chapter 28

Mary wasn't surprised to find that the whole island knew of Jack's impending arrival on Friday by the time they pulled up in the front yard. Maebelle waved from the porch and hurried down the stairs to meet them at the car.

"It is so wonderful. This whole thing is like a novel or something. I suppose this is just about the most exciting thing to happen around here in forever."

Mary got out of the car pulling a dress bag behind her. She and Maebelle made their way to the porch as Carl retrieved several boxes from the trunk and followed behind them. Bubba intercepted him and asked what was in the boxes.

"Well, I found out something today. It is impossible to buy a new dress without also getting new shoes, a purse, a slip, and a half dozen other things." Carl said as he re-balanced his load to climb the steps.

"The next thing you will learn is that it is all worth it when you see the finished product," Bubba said with a laugh and relieved Carl of the box that sat precariously on top of the stack.

The girls hurried into the bedroom so Mary could show Maebelle the things she had bought for the dance.

Carl helped Bubba prepare a dinner of flounder, beans, and cornbread.

"Carl, you are going to have the most sought-after lady at the Fireman's Ball this Saturday I guarantee you," Maebelle announced when she and Mary joined the others in the kitchen.

Mary blushed as she began setting the table for supper. When they were all seated, they joined hands, as usual, and Bubba thanked God for the blessings of the day and the delicious food.

Carl recounted how things had gone at the College of Charleston and that they had been invited back to speak again. Mary described finding the graves Buba had told her about. Carl made a quick trip out to his car and retrieved a large envelope containing the enlarged photos Mary had taken. The photographer for the newspaper had developed and printed them while the clothes were being purchased.

Maebelle stepped into her bedroom and returned with a large magnifying glass that they used to study the photos up close. The magic of custom film developing had brought out a lot of the details they had not seen before. Mary said she wanted to take them to Preston after supper.

"Oh, Buddy will love these. You can bet he won't quit until he has found everything there is to know about who is buried out there in the woods. As a matter of fact, why don't you and I run them over right now while the boys clean up? I have been meaning to visit Lottie for days now and this is the most convenient excuse," Maebelle suggested.

When they returned an hour later from their visit Mary and Maebelle found the boys sitting on the quaint lookout on top of Mary's place. Bubba waved and held up a large thermos, indicating there was coffee for all of them. A few moments later all four of them sat listening to the waves crash on the beach.

"We have talked about everything but the biggest news tonight; Jack's return," Maebelle said after a long stretch of silence.

"I am almost afraid to talk about it. It is like I'm really dreaming and if I say the wrong thing I'll wake up and find none of it is real. I mean, I didn't know Jack or Folly Beach even existed just a couple of weeks ago." Mary admitted and then suddenly blurted out. "Did I do the right thing? I am afraid...I mean what if he resents my prying into his life? It was such a long time ago and..." The words faded off as Mary leaned back in her chair and gave a sigh. Carl reached for her hand and gave it a squeeze.

"You said before it seemed like your mother wanted you to know about Jack? I guarantee she knew you would do just what you did. None of this is a mistake. It was meant to be. Do you see how all the pieces fell into place? Things like this don't just happen, at least I don't believe they do. "When something is meant to be, it will happen," Maebelle said with feeling.

"When Bubba and I first met I thought he was so handsome I just knew he wouldn't be interested in me, but look what happened."

Bubba looked at his wife with such adoration as she spoke that Mary was sure he had thought the same about himself at the beginning.

"Did Carl say you were crazy for trying to locate your mother's old love from over thirty years ago? Obviously not, because he is right here. Did the people on the island think you were nuts for trying to find someone that hadn't stepped foot on Folly for three decades? No. They just said OK, we will help you find him. And Friday morning he will be tying his boat up at Andres' dock and you will get to tell him what happened all those years ago. That my dear is a miracle, not a mistake," Maebelle said with finality as she put an end to Mary's worry.

"Thank you Maebelle. You have been like a mother to me. I can never thank you and Bubba enough for all you have done."

"Mary dear, your coming into our life is a gift," Maebelle said and Bubba said he agreed with his wife.

They sat for a long time without speaking, just enjoying each other's company. At about midnight Bubba and Maebelle headed home. Mary and Carl took a moonlight walk on the beach. Mary played a hundred different scenarios of her meeting with Jack over and over in her mind as she and Carl walked silently hand in hand.

Back at the house, Mary once again fell asleep on the sofa, curled up against Carl. She woke up the next morning on top of her bed covered with a warm blanket.

When she came out of the bedroom, she didn't find Carl on the sofa or in his bed. She ventured onto the porch to see if he was there. Carl wasn't there either, so Mary started climbing the stairs to the Widow's Walk. She stopped when she caught sight of Carl, Maebelle, and Bubba engaged in a serious conversation on the porch next door. She watched, wondering what they might be talking about, and was just about to call over to them when Carl shook Bubba's hand and gave Maebelle a hug. They walked back into their house and when Carl turned to leave, he saw Mary on the porch. Without missing a beat, he smiled, waved at her, and jogged over to join Mary on the porch.

"Did you have a decent night's sleep? We have been invited to breakfast with the neighbors. Are you hungry?" Carl asked and kissed Mary on the cheek.

"What were you three talking about on the porch?" Mary asked.

"Oh, nothing much. I need to go to Charleston today for a bit and post some information on a couple of the stories I am working on. Maebelle told me she could use your help at the library today. She said something about a bookmobile."

"She doesn't need my help. Maebelle is just trying to keep me busy so I don't spend every minute today thinking about Friday," Mary speculated.

"And?"

"And it's not working. All I can think about is Jack's boat pulling into Andres and what I am going to say," Mary admitted.

"Try Hi, I am Margaret's daughter and I just wanted to tell you what happened more than thirty years ago and proceed from there."

Mary gave him a hip bump and said sarcastically, "Gee, thanks, I hadn't thought of that. Let's go next door, but I'm not sure I can eat anything. I am so nervous."

"You might get pretty hungry by the time the boat arrives," Carl said.

As they were heading down the stairs Chuck came out on the porch and waved at them. "Hey, you two. I think it's pretty cool that you found Jack and all. I hear he is docking Friday morning."

"That's the plan," Carl agreed.

"So maybe I'll get to meet him before I leave," Chuck said as he walked down the stairs.

"Leave. Where are you headed?" Mary asked.

"Taking my boat down to Florida. My parents live near Jacksonville so I figured I would shrimp out of there for a while. I'm on the way over to Andres to fuel up and get everything ready."."

"It's a little sudden, isn't it?" Mary continued questioning.

"Well, yeah, but I figure it is time to move on. Chuck replied, "I know you know the family and all," as he rolled his motorcycle out from under the house.

"You are staying for the Fireman's Ball?" Carl asked as he walked over to where Chuck was now straddling his bike.

"I guess I could leave the next day. I guess Abigail might want to go."

Carl offered his hand and Chuck took it. "Thanks again for helping me the other night on the beach."

The two men shook hands warmly and before Chuck started his motorcycle he called over to Mary, "I am glad things worked out for you and what you said the other day, you know after the hurricane and all, I think it is about time to grow up. At least a little, anyway."

Chuck grinned as he kicked his motorcycle to life and waved over his shoulder as he accelerated out of the yard.

"What was that all about?" Carl asked as he rejoined Mary.

"I'll tell you all about it later. Right now, let's eat. I'm hungry."

"Whatever happened to being too nervous to eat?" Carl kidded as Mary took his arm and guided him across the yard. Mary just smiled as she watched the motorcycle disappear as the rider turned the corner, thinking maybe more than one miracle was happening on this magical island.

After cleaning up, Mary walked Carl to his car.

"Keep busy and I'll be back soon. By this time Friday, everything you have been working for will come to pass. I am proud of you Mary, I really am," Carl said and kissed her before getting in his car and backing out of the yard.

Mary stood for a long while after the Camaro had been lost from sight. Carl had been right. Friday, everything would be different, for better or worse. As she turned back toward Maebelle's house her friend came through the screen door.

"Are you ready to be an assistant librarian?" Maebelle asked.

"Lead the way," Mary responded, thankful to Maebelle that she would have something to occupy her mind during what she figured would be a very long day.

It was around noon when Carl crossed the Folly Beach bridge back to the island. He pulled into the parking area next to the library. He could see Mary and Maebelle busy inside through the window.

"My two favorite librarians. I have food," Carl announced as he came through the door carrying a large bag. "It's not Leus, but I have Chinese as well as a couple of Po-boys. I called Bubba from the car and he is on the way."

They heard Bubba's truck pull up as he finished his announcement. A moment later he entered the building carrying paper plates, napkins, and plasticware.

"How did you keep this hot?" Bubba asked as he took a big bite of one of the sandwiches.

"I had them wrap everything in foil and I put it on top of the engine. It works perfectly every time." Carl said with a grin.

"Carl is a man of many talents and ideas," Mary laughed.

"You can't succeed unless you are willing to fail," Bubba philosophized as he raised his paper cup to Carl. "A culinary delight, young man."

"Mary and I have another hour and we should be finished. That is if Mary doesn't mind staying a little longer," Maebelle said.

"I am en route to the Blanton place to help Preston put up a replacement antenna for his radio. We could use your help if you are willing," Bubba said to Carl, who was busy shoving trash into the bag he had brought the food in.

"Count me in, I want a chance to talk to Preston again," Carl readily agreed.

"We will see you back at the house in a bit," Bubba told the girls as they headed out the door.

Bubba saw Jesse Porter talking to Preston in the empty lot next to Preston's radio shack when he pulled into the empty lot. After shaking hands all around, they got right to work assembling and erecting the new antenna tower. When Preston tried the radio he said he was getting a much stronger signal.

After they were done Jesse asked Carl, "You aren't afraid of heights, are you?"

"Me? No. Why?" Carl answered

"Then, why don't we go climbing?" Jesse asked.

"Climbing?" Carl asked, wondering what there was on the relatively flat island for him to climb.

"Hop into my truck and I'll show you."

Jesse drove back toward his house after promising Bubba he would deliver Carl in good condition to his house. Parking in his yard, Jesse started off down the road next to his house at a brisk walk. A minute later they stood at the foot of the Folly Beach water tower.

"It is time for my monthly inspection of the hatch on top of the tower." Mr. Porter said as he unlocked a ladder and pulled it down, allowing them access to the main ladder that went to the catwalk encircling the big ball that was the tank holding fresh water for the township.

Despite being younger and having a much longer arm reach, Carl found himself struggling to keep pace with the one-handed head of the water department. It was quite a climb and Carl's breathing had quickened by the time he clambered onto the catwalk. Jesse Porter seemed like a man that had just gotten out of his easy chair and walked across the room.

Jesse handed Carl a heavy leather belt with a three-foot-long rope connected to it. On the other end was a large snap hook. They fastened the belts around their waist and Carl draped the rope over his shoulder, mimicking the other man's motions.

"You ready?"

"Ready."

"When you get to the top there are a couple of swivel rings on each side of the top hatch and one in the middle. I'll go ahead and check the hatch. When I call down, come up and hook onto the middle ring." Jesse instructed. He then shot up the narrow ladder that followed the curve of the huge water container.

When Mr. Porter got near the top Carl could no longer see him. After a few minutes, he heard Jesse call his name and he began climbing the ladder. As he came over the curve of the tower Carl saw Jesse Porter standing on top of the water tank. He had his safety line snapped into one of the rings.

"When you get to the top rung of the ladder reach over and hook up to the ring before you stand up. Sometimes people get dizzy the first time." Jesse instructed Carl as he neared the end of the ladder.

Carl did as he was told, standing at the very top of the water tower. He wasn't dizzy, but the curve of the tank made him feel like he could easily slide off. Carl looked around and whistled.

"Quite a view from here. Thanks for bringing me up here. I bet the local kids try to get up here a lot."

"Oh, there are some. In fact, Johnny, that's Frenchie's second oldest son, used to climb up here every now and then and just sit. He joined the Air Force just this summer but should be back for a visit at Christmas I imagine. He would like to meet you and Mary since he likes to write and tell stories," Jesse said.

"We will be back, that's for sure and maybe we will get to meet him. Was he one of your boys?" Carl asked.

"Is one of my boys. They all are, no matter how much time passes. Since his father was away chasing shrimp for long periods of time, Johnny and I became close when he was young. God's been kind to me that way."

Carl looked at the battered figure standing there on the water tower and saw a very special man. A man that continued to mold the lives of the youth that he mentored. One that had found his place in life despite all that had happened to him, and was content with it. Carl thought that was as much as anyone could hope for their life.

They sat for a while, on top of the world, and Mr. Porter pointed out landmarks like Maebelle's house and the dance pier. Jesse recounted some of the adventures he and his boys had camping on the secluded islands that abounded in the area. He spoke about abandoned houses, the wild horses on Long Island, and how he had taught the boys to get the animals into the marsh, so they could put bridles on them.

Carl glanced at this watch and got to his feet. "I better get back before Mary and Maebelle organize the rescue squad to search for me."

"It sure got late fast. I better get you back since it would be embarrassing for you to be rescued, you being a member of the rescue squad yourself," Jesse said as scurried down the ladder. Jesse was on the ground before Carl was halfway down.

Chapter 29

When Carl woke up early on Friday morning, he could hear Mary in the kitchen. It was the first time he remembered her rising before him. Most of the time when he would call and let her know he was on the way to pick her up for work she had to pretend that she hadn't been asleep when the phone rang.

They had spent most of the day before doing odd jobs around the two houses. Carl had helped Bubba change the oil in his truck and then spent some time working on Chuck's motorcycle. Chuck was impressed with how much Carl knew about British bikes.

"These Triumph TR6Cs are a little touchy about carb adjustment and the coil should be replaced with a better one. The factory ones are prone to flooding," Carl told Chuck as he made adjustments.

Mary helped Maebelle at the library for a while and then rode with her on a couple of errands off-island.

"Girl, you are like a cat sitting in a frying pan. Don't fret so, everything will be okay. You'll see." Maebelle told Mary as they pulled into the yard.

That evening they played Monopoly until they couldn't keep their eyes open. It had been guys against girls, and the girls won because of Maebelle's shrewd property purchases.

After splashing water on his face, Carl slipped into jeans and a sweatshirt and joined Mary. From her movements and demeanor, it was obvious she hadn't gotten much sleep during the night despite the long game.

"Coffee ready?" He asked as he came in and sat at the kitchen table.

Without a word, Mary took a cup from the cupboard and set it in front of him. Taking the coffee pot, she only poured a half cup before the pot ran dry.

"Oops, I guess someone already drank most of it," Mary confessed with a sigh.

Carl rose and took the coffee pot from her and carried it to the sink. "Sit down and I'll make a brand-new pot. Are you excited? In a couple of hours, you will be face to face with Jack."

"Thanks, that is just what I needed to hear. Maebelle said the same thing when she came over a few minutes ago. She told me Preston had called her and said the boat should be docked by 10 o'clock." Mary sat and placed her hands over her face and groaned.

Carl finished filling the pot, put it on the stove, and joined Mary at the table. He took her hands in his and leaned forward, kissing her lightly on the forehead.

Mary felt her tense shoulders relax a bit, and she leaned back in the chair.

"If those students at the college could see me now. The fearless, objective, professional reporter; a wreck at the kitchen table," Mary said with a hint of a smile.

"Remember what I said when I came to your school years ago about how I chose whether to pursue a story or not?" Carl asked as he sipped his coffee.

Mary thought for a moment and then answered. "Consider the worst that could happen and the best that could happen. The one with the most weight wins. But…"

"There are no buts Mary. Just because you are part of the story doesn't change the results of the test. Whatever happens today, we both know which way the scales tip. Now go take a shower and get dressed. I'll have breakfast ready when you come out," Carl instructed as he pulled Mary to her feet and headed her toward the bedroom.

Soon Carl could hear Mary humming her favorite song and then the shower drowned out the sound. He walked to the front door and opened it, stepped out on the porch, and looked at the eastern sky. A bright red sky glowed as the sun began its morning journey.

"It is going to be a great day!" Carl said out loud and then turned back to the task of making breakfast.

A platter of flapjacks and bacon sat in the middle of the table when Mary emerged, dressed in jeans and a pink sweatshirt. Mary noticed that the table was set for four so she asked if they were having guests for breakfast.

"I figured it was time we had Bubba and Maebelle over. It seems like we are always eating at their place, so I thought this would be a pleasant change."

As Carl finished explaining they heard footsteps on the front porch. He went to the door and opened it before Bubba or Maebelle had a chance to knock.

"Come on in and get it while it's hot," Carl instructed as he ushered the other couple toward the kitchen.

Mary was completely composed now. She hugged both of the guests as they came in and seated them at the table. Carl had warmed the syrup in a pan of hot water which he set next to the pancakes.

A glass of milk sat in front of each setting and after Carl had said grace he took his glass and raised it.

"I would like to propose a toast to true love and new friends."

Glasses clinked and a chorus of "Here! "Here!" echoed around the small kitchen.

"Preston called just before we came over and said he had heard from Jack and he is about two hours out," Maebelle informed them.

"Well then, I suppose we should get to eating so we can be there when the *Miss Margaret* makes dock," Bubba said as he began forking pancakes onto his plate. Mary realized her apprehension had been replaced with excitement and she ate heartily. The rest of them followed her lead and the food quickly disappeared.

After cleaning up they were ready to head to Andres. Carl followed Bubba's truck across the bridge.

"Sure are a lot of cars here today," Carl said to Mary as they wove through the parking area behind the building where the alligator's residence was. They recognized many of the people they had met at the Baptist and the Catholic church. They all smiled and waved as Carl passed them.

"Do you think all these people are here for..." Mary hesitated for a moment and Carl took the lead.

"For you, Mary, they are here for you," Carl replied.

"Jack may turn his boat around and head back to Florida when he sees this crowd," Mary said out of worry.

Bubba had found a spot to park and waved through the window for Carl to pull up next to him. Bubba was out of his truck and opening the door for Maebelle when Carl pulled in and shut off his engine.

Maebelle came over to the car and told Mary through the window. "Don't worry dear, Bubba will see that everyone gives you some space. They are all just excited for you. Why don't you two stroll down to the dock and watch for Jack?"

Carl took Mary's hand and they walked slowly down the oyster shell road toward the dock. She clutched the Valentine's card, the reason she was there, tightly in her right hand. As they walked, everything that had happened since she had found it played like a movie at high speed in her mind. The life she led before embarking on this quest seemed to belong to someone else. Everything was different now and she knew that it would always be so. It was troubling in a way because Mary had always thought she had a fulfilling life. She liked her job and the people she worked with and now that she and Carl were more than just casual friends, she just didn't know.

Suddenly she pulled Carl to a stop and when he turned to her she said, "I want to pray."

"Exactly what I was thinking," Carl said with a smile and pulled her to him. He put his arm around her and for several minutes they stood there, in the middle of the road, eyes closed and heads bowed.

"Amen," Mary said quietly.

"Feel better now?" Carl asked.

"Much," Mary admitted.

"Then let's go. We have a boat to greet."

They rounded the curve in the road and the dock was before them. A lone shrimp boat was tied at the end near the ice house. No one was on the boat or around the dock. It was eerily quiet as they stood there away from all the people.

"Someone made sure you had your privacy," Carl mused and then he shaded his eyes with one hand and looked hard in the direction of the inlet to Folly River.

"Do you see something?" Mary asked.

"What time is it?"

"Nine-fifteen. Why?" Mary glanced at her watch and answered.

"Someone has been running full throttle and making good time I suppose."

Mary stepped onto a cable spool and followed Carl's gaze. A large shrimp boat was coming fast down the river; dual smokestacks pouring black smoke from the diesel engine and pushing a large bow wave.

"Do you think that is Carl's boat?"

"I can't see a name, but I am betting that is the *Miss Margaret*."

As the boat came closer they could hear the deep rumble of the big engine. One man stood on the bow and they could just make out a figure in the wheelhouse. As the shrimp boat drew closer Mary thought it was going to run right into the dock. Instead, the captain reversed the prop and opened the throttle again. The big boat shuddered and almost came to a full stop.

The *Miss Margaret* drew abreast to the far end of the dock. A man, they could now see that it was Frenchie on the bow, threw a rope deftly across one of the pilings. He quickly took out most of the slack and looped the rope around a large cleat. As the boat coasted in, the rope tightened and slowly pulled it to a gentle stop against the rail. Frenchie jumped onto the dock and finished securing the shrimp boat.

There was a sudden quiet as the engine was cut; only the quiet lapping of the wake from the boat against the shore was left. Frenchie spoke to the other man through the wheelhouse door for a moment and then started down the dock toward Carl and Mary.

Mary squeezed Carl's hand until he winced. Frenchie came up to them and before he could speak Mary hugged him hard, almost knocking his captain's hat off.

"Thank you so much," she said, releasing him and stepping back.

"For what? All I did was save bus fare by getting a ride back here," Frenchie protested.

"We know everything you did, Frenchie. You spent a lot of time and went out of your way to help find Jack. In fact, without your help, who knows how long it would have taken?" Carl disputed.

Frenchie smiled, shook his head, and started towards Andres. He announced over his shoulder, "By the way, Jack is waiting for you."

When Mary turned and looked she saw a man step out of the cabin and onto the dock. He was much taller than Frenchie with the same slender but sturdy build of a working man. Mary noticed that he looked just like an older version of the boy in the photos she had seen.

"Well, my dear, this is what you have been waiting for," Carl said as he motioned toward the boat and the man standing there waiting.

"Aren't you coming with me?" Mary asked, a little shakily.

"I'll be right here in case you need me, but I think this is something you need to do yourself. It will be fine, trust me." Carl said and gave her a nudge.

As Mary walked toward the boat Jack began moving in her direction. Carl could not help but visualize the westerns where the gunfighters met in the middle of the street for the fast draw contest. He hoped the results of this showdown would be more positive.

The two figures moved closer until they stopped a couple of feet apart. Mary said something Carl couldn't hear and then handed Jack the Valentine card she had been clutching in her hand. He removed the card from the envelope, and then sat on an overturned bucket to read it.

Carl assumed Jack must have read the card several times because he held it open for a long time. Then he slowly closed it and slipped the card back into the envelope. Jack stood and took a step closer to Mary, towering over her.

Carl tensed and then relaxed when Jack spread his arms and Mary stepped into them. For a long time, they embraced each other. When they started walking down the dock Mary motioned for Carl to join them.

"Jack, this is…" Mary hesitated, as she tried to think of the right words and then said, "My Carl."

Jack smiled, "Yes, I can see that. Why don't we go somewhere and talk? I want to know everything."

Mary took their arms, one on each side, and they started down the dock. They stopped when they looked out to the road and saw it full of people. There were dozens of them. Preston and his family stood with Frenchie and his wife Joyce. Mr. Porter was with his family and the pastor of the Baptist church stood with Father Williams. Most of the people Mary had met on her journey to find Jack were there.

Carl took the lead, Jack and Mary joining him as he moved off the dock and onto the road. The crowd parted as the three of them drew closer. Someone started clapping and soon everyone joined in.

Maebelle stood with Bubba on the side of the road behind the crowd. Mary took their hands and pulled them into their little group as they continued on to Andres.

They stopped near the alligator, who slept with his mouth half open. The reptile was totally disinterested in all that was going on.

"You three need some alone time, so why don't you go to your place? Bubba promised everyone they would hear everything, what you want them to know anyway, soon enough," Maebelle told them.

A minute later the Camaro crossed the bridge with Carl and Jack in the front and Mary sitting quietly in the back.

Jack seemed to be trying to soak the island back into his system during the short drive. A lot must have changed for him in the thirty years he had been absent. Mary wondered, "would he ever have come back if she hadn't summoned him?"

As they pulled into the yard Jack got a big smile on his face and asked, "You are staying in Margaret's old summer place?"

"Yes, that is Carl's doings. He thought it would only be appropriate for my stay there while I was here. Does your old place still look the same? I don't know who owns it now, Chuck's said his family rented it from someone out of town for years."

Jack surprised them by saying, "It still belongs to me. A rental agency has been taking care of it all these years. The money has been deposited into a trust of some type."

"I... didn't know," Mary stated, shocked to hear the news. She had figured Jack had cut all ties with Folly when he left.

Shortly, they were sitting on the Widows Walk in a small circle, drinking iced tea and eating cookies Maebelle had baked just the night before.

Chapter 30

"Mary, I want you to know I never stopped loving Margaret, your mother. When I didn't hear back from her I even went so far as to go to the bus station. I even bought a ticket to travel to see her." Jack said, pulling the Valentine from inside his shirt.

"What happened? Why didn't you go?" Mary asked, knowing everything would have been different if he had shown up at her mother's house.

For a long time, Jack seemed to ponder the question Mary had asked as he studied the drink in his hand.

"I think maybe I realized that your grandparents were right about us. We were two kids, from two different worlds, caught up in a summer romance."

Mary's reaction surprised two men. "No! That didn't matter to her. She wrote you letters, just like you sent her. She really loved you. My mother was willing to move down here and attend school to be with you."

"I have all the letters, Mary, in a box on the boat. I have read them a hundred times or more. Of course, Margaret loved me. We loved each other very much."

"Then it would have been fine and my grandparents had given their blessings," Mary objected.

"But Jack didn't know that," Carl reminded her. "Remember, he didn't get the Valentine."

"The last letter I wrote to Margaret was unfair to her. I put a lot of pressure on her to make a decision when I should have told her that however long it took I would wait. But I was just a kid, madly in love, who wanted his sweetheart with him. We were both pretty young."

"It is difficult for me to think of Mom as a young girl. I was so young myself when my father died, I don't even really remember him. She had to take on a lot and my grandmother depended on her too," Mary said.

"Anyway, I was waiting at the bus station when I started thinking about my own parents. In spite of how much I wanted to visit Margaret, I wasn't able to do it. My father was in pretty bad shape and as it turned out he died a couple of weeks later."

"I am so sorry. I didn't mean to get so weird. There were a lot of things going on in both of your lives at the time," Mary apologized.

"It's OK. Around six months later, my mother was killed by a drunk driver in North Charleston. He just never saw a red light. After that, I felt abandoned, which sounds stupid. The lawyer who handled the thing with my mother got a pretty big settlement and I was able to pay off the boat and all the other bills. He suggested I put the house in trust since I told him I was leaving but didn't want to sell it."

"Which explains why we didn't know you still owned the house. The records just showed a change of deed so we assumed it was sold," Carl reasoned.

"Where did you go?" Mary asked. Now that the initial shock of actually meeting her mother's old flame was over, Mary wanted to know all about his life.

"I sailed down the coast of Florida and into the Gulf. I was gone for about a year when I found out Margaret had gotten married. It was kind of like the final blow and I had to get even further away. I made it all the way to Argentina and stayed there for almost three years."

"How did you find out about the marriage?" Carl asked.

" There was a guy whose roots were in the DC area who received several local papers at a dock in Barton Rouge. I had told him about Margaret and when he saw the wedding announcement, he gave it to me."

Mary touched Jack's arm. "I am so sorry. It must have been terrible. I know only that they met in college and were married soon after. The more I learn, the more I think it might have been a rebound thing. It all just seems so, I don't know... sad."

Jack patted her hand and smiled warmly. "You look so much like your mother in a lot of ways. You are just as pretty as she was and she was a sensitive person just like you are."

"Thank you," Mary said and leaned back in her chair.

"I'm not just saying that to be polite. I see so much of her in you that I can understand why Carl here is so taken with you. Mary, I wish it had all been different, but it wasn't. The important thing is, I am sitting across from Margaret's daughter and I am happier than I have been in a very long time."

"What happened after your time in South America?" Carl asked.

"It took me about a year to work my way back up the coast to the Gulf. Since I had learned Spanish, I made Mexico my home port for years. After that, well, I just kept moving. I wore out two boats. This is the third *Miss Margaret*."

"You never met anyone and got married?" Mary asked tentatively.

"I won't say there were no women in my life, but they came up short. What it came down to was, no other woman could compare to Margaret and I wasn't willing to settle for second best."

"How did you find out Mary was looking for you?" Carl asked.

"It was pretty simple actually. I was tied up at a dock just down the coast from Miami when this other shrimp boat tied up next to me. I stepped over to the rail to tell him I was about to leave when Frenchie introduced himself and said someone was looking for me. You could have knocked me over with a feather when he said it was Margaret's daughter."

"He told you my mother had died?" Mary asked.

"That was the most miserable I had felt since I thought Margaret didn't love me anymore." Jack pulled a laminated paper out of his shirt pocket and showed it to Mary. It was a faded photo of him and Margaret sitting close together in a booth eating hamburgers.

"That was the last time we were together, right before she left Folly. Our waiter took it for us with Margaret's camera. She sent it to me when she got home." Jack put the photo back in his pocket and patted it lovingly.

"Thank you for coming back. I know you didn't have to and you had come a long way," Mary said gratefully.

Jack looked surprised and said, "Of course, I had to come. If I had gotten a message saying that Margaret's daughter was in Italy and she needed me, I would be crossing the Atlantic right now."

Mary leaned over, hugged Jack, and kissed him on the cheek. "Hearing you say that makes this whole thing worth it. I was afraid you might forget about my mother. I didn't want you to always believe she just decided to move on. I am sure she was a faithful wife to my father, but I don't think she ever loved anyone the way she loved you."

"Forget Margaret? My dear, that is impossible. It would be easier to forget to breathe. I am sure she was a wonderful wife to your father. I would say he was one of the luckiest men on earth." Jack laughed and then leaned back in his chair and got comfortable.

"Now, enough about me. I want to hear everything about you and Margaret."

For nearly two hours Mary regaled Jack with every significant detail she could remember about her mother's and her own life.

She explained how her father and grandfather had died just a few months apart. Margaret and her little girl moved in with her mother. When Mary's grandmother needed full-time care, they placed her in a care facility. After Margaret's untimely death, Mary found herself living alone.

"Mother was really pretty and I remember a couple of times she went out to dinner or the movies with a man, but it never amounted to anything. She would always say it was nothing special. He just didn't seem like the right one. I asked her once if there might be more than one right person and she said she didn't think so. I always assumed she meant my father. Now I know she meant you."

Mary told Jack how she had inherited the jewelry box with the key to the letters just as Bubba's truck pulled into their driveway.

"Lunch is served!" Maebelle called out to them, holding up a picnic basket. Bubba pulled a large platter from the truck and they headed in their direction.

"Some of the ladies at the church prepared food for you. There is fried chicken, potato salad, and freshly baked apple pie," Bubba announced, holding the platter up toward them.

"Well, bring it on up. Sounds like enough for all of us," Carl called as he headed down the stairs to see if they needed any help.

"We don't want to intrude," Maebelle said.

"That is ridiculous. There is no way either of you could intrude. I'll put on some more tea." Mary said and added, "It is so pleasant out here, why don't we eat on the porch? Carl, I saw a folding table on the back porch."

Carl retrieved the table and Jack helped Bubba set out the food while Carl brought a couple of chairs from the kitchen for more seating. By the time everything was set, Mary and Maebelle appeared with freshly brewed iced tea.

After grace, they dug into the food. A few minutes later, Mary excused herself and headed to her bedroom. She sat on the bed and held the phone in her lap. Her grandmother had a private phone in her room, although she often didn't answer it. This time, though, she picked it up right away.

"Grams, it's Mary. I wanted to see how you were doing today," Mary said and almost dropped the phone when her grandmother responded.

"Mary dear, I am so glad you called. That good-looking boyfriend of yours was here the other day for a visit. You should marry him if he ever asks you."

Mary was so stunned that she didn't respond right away. Most of the time her grandmother didn't even know who she was. Carl had said she didn't respond when he visited her before he left to come to her. Mary realized

Grams was sometimes aware of things even if she didn't show it.

"I am down at Folly Beach and Carl is here too. We will be coming back in a couple of days and I'll come to see you as soon as I get home."

"That's great dear, and bring your boyfriend along with you. We can play bingo.

After a moment of hesitation, Mary asked, "Do you remember a friend of Mom's named Jack?"

With no sign of uncertainty, her grandmother answered, "Oh yes, Jack was your mother's beau. Your grandfather didn't like him too much, but I thought he was a very sweet boy. Margaret should have married him instead of Steven Lassiter. Your father was a nice man, mind you, but Mary never stopped loving that boy. Mary, I am so glad you called. I have to go now. They are about to start bingo and I almost won on Tuesday."

Before Mary could answer the phone clicked and went dead. As she hung up the receiver Mary shook her head in amazement. It was the first time in a year that Grams had carried on a normal conversation.

When Mary came out of the bedroom Carl was watching for her. When he saw the look on her face, he slid from the chair and walked over to her.

"Is everything alright?"

Mary recounted most of the conversation to him and she could see that Carl was happy with the news. Noticing the banter had stopped at the table, they took their seats again. Mary told them she had called her grandmother and she was having a very good day.

"So, what's next?" Bubba asked, spearing a pickle from a bowl in the middle of the table. He addressed his questions to the three people across the table from him.

Mary sat between Carl on her right and Jack on her left and she glanced at both of them.

"I have spent a lot of years on the water, sleeping in a bunk on my boat, and think it is about time I had a real bed. Someone once told me you can leave Folly but she will never leave you. Since I have a house right next door, I think I'll hang around for a while," Jack announced.

"What about you and Carl? Will you be heading back up north now that you have delivered your Valentine?" Maebelle asked Mary.

"I did what I set out to do with a lot of help," Mary said, smiling at Maebelle and Bubba. "This place and all the people are amazing, but our jobs and homes are in DC. My grandmother is there and she needs me. I know it sounds silly, but Folly feels more like home than DC ever did. I am sure Carl and I'll be coming back to visit often."

"I hope you do, Mary. I lost your mother due to a silly mistake and I have a chance to reconnect with her through you. I don't want to lose that," Jack said with sincerity.

"Well, whatever happens, I am sure everything will turn out the way it should. Right now, though we need to make plans for the next couple of days." Maebelle said as she once again took charge of the situation at hand. "Chuck, the young man that is living in the house right now, will be leaving sometime on Sunday I imagine. We have an extra bedroom so Jack can stay with us until we can get him ready to move in."

"No need for that, I can just sleep on my boat for a couple more days."

"Nonsense, you will stay with us. Besides, it will be much easier for you to get ready for the dance tomorrow night if you are here," Maebelle insisted. Jack was pretty sure that arguing with her would be of no avail.

"What dance are we talking about?" Jack asked.

He was informed about the Fireman's Ball the next evening and said it sounded like fun.

"Margaret and I used to enjoy dancing often. I just request at least one dance with Mary."

"Then it is settled." Maebelle laughed and began to clear the remains of their feast.

"There will be a lot of handshakes and questions, but I'll do my darndest to give you some breathing room." Bubba injected.

"That's fine. If I am going to be living here again, I expect getting to know everyone will be something that will happen in time."

While Mary and Maebelle cleaned up and prepared the room, Carl and Bubba took Jack to get some of his things off the boat.

Most of the people that had been at Andres for the welcome home event were gone, although the usual half dozen were still there playing checkers and talking.

Mr. Porter and Preston were discussing something over by the alligator enclosure and Bubba pulled his truck to a stop next to them. The two men had played a vital role in the hunt for Jack, so Bubba thought he might like to talk with them.

Carl and Bubba walked around the front and got some cold drinks. When they returned the three men were standing next to the Water Department truck and Jack was thanking them again for all they had done.

"I am giving Preston a ride home and then I have a plumbing job to do. We will see you at the dance tomorrow," Jesse stated as he climbed into the cab of the truck.

The others continued on to the dock and loaded some of Jack's belongings into the back of Bubba's truck. After double-checking the ropes, Jack ventured into the cabin and returned with a leather bag. It contained the letters he had received from Mary's mother all those years ago.

By the time they returned to the house the women had changed the linen and had the spare room ready for Jack to move in.

"You didn't have to put yourself through all this trouble for a couple of days," Jack said.

"If you knew Maebelle you wouldn't even think of that. If we were going to tear this place down, she would spend a week cleaning before the bulldozer started," Bubba enlightened him.

Later that evening they all took a long walk on the beach while Jack told them more stories of his seafaring adventures.

"Look!" Mary pointed to where a shooting star was crossing the darkening sky.

"You get a wish when you see one of those," Maebelle informed her.

Mary bit her lower lip and stared at the sand, then she announced, "Ok, I got it."

"What is it?" Carl asked.

"She can't tell or it won't come true," Bubba said. He and Maebelle walked behind the others holding hands and enjoying the evening.

"Then mum is the word," Mary said, biting her lip.

When they returned to the house Jack gave Mary the bag containing the letters he had received from her mother. He told her he figured she might want to read them, and of course, she did.

Late into the night, she sat propped up in bed with the letters lying around her. She had arranged them chronologically as she was sure Carl would have guessed she would do. There were also dozens of photos, organized in order of when they were taken.

As Mary read she was transported into her mother's life as it had been so many years before. Each letter and photo was another piece of the puzzle that dropped into place.

Chapter 31

The morning of the Fireman's Ball dawned clear, cool, and with the promise of a beautiful day. When Mary entered the living room she saw that the front door was partly open as was the door to Carl's room. She walked out onto the front porch where she heard voices coming from overhead.

Mary craned her neck and saw Carl and Jack sitting on the Widows Walk talking. They were sharing a joke of some kind. Jack let out a loud laugh and slapped Carl on the back.

It was one of those things she had seen so often the last few years, the way Carl was able to make friends so easily. His ability to put people at ease was one of the reasons Carl was such a successful journalist. Where others trying to get information on a story were chased away by angry citizens Carl would get invited to supper.

"You must be an early riser like Carl," Mary said to Jack as she climbed the stairs to where they sat.

"Morning Mary," he said as he stood and smiled at her. "One of the habits developed from running a shrimp boat. I am usually out on the water by five every morning."

"OK, I just took shrimp boat captain off my possible list of future jobs," Mary laughed and said she would have breakfast ready in half an hour. They offered to help but Mary told them to stay where they were and that she would call them when breakfast was ready.

About the time they were through eating there was a knock on the door. Carl called for whoever it was to come on in. Maebelle entered and when she had reached the kitchen Mary handed her a cup of coffee.

"Mary, some of the women are heading over to the Pier and putting up some decorations for tonight. I thought I would check and see if you would like to help," Maebelle said between sips.

"Sure. I would be glad to. What time do I need to be there?"

"I'm planning on walking, so whenever you're ready, come on over. A couple of hours is all we will need if enough women show up. What about you two boys? Do you have anything planned for today?"

"Jack said he wanted to get something to wear tonight besides rubber boots and jeans, so I figured I would drive him into town to pick up a few things," Carl said.

"Bubba has a couple of errands to run today. Why don't we plan on meeting around one for lunch at the Sandbar restaurant?" Maebelle suggested and then realized neither of them would know where it was. She grabbed a pen and a piece of paper from one of the kitchen drawers and drew a simple map showing them where the restaurant was located.

After Mary left, Carl and Jack headed down the steps. Chuck came riding up on his motorcycle, which was running a lot smoother after Carl's manipulations. He dismounted and came over to them, shaking Jack's hand when he reached the Camaro.

"You must be the famous Jack. I saw the *Miss Margaret* when I tied up at Andres this morning. Sorry, I wasn't here to greet you when you arrived, but I took my boat over to Shem Creek the night before last. I heard there was quite a crowd to greet you."

"Well, I am Jack Young. You must be Chuck. I want to thank you for taking care of my house. It looks in good shape."

Chuck was glad he had carted away all the trash that had been generated by the hurricane party.

"I have everything pretty much sorted out. The furniture was all there when my family moved in a while ago. Anyway, I'll be leaving for Florida tomorrow morning and will be sleeping on the boat tonight." Chuck informed Carl.

"You coming to the ball tonight?" Carl asked as Chuck headed back to his place.

"Yeah, for sure. I want to dance with Mary before I leave."

"Sheesh. I'll be lucky to get a dance myself," Carl muttered as they got in his car.

Jack laughed and slapped the other man on the shoulder and said, "That's what happens when you take the prettiest girl in town to the dance."

Carl pulled up in the parking lot of the Sandbar Restaurant a few minutes before one o'clock with a trunk load of boxes. Bubba's truck stopped beside them less than a minute later.

Maebelle had called that morning and reserved a table in the corner, overlooking the river. The place was full and tongues wagged as they walked in and were escorted to their table.

"My thinking was that the more you were out in public, the quicker things would return to normal. Besides, they are all well-wishers," Maebelle explained and waved at a couple sitting across the room.

"Oh, it doesn't bother me. Sometimes, when I was in South America, I was the only gringo for a hundred miles," Jack said and then surprised them by standing and addressing the room.

"I want to thank you for welcoming me back to the island yesterday. I plan on staying around for a long while and hope to get the chance to meet each and every one of you." Like magic, the room quieted as the patrons returned to their meals.

"You ever considered politics?" Carl asked with a chuckle.

"Or maybe a journalist. Carl went to a biker bar once to gather some information for a story. I was waiting in his car in case I had to call the police. Instead, Carl was wearing a vest from the club when he emerged. He even rode with the leader of the gang on a borrowed motorcycle," Mary told the others at the table.

"Hey, they were nice guys. In their own way, that is. Some of them could use a bath more often," Carl explained.

"It sounds like being in the newspaper business can be kind of dangerous," Bubba concluded.

"It does have its moments. "Like the time Mary went undercover as a drug dealer's girlfriend that she failed to tell me about," Carl said in a somewhat scolding tone.

"Yeah, well that probably wasn't my most brilliant idea. But my hero rescued me. Carl came with the police, busted in the door, and shot a hole in the ceiling with a shotgun," Mary smiled and patted Carl on the hand.

"Shucks, little lady. It wasn't anything," Carl said in a flawless John Wayne imitation.

Everyone laughed and Jack decided he liked Carl even more. A shotgun. He was glad Margaret's little girl had someone he could trust to take care of her.

They ate an excellent meal and then returned home to start preparing for the dance. Carl helped Jack carry his boxes from the Camaro to his temporary living quarters at Maebelle's. It was a good load since Jack had little in the way of "land" clothes.

Jack picked out what he needed and he and Carl walked next door while Mary stayed there since she and Maebelle were helping each other get ready.

Since they both knew it would take the women a lot longer to get ready than it would for them, they decided to kill some time. There were a couple of bicycles under the house and a ride sounded like a terrific idea. First Carl took Jack down the same dirt road he and Mary had traveled in their search for the old graves. They then rode down West Ashley all the way to the end of the road. They then walked across the dunes to the very end of the island.

Jack pointed out Bird Key, which sat in the middle of the channel, and Kiawah Island on the other side of the inlet. He explained that this was one end of Folly River and that the other end came out at the Morris Island Lighthouse.

"Tell me about Mary. What is she like?" Jack asked as they stared across the channel.

"Mary is beautiful, but you can see that for yourself. She is strong and determined. If Mary decides to do something, well, don't try to stop her."

"I guess the fact that I am here is proof of that," Jack said with a chuckle.

"Mary has a heart for people. If she walks past an alley and sees a bum sleeping there, in ten minutes she is back with a bag of food and the biggest coffee she can buy. The reason she was pretending to be a drug dealer's girlfriend was that she knew drugs were being sold right outside a school building. She was determined to stop it, and she did," Carl said with obvious pride.

"I wish I had known her sooner. Margaret's daughter seems like a very special young lady."

"Jack, I was all for her coming here to try and find you, but it was difficult. When she walked through that turnstile at the airport she took my heart with her. I had to come down here and be with her."

"Mary is very fortunate to have you, Carl," Jack said with genuine appreciation.

"Promise me you will stay in Mary's life. She needs a connection to her mother's past. It is really important to her."

"Carl, my friend, Mary couldn't get rid of me now if she wanted to," Jack said.

After consulting his watch, Carl suggested they head back and start getting ready for the Fireman's Ball.

"It wouldn't be right if the girls were ready before we were."

Jack agreed and they made quick time on their trip back, occasionally exchanging waves with some of the well-wishers that had been at the dock the day before.

Bubba was sitting on the front porch reading a newspaper when they rode up.

"Got kicked out of the house, and if you know what is healthy for you, you won't try to go in until you are summoned," Bubba explained and held up a clothes bag, indicating he was planning on dressing next door.

"Come on over, Bubba. We have plenty of room," Carl invited.

Jack showered, shaved, and dressed in Mary's room while Carl got ready in the room Carl had been using. Bubba changed in the living room and was once again reading his paper when the others emerged ready to attend the annual ball.

Carl was dressed in gray slacks and a dark blue blazer and Jack had bought an outfit the exact opposite with dark slacks and a gray jacket. Neither of them wore a tie since Bubba had said it wasn't necessary.

Bubba kept watching his house through the window until he finally saw Maebelle's hand appear out the screen door, waving in his direction.

"Well boys, it's show time. Let's go check out the ladies," Bubba ordered as he headed for the door.

Maebelle stood in the middle of the living room wearing a flattering ankle-length black dress with diamond earrings and a necklace.

"Maebelle, you look terrific," Jack said and he meant it.

"Thank you, kind sir. I think someone besides Mary is liable to garner a lot of dance invitations tonight. You clean up very nicely, Mr. Jack Young," Maebelle said, returning the compliment.

Jack blushed and Bubba asked, "What about me?"

Maebelle came over to him and kissed him. "Don't worry, my darling husband. You are stuck with me forever."

"Good, I was getting worried there for a minute."

Maebelle released her husband and swept her arm toward the bedroom door. "Now, gentlemen, I want you to meet the real star of the Fireman's Ball; Miss Mary Lassiter."

The door opened and Mary stepped tentatively out of the room. Three pairs of male eyes centered on her and simultaneously, "Wow!", came from each of them.

Mary wore a fitted red dress that stopped four inches above the knee. Maebelle had fixed her hair so that it cascaded in curls to her shoulders. Simple pearl earrings and red pumps gave Mary an understated but elegant look.

Carl had accompanied Mary to a number of events where she had dressed up, but this time, her beauty had sucked the very air from his lungs.

Jack was the first to speak. "You are a stunning replica of your mother, Mary. If possible, you are even more beautiful. But there is one thing missing." With that, he crossed the room to Mary's side. He pulled a pearl necklace from his pocket, stepped behind Mary, and fastened it around her slender neck. Mary touched the small round beads with her fingers and felt the smoothness.

Maebelle retrieved a small mirror from the bedroom so Mary could see how it looked. It only took a glance to see that the pearls were exquisite and flawless, as well as very expensive.

Before Mary could object Jack said, "A pearl diver worked on the boat for me in Mexico for a while. He gathered these for me and I had them made into a necklace. I had hoped to send them to Margaret someday as a wedding gift, but I chickened out time after time. I never thought anyone else would be worthy of them until today. So please accept them as a gift from me."

Mary hugged Jack tightly and then stepped back as Maebelle handed her a Kleenex.

"Now don't ruin your makeup," Maebelle ordered. " We should leave in a few minutes if everyone is ready.

There will be a big crowd and Bubba likes to be at the front of the line for the buffet."

"One year Billy Simpson got to the fried oysters first and ate about fifteen pounds and there was hardly any left for me," Bubba explained.

"I like my share of oysters, so I suggest we get this show on the road," Jack laughed.

As it would take no more time to walk than it would have to load up and drive, the group decided to take that route. It was a pleasant evening and they could hear the band already playing as they neared the Pier. It was a local band and one of the singers was also a volunteer fireman. Mary commented that the drummer sounded especially talented.

On the island, people were coming from every direction, and nearly everyone seemed to be a member of the Auxiliary Fire Department or their guests. Many of them seemed to gain admission by showing a badge so Carl pulled his out and led their group inside.

Maebelle heard her name called over the noise and saw Chuck waving at her from the side of the room nearest the buffet tables. He had saved them a table.

Carl noticed how every eye, male and female, seemed to be drawn in their direction as they worked through the crowd. He figured it was because of Jack and Mary, who clung to his arm as they moved toward the table. Carl's thoughts were confirmed by an occasional soft whistle as they passed tables filled with other guests. Glancing at Mary, who was smiling and waving at Mr. Porter and his family, Carl thought she looked happier than he had ever seen her.

"I got us as close to the food as possible," Chuck said to Bubba as they finally reached the table. Bubba just grinned and slapped him on the back.

"I always liked that boy," Bubba whispered to Maebelle, who just rolled her eyes.

While they ate, a number of people came by and introduced themselves, wishing Jack well on his return to Folly. They always expressed the wish that Mary and Carl would return often to visit.

Once everyone had been through the food line, the band began to play, in earnest this time. The dance floor filled quickly with enthusiastic dancers.

"From all the looks coming this way, I think it would be a wise idea to get my dance in right away," Jack suggested as a slow dance began. He stood and offered Mary his hand and they made their way into the crowd.

Mary quickly found that the man her mother had loved when she was young was an excellent dancer. He moved Mary around the floor with ease and grace. When the song was over they started back to the table as a much faster song began.

Mary suddenly found Chuck at her side. "My turn now."

Jack returned to the table alone and said, "Sorry pal, but your date was waylaid on the way back here."

Carl smiled as he leaned back in his chair to watch. Her movements, her laughter, and the way she lit up the room made him happy.

For half an hour, Mary's attempts to return to the table were thwarted. She was the belle of the ball, there was no doubt. The way was finally clear and Mary almost made it back to Carl when a boy of about seventeen caught up with her. It was probably a bet of some kind because Carl could see a group of boys around the same age laughing and pointing in their direction.

Jack guided one of his many partners of the evening to intercept them. He tapped the shoulder of the youth and they exchanged partners. Jack managed to maneuver over to where Jack sat and then presented Mary to him just as a romantic waltz was starting.

"I was beginning to wonder if I would ever get my chance. Are you having a good time?" Mary's answer was to lay her head against his shoulder and pull him closer to her. As they glided across the floor their world became just the two of them.

When the band stopped, they just stood for a long time, swaying to their own music. Mary raised her head and saw him gazing at her. He gave her the slightest hint of a kiss.

"You two seem to be enjoying the ball," Maebelle said as she and Bubba passed by. They had been on the floor since the first cord began.

"Let's go outside for a breath of air," Carl suggested, taking Mary's hand and leading her across the room.

"You two don't be too long. The awards ceremony will be coming up in a bit." Bubba called after them. Carl gave the signal that he had heard and they moved toward the door.

Chapter 32

Carl draped his jacket over Mary's shoulders as they strolled down the boardwalk in the cool breeze. Carl guided Mary off the concrete and onto the sand that surrounded what was left of the amusement park rides.

"Where are we going?" Mary asked as she stopped long enough to slip off her shoes, which were not really meant for walking on the sand.

"Right here," Carl answered as they stopped in front of the canvas-enclosed carousel. Big yellow letters announced Merry-Go-Round across the material. Saying nothing else,

Carl reached out and parted the canvas. He held it back and motioned for Mary to enter. She could see that lights were on behind the cover and music was playing softly from the big speakers mounted overhead.

"What is this all about?" She asked as she stepped up on the platform.

"I wanted a moment of private time with you, away from the crowd."

"Yes, but how..." Mary began.

"I know people," Carl said modestly, guiding her towards a booth with ornate high-backed seats. Once she was seated, he slid in beside her.

"Is there anyone you don't know?"

Carl didn't answer. Instead, he took Mary's hand in his and said, "I have a couple of things to ask you, Mary."

"What things?" Mary asked, feeling goosebumps rise on her arms.

"Well, first. How would you like to live here, on Folly Beach? Would you miss the hustle and bustle of DC?"

"What are you asking, Carl? Our jobs, our homes, my grandmother are back in DC," Mary stated the obvious.

"All valid points," Carl agreed, "but I have answers to all of those. First, remember when Professor Kingsberry and I took that walk after the program the other day? Well, he had something to ask me. He told me he was taking a two-year sabbatical starting in a couple of months. He has taught journalism for more than thirty years, but has never actually worked at a newspaper or magazine, something he has always wanted to do."

"What does that have to do with you?"

"I am coming to that. He asked me if I would consider taking his position while he was away."

"You. A professor?" Mary asked, confused by what Carl was suggesting.

"Well, it isn't that difficult to believe, is it?"

"Yes, I mean no. But you love being out in the field chasing stories and writing," Mary explained.

"True and the second part of the story is that it seems as though professors have a lot of free time. The News and Courier said they would be glad to use me on a part-time basis and I even get to work with my old partner."

"What old partner?" Mary asked, confused for a moment. She was sure Carl had told her before that she was the first person he had ever teamed up with. Then suddenly her eyes opened wide and she asked.

"Me! We would be working together at the newspaper?"

"Not exactly. You would be the lead reporter and I would help you when I had the time," Carl explained.

"So," Mary began slowly, "I would be your boss?"

"In a manner of speaking, yes."

"I kind of like this part, but there is still the issue of our homes in DC. It would be quite a commute." Mary decided to play along with Carl's joke.

Carl grinned and said, "Maebelle told you she was managing the rental house we are staying in, right? She neglected to tell you that she and Bubba are also the owners. They bought both houses when they moved to Folly. We were talking about that when you saw us on the porch a couple of days ago. They said we could buy the place we are staying in right now if we wanted it, at a very good price too."

"Buy the house? Carl, this is crazy."

"Not really. If we both sold our places, we would have enough to buy your mother's summer retreat, with a good bit left over," Carl explained to Mary as she sat there shaking her head.

Before she could object again Carl moved on. "Now the issue of Grams. There is a place on James Island that just recently opened. It is a restored southern mansion set up for people just like your grandmother. They have a full staff, even a doctor that lives on the premises, and only ten residents at a time. They have developed a whole program that is groundbreaking. Best of all," Carl hurried on before Mary could interrupt, "it is less than six miles from here."

"It sounds wonderful, but it must cost a fortune, and how long is the waiting list?" Mary asked, her head spinning as she realized Carl wasn't joking.

"Remember when Jack and I drove to Charleston to buy him some new clothes for the dance? I took him by the place to get his opinion and he loved it. He said he wanted to speak to the owner of the facility if I didn't mind checking out the grounds. And let me tell you it is amazing. They have their own fishing dock, walking paths, and an incredible Azalea garden with a huge gazebo in the middle. When I got back to the house Jack was shaking hands with the owner and told me everything was settled."

"What do you mean by settled?"?" Mary asked, still trying to grasp all that Carl was saying.

"Jack got Grams in. He wrote a check for a full year right then and there. Seems that all those years he lived on his boat he put aside a fortune, not to even mention several bags of very expensive pearls. When I objected, he just laughed and said he had always liked Margaret's mother and he was doing it for her. He said he would take care of her for as long as she lived and that was all there was to it," Carl concluded.

Mary closed her eyes and sank back into the seat. Carl moved from the seat beside her and stood over by one of the wooden horses. He knew her head must be spinning with everything he had told her, so he gave her space.

Minutes ticked by, with the music from the Pier mixing with the melody from the carousel. Finally, Mary opened her eyes, looked at him, and asked, "You do know this is crazy, don't you?"

"Yes", Carl agreed, "but the right kind of crazy. The question is, why not? You asked me the other day if I ever considered living somewhere other than DC. The answer is yes, I am ready to move and live here. Think about it, Mary. It would be a great adventure! What do you say?"

Mary said nothing but he could see the wheels turning, organizing all he had proposed.

"Before you answer, there is one other thing. I have one more question, the most important one." Carl dropped to one knee, right in front of Mary. He took both her hands in his and said, "I thought I fell in love with you after I got to know you, but I was wrong."

When a puzzled look entered Mary's eyes Carl pulled a small box from his pocket. He opened it and a diamond ring sparkled in the carousel lights.

"I didn't fall in love with you; I always loved you. Before we ever met you were the one I loved. When I asked God to give me the perfect partner and wife, I didn't realize He already had. It was just a matter of our meeting."

Mary leaned forward and he could feel her breath on his face when she whispered, "Carl, are you asking me to marry you?"

"I am, and I'll never stop asking until you agree."

"In that case, my dear Carl, the answer is yes," Mary smiled and held out her hand for him to put the ring on her finger. Mary rushed into his arms and he held her close to him.

"Let's take a ride," Carl suggested and pointed to one of the horses that stood there waiting. He took hold of her waist and set Mary sidesaddle on one of the waiting horses. Carl pressed a button and the ride started moving. The horses started their up-and-down motion as the ride picked up speed. Carl jumped on the horse across from Mary. They made several revolutions before Mary spoke.

"I had to say yes, you know. Grams told me I should marry you when I talked to her the other day," Mary confided in him as she looked at her ring.

"Smart woman, your grandmother. I would have been in big trouble if you had said no because I wouldn't have had any place to live. I'm not sure Maebelle would have let me stay in your spare bedroom forever." Carl laughed.

"We better get back to the party before people begin to talk," Carl said with a grin as he slid off his horse. He held up his arms and Mary slid into them as her horse reached the bottom.

Mary looked around, studying the design of the merry-go-round, and then asked. "How old is this ride?"

"Right at fifty years old, so I am told. Most of the time it has set right here and yes, it was here when Jack asked your mother to marry him. So the circle is complete. The Valentine card that got you here brought us all together; Jack, Maebelle, and Bubba, all of the people on this island that helped, and you and I," Carl answered. He then turned off the ride and as the music died, they stepped back out into the night.

"I don't hear the band anymore. I wonder what is going on?" Carl asked as they hurried back to the dance. Their view of the dance space was blocked by a wall behind the bandstand, so they couldn't see anything until they turned the corner.

The people inside were sitting quietly in their chairs and every eye was on them as they entered the dance space. Then a slow, soft drum roll began from the bandstand.

"What's going on?" Mary asked, mystified. In answer to her question, Carl raised the left hand he had been holding and turned it so that the overhead lights made the diamond glitter.

"She said YES!" Carl's voice boomed across the room, and in one motion all of them were on their feet and applauding.

It was then that Mary knew, like Jack, that she had come home.

THE END

Folly Beach: Homecoming

Ramblings from the Author

It is my sincere hope that you have enjoyed reading this novel as much as I enjoyed writing it.

1969 was the year I left Folly to go into the Air Force. I got married soon after and then was off to Vietnam. I stayed in the Service for a little over eight years and eventually ended up in the upstate of South Carolina. I currently live in Greer, SC. God has been good to me, more so than I have ever deserved, and I praise Him for that.

I don't get to visit Folly nearly as often as I like, but it is always right there in my heart. Every time I do get to visit I am struck by the changes that have taken place. Seeing the Welcome sign long before the bridge seems odd, as do all the condos. The old Folly is still there, though, all you have to do is turn off of Center Street and drive a few blocks to see it. Whatever changes may come; in my mind, I am that little barefoot boy with my toes in the sand and my head in the clouds. May it always be so.

John C. Lasne'

John C. Lasne'

The Folly Beach I remember from my youth and the one that lives in my heart.

Circa 1967

Made in the USA
Middletown, DE
18 July 2025